The Lust Lizard of Melancholy Cove

ALSO BY CHRISTOPHER MOORE

The Lust Lizard of Melancholy Cove

Christopher Moore

SPIKE
AN AVON BOOK

Avon Books, Inc.
1350 Avenue of the Americas
New York, New York 10019

Library of Congress Cataloging in Publication Data:
Moore, Christopher, 1957–
The lust lizard of Melancholy Cove / Christopher Moore.—1st ed.
p.   cm.
"An Avon book."
I. Title.
PS3563.O594L87   1999   98-46850
813'.54—dc21   CIP

First Spike Printing: April 1999

SPIKE TRADEMARK REG. U.S. PAT. OFF. AND IN OTHER COUNTRIES, MARCA REGISTRADA,
HECHO EN U.S.A.

Printed in the U.S.A.

FIRST EDITION

QPM   10 9 8 7 6 5 4 3 2 1

www.spikebooks.com

This one's for Mom

Acknowledgments

My thanks to Dr. Kenneth Berv and Dr. Roger Wunderlich for their advice on mental health and pyschoactive drugs; to Galen and Lynn Rathbun for help with biology and rat tagging information; to Charlee Rodgers, Dee Dee Leichtfuss, and Jean Brody for manuscript readings and comments; to Nick Ellison for agent stuff; to Rachel Klayman for patience and precision in her editing; and finally to all those people who were willing to share their experiences with antidepressants and other psychotropic drugs—you know who you are, you crazy fucks. (Just kidding.)

The Lust Lizard of Melancholy Cove

prologue

September in Pine Cove is a sigh of relief, a nightcap, a long-deserved nap. Soft autumn light filters through the trees, the tourists go back to Los Angeles and San Francisco, and Pine Cove's five thousand residents wake up to discover that they can once again find a parking place, get a table in a restaurant, and walk the beaches without being conked by an errant Frisbee.

September is a promise. Rain will come at last and turn the golden pastures around Pine Cove green, the tall Monterey pines that cover the hills will stop dropping their needles, the forests of Big Sur will stop burning, the grim smile developed over the summer by the waitresses and clerks will bloom into something resembling real human expression, children will return to school and the joy of old friends, drugs, and weapons that they missed over the summer, and everyone, at last, will get some rest.

Come September, Theophilus Crowe, the town constable, lovingly clips the sticky purple buds from his sensimilla plants. Mavis, down at the Head of the Slug Saloon, funnels her top-shelf liquors back into the well from whence they came. The tree service guys, with their chain saws, take down the dead and dying pines lest they crash through someone's roof with the winter storms. Woodpiles grow tall and wide around Pine Cove homes and the chimney sweep goes to a twelve-hour workday. The sunscreen and needless souvenir shit shelf at Brine's Bait, Tackle, and Fine Wines is cleared and restocked with candles, flashlight batteries, and lamp oil. (Monterey pine trees have notoriously shallow root systems and an affinity for falling on power lines.) At the Pine Cove Boutique, the hideous reindeer sweater is marked up for winter to await being marked back down for the tenth consecutive spring.

In Pine Cove, where nothing happens (or at least nothing has happened for a long time), September is an event: a quiet celebration. The people like their events quiet. The reason they came here from the cities in the first place was to get away from things happening. September is a celebration of sameness. Each September is like the last. Except for this year.

This year three things happened. Not big things, by city standards, but three things that coldcocked the beloved status quo nonetheless: forty miles to the south, a tiny and not very dangerous leak opened in a cooling pipe at the Diablo Canyon Nuclear Power Plant; Mavis Sand advertised in *Songwriter* magazine for a Blues singer to play through the winter at the Head of the Slug Saloon; and Bess Leander, wife and mother of two, hung herself.

Three things, omens if you will. September is a promise of what is to come.

Admitting You Have a Problem

"Dear, dear, how queer everything is today! And yesterday everything went on just as usual. I wonder if I've been changed in the night? Let me think: Was I the same when I got up this morning? I almost think I can remember feeling a little different. But if I'm not the same, the next question is: Who in the world am I? Ah, that's the great puzzle!"

—LEWIS CARROLL,
Alice's Adventures in Wonderland

one

Theophilus Crowe

As dead people went, Bess Leander smelled pretty good: lavender, sage, and a hint of clove. There were seven Shaker chairs hung on pegs on the walls of the Leanders' dining room. The eighth was overturned under Bess, who hung from the peg by a calico cloth rope around her neck. Dried flowers, baskets of various shapes and sizes, and bundles of dried herbs hung from the open ceiling beams.

Theophilus Crowe knew he should be doing cop stuff, but he just stood there with two emergency medical technicians from the Pine Cove Fire Department, staring up at Bess as if they were inspecting the newly installed angel on a Christmas tree. Theo thought the pastel blue of Bess's skin went nicely with her cornflower-blue dress and the patterns of the English china displayed on simple wooden shelves at the end of the room. It was 7 A.M. and Theo, as usual, was a little stoned.

Theo could hear sobs coming from upstairs, where Joseph Leander held his two daughters, who were still in their nightgowns. There was no evidence of a masculine presence anywhere in the house. It was Country Cute: bare pine floors and bent willow baskets, flowers and rag dolls and herb-flavored vinegars in blown-glass bottles; Shaker antiques, copper kettles, embroidery samplers, spinning wheels, lace doilies, and porcelain placards with prayers from the Dutch. Not a sports page or remote control in sight. Not a thing out of place or a speck of dust anywhere. Joseph Leander must have walked very light to live in this house without leaving tracks. A man less sensitive than Theo might have called him whipped.

"That guy's whipped," one of the EMTs said. His name was Vance McNally. He was fifty-one, short and muscular, and wore his hair slicked back with oil, just as he had in high school. Occasionally, in his capacity as an EMT, he saved lives, which was his rationalization for being a dolt the rest of the time.

"He just found his wife hanging in the dining room, Vance," Theo pronounced over the heads of the EMTs. He was six-foot-six, and even in his flannel shirt and sneakers he could loom large when he needed to assert some authority.

"She looks like Raggedy Ann," said Mike, the other EMT, who was in his early twenties and excited to be on his first suicide call.

"I heard she was Amish," Vance said.

"She's not Amish," Theo said.

"I didn't say she was Amish, I just said I heard that. I figured she wasn't Amish when I saw the blender in the kitchen. Amish don't believe in blenders, do they?"

"Mennonite," Mike said with as much authority as his junior status would afford.

"What's a Mennonite?" Vance asked.

"Amish with blenders."

"She wasn't Amish," Theo said.

"She looks Amish," Vance said.

"Well, her husband's not Amish," Mike said.

"How can you tell?" Vance said. "He has a beard."

"Zipper on his jacket," Mike said. "Amish don't have zippers."

Vance shook his head. "Mixed marriages. They never work."

"She wasn't Amish!" Theo shouted.

"Think what you want, Theo, there's a butter churn in the living room. I think that says it all."

Mike rubbed at a mark on the wall beneath Bess's feet where her black buckled shoes had scraped as she convulsed.

"Don't touch anything," Theo said.

"Why? She can't yell at us, she's dead. We wiped our feet on the way in," Vance said.

Mike stepped away from the wall. "Maybe she couldn't stand anything touching her floors. Hanging was the only way."

Not to be outdone by the detective work of his protégé, Vance said, "You know, the sphincters usually open up on a hanging victim—leave an awful mess. I'm wondering if she actually hanged herself."

"Shouldn't we call the police?" Mike said.

"I am the police," Theo said. He was Pine Cove's only constable, duly elected eight years ago and reelected every other year thereafter.

"No, I mean the real police," Mike said.

"I'll radio the sheriff," Theo said. "I don't think there's anything you can do here, guys. Would you mind calling Pastor Williams from the Presbyterian church to come over? I need to talk to Joseph and I need someone to stay with the girls."

"They were Presbyterians?" Vance seemed shocked. He had really put his heart into the Amish theory.

"Please call," Theo said. He left the EMTs and went out through the kitchen to his Volvo, where he switched the radio over to the frequency used by the San Junipero Sheriff's Department, then sat there staring at the mike. He was going to catch hell from Sheriff Burton for this.

"North Coast is yours, Theo. All yours," the sheriff had said. My deputies will pick up suspects, answer robbery calls, and let the Highway Patrol investigate traffic accidents on Highway 1, that's it. Otherwise, you keep them out of Pine Cove and your little secret stays secret." Theo was forty-one years old and he still felt as if he was hiding from the junior high vice principal, laying low. Things like this weren't supposed to happen in Pine Cove. Nothing happened in Pine Cove.

He took a quick hit from his Sneaky Pete smokeless pot pipe before keying the mike and calling in the deputies.

Joseph Leander sat on the edge of the bed. He'd changed out of his pajamas into a blue business suit, but his thinning hair was still sticking out in sleep horns on the side. He was thirty-five, sandy-haired, thin but working on a paunch that strained the buttons of his vest. Theo sat across from him on a chair, holding a notepad. They could hear the sheriff's deputies moving around downstairs.

"I can't believe she'd do this," Joseph said.

Theo reached over and squeezed the grieving husband's bicep. "I'm really sorry, Joe. She didn't say anything that would indicate she was thinking about doing something like this?"

Joseph shook his head without looking up. "She was getting better. Val had given her some pills and she seemed to be getting better."

"She was seeing Valerie Riordan?" Theo asked. Valerie was Pine Cove's only clinical psychiatrist. "Do you know what kind of pills?"

"Zoloft," Joseph said. "I think it's an antidepressant."

Theo wrote down the name of the drug on his notepad. "Then Bess was depressed?"

"No, she just had this cleaning thing. Everything had to be cleaned every day. She'd clean something, then go back five minutes later and clean it again. She was making life miserable for the girls and me. She'd make us take our shoes and socks off, then wash our feet in a basin before we came into the house. But she wasn't depressed."

Theo wrote down "crazy" on his notepad. "When was the last time Bess went to see Val?"

"Maybe six weeks ago. When she first got the pills. She really seemed to be doing better. She even left the dishes in the sink overnight once. I was proud of her."

"Where are her pills, Joseph?"

"Medicine cabinet." Joseph gestured to the bathroom.

Theo excused himself and went to the bathroom. The brown prescription bottle was the only thing in the medicine cabinet other than disinfectants and some Q-Tips. The bottle was about half-full. "I'm going to take these with me," Theo said, pocketing the pills. "The sheriff's deputies are going to ask you some of these same questions, Joseph. You just tell them what you told me, okay?

Joseph nodded. "I think I should be with the girls."

"Just a bit longer, okay? I'll send up the deputy in charge."

Theo heard a car start outside and went to the window to see an ambulance pulling away, the lights and siren off. Bess Leander's body riding off to the morgue. He turned back to Joseph. "Call me if you need anything. I'm going to go talk to Val Riordan."

Joseph stood up. "Theo, don't tell anyone that Bess was on antidepressants. She didn't want anyone to know. She was ashamed."

"I won't. Call me if you need me." Theo left the room. A sharply dressed plainclothes deputy met him at the bottom of the steps. Theo saw by the badge on his belt that he was a detective sergeant.

"You're Crowe. John Voss." He extended his hand and Theo shook it. "We're supposed to take it from here," Voss said. "What have you got?"

Theo was at once relieved and offended. Sheriff Burton was going to push him off the case without even talking to him. "No note," Theo said. "I called you guys ten minutes after I got the call. Joseph said she wasn't depressed, but she was on medication. He came down-stairs to have breakfast and found her."

"Did you look around?" Voss asked. "This place has been scoured. There isn't a smudge or a spot anywhere. It's like someone cleaned up the scene."

"She did that," Theo said. "She was a clean freak."

Voss scoffed. "She cleaned the house, then hung her-self? Please."

Theo shrugged. He really didn't like this cop stuff. "I'm going to go talk to her psychiatrist. I'll let you know what she says."

"Don't talk to anybody, Crowe. This is my investiga-tion."

Theo smiled. "Okay. But she hung herself and that's all there is. Don't make it into anything it's not. The fam-ily is in pretty bad shape."

"I'm a professional," Voss said, throwing it like an insult, implying that Theo was just dicking around in law enforcement, which, in a way, he was.

"Did you check out the Amish cult angle?" Theo asked, trying to keep a straight face. Maybe he shouldn't have gotten high today.

"What?"

"Right, you're the pro," Theo said. "I forgot." And he walked out of the house.

In the Volvo, Theo pulled the thin Pine Cove phone directory out of the glove compartment and was looking up Dr. Valerie Riordan's number when a call came in on the radio. Fight at the Head of the Slug Saloon. It was 8:30 A.M.

Mavis

It was rumored among the regulars at the Head of the Slug that under Mavis Sand's slack, wrinkled, liver-spotted skin lay the gleaming metal skeleton of a Terminator. Mavis first began augmenting her parts in the fifties, first out of vanity: breasts, eyelashes, hair. Later, as she aged and the concept of maintenance eluded her, she began having parts replaced as they failed, until almost half of her body weight was composed of stainless steel (hips, elbows, shoulders, finger joints, rods fused to vertebrae five through twelve), silicon wafers (hearing aids, pacemaker, insulin pump), advanced polymer resins (cataract replacement lenses, dentures), Kevlar fabric (abdominal wall reinforcement), titanium (knees, ankles), and pork (ventricular heart valve). In fact, if not for the pig valve, Mavis would have jumped classes directly from animal to mineral, without the traditional stop at vegetable taken by most. The more inventive drunks at the Slug (little more than vegetables themselves) swore that sometimes, between songs on the jukebox, one could hear tiny but powerful servomotors whirring Mavis around behind the bar. Mavis was careful never to crush a beer can or move a full keg in plain sight of the customers lest she feed the rumors and ruin her image of girlish vulnerability.

When Theo entered the Head of the Slug, he saw ex-scream-queen Molly Michon on the floor with her teeth locked into the calf of a gray-haired man who was screeching like a mashed cat. Mavis stood over them both, brandishing her Louisville Slugger, ready to belt one of them out of the park.

"Theo," Mavis shrilled, "you got ten seconds to get this wacko out of my bar before I brain her."

"No, Mavis." Theo raced forward and knocked Mavis's bat aside while reaching into his back pocket for his handcuffs. He pried Molly's hands from around the man's ankle and shackled them behind her back. The gray-haired man's screams hit a higher pitch.

Theo got down on the floor and spoke into Molly's ear. "Let go, Molly. You've got to let go of the man's leg."

An animal sound emanated from Molly's throat and bubbled out through blood and saliva.

Theo stroked her hair out of her face. "I can't fix the problem if you don't tell me what it is, Molly. I can't understand you with that guy's leg in your mouth."

"Stand back, Theo," Mavis said. "I'm going to brain her."

Theo waved Mavis away. The gray-haired man screamed even louder.

"Hey!" Theo shouted. "Pipe down. I'm trying to have a conversation here."

The gray-haired man lowered his volume.

"Molly, look at me."

Theo saw a blue eye look away from the leg and the bloodlust faded from it. He had her back. "That's right, Molly. It's me, Theo. Now what's the problem?"

She spit out the man's leg and turned to look at Theo. Mavis helped the man to a bar stool. "Get her out of here," Mavis said. "She's eighty-sixed. This time forever."

Theo kept his eyes locked on Molly's. "Are you okay?"

She nodded. Bloody drool was running down her chin. Theo grabbed a bar napkin and wiped it away, careful to keep his fingers away from her mouth.

"I'm going to help you up now and we're going to go outside and talk about this, okay?"

Molly nodded and Theo picked her up by the shoulders, set her on her feet, and steered her toward the door. He looked over his shoulder at the bitten man. "You okay? You need a doctor?"

"I didn't do anything to her. I've never seen that woman before in my life. I just stopped in for a drink."

Theo looked at Mavis for confirmation. "He hit on her," Mavis said. "But that's no excuse. A girl should appreciate the attention." She turned and batted her spiderlike false eyelashes at the bitten man. "I could show you some appreciation, sweetie."

The bitten man looked around in a panic. "No, I'm fine. No doctor. I'm just fine. My wife's waiting for me."

"As long as you're okay," Theo said. "And you don't want to press charges or anything?"

"No, just a misunderstanding. Soon as you get her out of here, I'll be heading out of town."

There was a collective sigh of disappointment from the regulars who had been placing side bets on who Mavis would hit with her bat.

"Thanks," Theo said. He shot Mavis a surreptitious wink and led Molly out to the street, excusing himself and his prisoner as they passed an old Black man who was coming through the door carrying a guitar case.

"I 'spose a man run outta sweet talk and liquor, he gots to go to mo' di-rect measures," the old Black man said to the bar with a dazzling grin. "Someone here lookin fo' a Bluesman?"

Molly Michon

Theo put Molly into the passenger side of the Volvo. She sat with her head down, her great mane of gray-streaked blonde hair hanging in her face. She wore an oversized green sweater, tights, and high-top sneakers, one red, one blue. She could have been thirty or fifty—and she told Theo a different age every time he picked her up.

Theo went around the car and climbed in. He said, "You know, Molly, when you bite a guy on the leg, you're right on the edge of 'a danger to others or yourself,' you know that?"

She nodded and sniffled. A tear dropped out of the mass of hair and spotted her sweater.

"Before I start driving, I need to know that you're calmed down. Do I need to put you in the backseat?"

"It wasn't a fit," Molly said. "I was defending myself. He wanted a piece of me." She lifted her head and turned to Theo, but her hair still covered her face.

"Are you taking your drugs?"

"Meds, they call them meds."

"Sorry," Theo said. "Are you taking your meds?"

She nodded.

"Wipe your hair out of your face, Molly, I can barely understand you."

"Handcuffs, whiz kid."

Theo almost slapped his forehead: idiot! He really needed to stop getting stoned on the job. He reached up and carefully brushed her hair away from her face. The expression he found there was one of bemusement.

"You don't have to be so careful. I don't bite."

Theo smiled. "Well, actually . . ."

"Oh fuck you. You going to take me to County?"

"Should I?"

"I'll just be back in seventy-two and the milk in my refrigerator will be spoiled."

"Then I'd better take you home."

He started the car and circled the block to head back to the Fly Rod Trailer Court. He would have taken a back way if he could, to save Molly some embarrassment, but the Fly Rod was right off Cypress, Pine Cove's main street. As they passed the bank, people getting out of their cars turned to stare. Molly made faces at them out the window.

"That doesn't help, Molly."

"Fuck 'em. Fans just want a piece of me. I can give 'em that. I've got my soul."

"Mighty generous of you."

"If you weren't a fan, I wouldn't let you do this."

"Well, I am. Huge fan." Actually, he'd never heard of her until the first time he was called to take her away from H.P.'s Cafe, where she had attacked the espresso machine because it wouldn't quit staring at her.

"No one understands. Everyone takes a piece of you, then there's nothing left for you. Even the meds take a piece of you. Do you have any idea what I'm talking about here?"

Theo looked at her. "I have such a mind-numbing fear of the future that the only way I can function at all is with equal amounts of denial and drugs."

"Jeez, Theo, you're really fucked up."

"Thanks."

"You can't go around saying crazy shit like that."

"I don't normally. It's been a tough day so far."

He turned into the Fly Rod Trailer Court: twenty run-down trailers perched on the bank of Santa Rosa Creek, which carried only a trickle of water after the long, dry summer. A grove of cypress trees hid the trailer park from the main street and the view of passing tourists. The chamber of commerce had made the owner of the park take down the sign at the entrance. The Fly Rod was a dirty little secret for Pine Cove, and they kept it well.

Theo stopped in front of Molly's trailer, a vintage fifties single-wide with small louvered windows and streaks of rust running from the roof. He got Molly out of the car and took off the handcuffs.

Theo said, "I'm going to see Val Riordan. You want me to have her call something in to the pharmacy for you?"

"No, I've got my meds. I don't like 'em, but I got 'em." She rubbed her wrists. "Why you going to see Val? You going nuts?"

"Probably, but this is business. You going to be okay now?"

"I have to study my lines."

"Right." Theo started to go, then turned. "Molly, what were you doing at the Slug at eight in the morning?"

"How should I know?"

"If the guy at the Slug had been a local, I'd be taking you to County right now, you know that?"

"I wasn't having a fit. He wanted a piece of me."

"Stay out of the Slug for a while. Stay home. Just groceries, okay?"

"You won't talk to the tabloids?"

He handed her a business card. "Next time someone tries to take a piece of you, call me. I always have the cell phone with me."

She pulled up her sweater and tucked the card into the waistband of her tights, then, still holding up her sweater, she turned and walked to her trailer with a slow sway. Thirty or fifty, under the sweater she still had a figure. Theo watched her walk, forgetting for a minute who she was. Without looking back, she said, "What if it's you, Theo? Who do I call then?"

Theo shook his head like a dog trying to clear water from its ears, then crawled into the Volvo and drove away. I've been alone too long, he thought.

two

The Sea Beast

The cooling pipes at the Diablo Canyon Nuclear Power Plant were all fashioned from the finest stainless steel. Before they were installed, they were x-rayed, ultrasounded, and pressure-tested to be sure that they could never break, and after being welded into place, the welds were also x-rayed and tested. The radioactive steam from the core left its heat in the pipes, which leached it off into a seawater cooling pond, where it was safely vented to the Pacific. But Diablo had been built on a breakneck schedule during the energy scare of the seventies. The welders worked double and triple shifts, driven by greed and cocaine, and the inspectors who ran the X-ray machines were on the same schedule. And they missed one. Not a major mistake. Just a tiny leak. Barely noticeable. A minuscule stream of harmless, low-level radiation wafted out with the tide and drifted over the continental shelf, dissipating as it went, until even the most sensitive instruments would have missed it. Yet the leak didn't go totally undetected.

In the deep trench off California, near a submerged volcano where the waters ran to seven hundred degrees Fahrenheit and black smokers spewed clouds of mineral soup, a creature was roused from a long slumber. Eyes the size of dinner platters winked out the sediment and sleep of years. It was instinct, sense, and memory: the Sea Beast's brain. It remembered eating the remains of a sunken Russian nuclear submarine: beefy little sailors tenderized by the pressure of the depths and spiced with piquant radioactive marinade. Memory woke the beast, and like a child lured from under the covers on a snowy morning by the smell of bacon frying, it flicked its great tail, broke free from the ocean floor, and began a slow ascent into the current of tasty treats. A current that ran along the shore of Pine Cove.

Mavis

Mavis tossed back a shot of Bushmills to take the edge off her frustration at not being able to whack anyone with her baseball bat. She wasn't really angry that Molly had bitten a customer. After all, he was a tourist and rated above the mice in the walls only because he carried cash. Maybe the fact that something had actually happened in the Slug would bring in a little business. People would come in to hear the story, and Mavis could stretch, speculate, and dramatize most stories into at least three drinks a tell.

Business had been slowing over the last couple of years. People didn't seem to want to bring their problems into a bar. Time was, on any given afternoon, you'd have three or four guys at the bar, pouring down beers as they poured out their hearts, so filled with self-loathing that they'd snap a vertebra to avoid catching their own reflection in the big mirror behind the bar. On a given evening, the stools would be full of people who whined and growled and bitched all night long, pausing only long enough to stagger to the bathroom or to sacrifice a quarter to the jukebox's extensive self-pity selection. Sadness sold a lot of alcohol, and it had been in short supply these last few years. Mavis blamed the booming economy, Val Riordan, and vegetables in the diet for the sadness shortage, and she fought the insidious invaders by running two-for-one happy hours with fatty meat snacks (The whole point of happy hour was to purge happiness, wasn't it?), but all her efforts only served to cut her profits in half. If Pine Cove could no longer produce sadness, she would import some, so she advertised for a Blues singer.

The old Black man wore sunglasses, a leather fedora, a tattered black wool suit that was too heavy for the weather, red suspenders over a Hawaiian shirt that sported topless hula girls, and creaky black-on-white wing tips. He set his guitar case on the bar and climbed onto a stool.

Mavis eyed him suspiciously and lit a Tarryton 100. She'd been taught as a girl not to trust Black people.

"Name your poison," she said.

He took off his fedora, revealing a gleaming brown baldness that shone like polished walnut. "You gots some wine?"

"Cheap-shit red or cheap-shit white?" Mavis cocked a hip, gears and machinery clicked.

"Them cheap-shit boys done expanded. Used to be jus' one flavor."

"Red or white?"

"Whatever sweetest, sweetness."

Mavis slammed a tumbler onto the bar and filled it with yellow liquid from an icy jug in the well. "That'll be three bucks."

The Black man reached out—thick sharp nails skating the bar surface, long fingers waving like tentacles, searching, the hand like a sea creature caught in a tidal wash—and missed the glass by four inches.

Mavis pushed the glass into his hand. "You blind?"

"No, it be dark in here."

"Take off your sunglasses, idjit."

"I can't do that, ma'am. Shades go with the trade."

"What trade? Don't you try to sell pencils in here. I don't tolerate beggars."

"I'm a Bluesman, ma'am. I hear ya'll lookin for one."

Mavis looked at the guitar case on the bar, at the Black man in shades, at the long fingernails of his right hand, the short nails and knobby gray calluses on the fingertips of his left, and she said, "I should have guessed. Do you have any experience?"

He laughed, a laugh that started deep down and shook his shoulders on the way up and chugged out of his throat like a steam engine leaving a tunnel. "Sweetness, I got me more experience than a busload o' hos. Ain't no dust settled a day on Catfish Jefferson since God done first dropped him on this big ol' ball o' dust. That's me, call me Catfish."

He shook hands like a sissy, Mavis thought, just let her have the tips of his fingers. She used to do that before she had her arthritic finger joints replaced. She didn't want any arthritic old Blues singer. "I'm going to need someone through Christmas. Can you stay that long or would your dust settle?"

"I 'spose I could slow down a bit. Too cold to go back East." He looked around the bar, trying to take in the dinge and smoke through his dark glasses, then turned back to her. "Yeah, I might be able to clear my schedule if"—and here he grinned and Mavis could see a gold tooth there with a musical note cut in it—"if the money is right," he said.

"You'll get room and board and a percentage of the bar. You bring 'em in, you'll make money."

He considered, scratched his cheek where white stubble sounded like a toothbrush against sandpaper, and said, "No, sweetness, you bring 'em in. Once they hear

Catfish play, they come back. Now what percentage did you have in mind?"

Mavis stroked her chin hair, pulled it straight to its full three inches. "I'll need to hear you play."

Catfish nodded. "I can play." He flipped the latches on his guitar case and pulled out a gleaming National steel body guitar. From his pocket he pulled a cutoff bottleneck and with a twist it fell onto the little finger of his left hand. He played a chord to test tune, pulled the bottleneck from the fifth to the ninth and danced it there, high and wailing.

Mavis could smell something like mildew, moss maybe, a change in humidity. She sniffed and looked around. She hadn't been able to smell anything for fifteen years.

Catfish grinned. "The Delta," he said.

He launched into a twelve-bar Blues, playing the bass line with his thumb, squealing the high notes with the slide, rocking back and forth on the bar stool, the light of the neon Coors sign behind the bar playing colors in the reflection of sunglasses and his bald head.

The daytime regulars looked up from their drinks, stopped lying for a second, and Slick McCall missed a straight-in eight-ball shot on the quarter table, which he almost never did.

And Catfish sang, starting high and haunting, going low and gritty.

"They's a mean ol' woman run a bar out on the Coast.
I'm telling you, they's a mean ol' woman run a bar out on
the Coast.
But when she gets you under the covers,
That ol' woman turn your buttered bread to toast."

And then he stopped.

"You're hired," Mavis said. She pulled the jug of

white cheap-shit out of the well and sloshed some into Catfish's glass. "On the house."

Just then the door opened and a blast of sunlight cut through the dinge and smoke and residual Blues and Vance McNally, the EMT, walked in and set his radio on the bar.

"Guess what?" he said to everyone and no one in particular. "That pilgrim woman hung herself."

A low mumble passed through the regulars. Catfish put his guitar in its case and picked up his wine. "Sho' 'nuff a sad day startin early in this little town. Sho' 'nuff."

"Sho' 'nuff," said Mavis with a cackle like a stainless-steel hyena.

Valerie Riordan

Depression has a mortality rate of fifteen percent. Fifteen percent of all patients with major depression will take their own lives. Statistics. Hard numbers in a very squishy science. Fifteen percent. Dead.

Val Riordan had been repeating the figures to herself since Theophilus Crowe had called, but it wasn't helping her feel any better about what Bess Leander had done. Val had never lost a patient before. And Bess Leander hadn't really been depressed, had she? Bess didn't fit into the fifteen percent.

Val went to the office in the back of her house and pulled Bess Leander's file, then went back to the living room to wait for Constable Crowe. At least it was the local guy, not the county sheriffs. And she could always fall back on patient confidentiality. Truth was, she had no idea why Bess Leander might have hung herself. She had only seen Bess once, and then for only half an hour. Val had made the diagnosis, written the scrip, and collected a check for the full hour session. Bess had called in twice, talked for a few minutes, and Val had sent her a bill for the time rounded to the next quarter hour.

Time was money. Val Riordan liked nice things.

The doorbell rang, Westminster chimes. Val crossed the living room to the marble foyer. A thin tall figure was refracted through the door's beveled glass panels: Theophilus Crowe. Val had never met him, but she knew of him. Three of his ex-girlfriends were her patients. She opened the door.

He was dressed in jeans, sneakers, and a gray shirt with black epaulets that might have been part of a uniform at one time. He was clean-shaven, with long sandy hair tied neatly into a ponytail. A good-looking guy in an Ichabod Crane sort of way. Val guessed he was stoned. His girlfriends had talked about his habits.

"Dr. Riordan," he said. "Theo Crowe." He offered his hand.

She shook hands. "Everyone calls me Val," she said. "Nice to meet you. Come in." She pointed to the living room.

"Nice to meet you too," Theo said, almost as an afterthought. "Sorry about the circumstances." He stood at the edge of the marble foyer, as if afraid to step on the white carpet.

She walked past him and sat down on the couch. "Please," she said, pointing to one of a set of Hepplewhite chairs. "Sit."

He sat. "I'm not exactly sure why I'm here, except that Joseph Leander doesn't seem to know why Bess did it."

"No note?" Val asked.

"No. Nothing. Joseph went downstairs for breakfast this morning and found her hanging in the dining room."

Val felt her stomach lurch. She had never really formed a mental picture of Bess Leander's death. It had been words on the phone until now. She looked away from Theo, looked around the room for something that would erase the picture.

"I'm sorry," Theo said. "This must be hard for you. I'm just wondering if there was anything that Bess might have said in therapy that would give a clue."

Fifteen percent, Val thought. She said, "Most suicides don't leave a note. By the time they have gone that far into depression, they aren't interested in what happens after their death. They just want the pain to end."

Theo nodded. "Then Bess was depressed? Joseph said that she appeared to be getting better."

Val cast around her training for an answer. She hadn't really diagnosed Bess Leander, she had just prescribed what she thought would make Bess feel better. She said, "Diagnosis in psychiatry isn't always that exact, Theo. Bess Leander was a complex case. Without compromising doctor-patient confidentiality, I can tell you that Bess suffered from a borderline case of OCD, obsessive compulsive disorder. I was treating her for that."

Theo pulled a prescription bottle out of his shirt pocket and looked at the label. "Zoloft. Isn't that an antidepressant? I only know because I used to date a woman who was on it."

Right, Val thought. Actually, you used to date at least three women who were on it. She said, "Zoloft is an SSRI like Prozac. It's prescribed for a number of conditions. With OCD the dosage is higher." That's it, get clinical. Baffle him with clinical bullshit.

Theo shook the bottle. "Could someone O.D. on it or something? I heard somewhere that people do crazy things sometimes on these drugs."

"That's not necessarily true. SSRIs like Zoloft are often prescribed to people with major depression. Fifteen percent of all depressed patients commit suicide." There, she said it. "Antidepressants are a tool, along with talk therapy, that psychiatrists use to help patients. Sometimes the tools don't work. As with any therapy, a third get better, a third get worse, and a third stay the same. Antidepressants aren't a panacea." But you treat them like they are, don't you, Val?

"But you said that Bess Leander had OCD, not depression."

"Constable, have you ever had a stomachache and a runny nose at the same time?"

"So you're saying she was depressed?"

"Yes, she was depressed, as well as having OCD."

"And it couldn't have been the drugs?"

"To be honest with you, I don't even know if she was taking the drug. Have you counted them?"

"Uh, no."

"Patients don't always take their medicine. We don't order blood level tests for SSRIs."

"Right," Theo said. "I guess we'll know when they do the autopsy."

Another horrendous picture flashed in Val's mind: Bess Leander on an autopsy table. The viscera of medicine had always been too much for her. She stood.

"I wish I could help you more, but to be honest, Bess Leander never gave me any indication that she was suicidal." At least that was true.

Theo took her cue and stood. "Well, thank you. I'm sorry to have bothered you. If you think of anything, you know, anything that I can tell Joseph that might make it easier on him . . ."

"I'm sorry. That's all I know." Fifteen percent. Fifteen percent. Fifteen percent.

She led him to the door.

He turned before leaving. "One more thing. Molly Michon is one of your patients, isn't she?"

"Yes. Actually, she's a county patient, but I agreed to treat her at a reduced rate because all the county facilities are so far away."

"You might want to check on her. She attacked a guy at the Head of the Slug this morning."

"Is she in County?"

"No, I took her home. She calmed down."

"Thank you, Constable. I'll call her."

"Well, then. I'll be going."

"Constable," she called after him. "Those pills you have—Zoloft isn't a recreational drug."

Theo stumbled on the steps, then composed himself. "Right, Doctor, I figured that out when I saw the body hanging in the dining room. I'll try not to eat the evidence."

"Good-bye," Val said. She closed the door behind him and burst into tears. Fifteen percent. She had fifteen hundred patients in Pine Cove on some form of antidepressant or another. Fifteen percent would be more than two hundred people dead. She couldn't do that. She wouldn't let another of her patients die because of her noninvolvement. If antidepressants wouldn't save them, then maybe she could.

 *three*

Theo

Theophilus Crowe wrote bad free-verse poetry and played a jimbai drum while sitting on a rock by the ocean. He could play sixteen chords on the guitar and knew five Bob Dylan songs all the way through, allowing for a dampening buzz any time he had to play a bar chord. He had tried his hand at painting, sculpture, and pottery and had even played a minor part in the Pine Cove Little Theater's revival of *Arsenic and Old Lace*. In all these endeavors, he had experienced a meteoric rise to mediocrity and quit before total embarrassment and self-loathing set in. Theo was cursed with an artist's soul but no talent. He possessed the angst and the inspiration, but not the means to create.

If there was any single thing at which Theo excelled, it was empathy. He always seemed to be able to understand someone's point of view, no matter how singular or farfetched, and in turn could convey it to others with a succinctness and clarity that he seldom found in expressing his own thoughts. He was a born mediator, a peacemaker, and it was this talent, after breaking up numerous fights at the Head of the Slug Saloon, that got Theo elected constable. That and heavy-handed endorsement of Sheriff John Burton.

Burton was a hard-line right-wing politico who could

spout law and order (accent on order) over brunch with the Rotarians, lunch with the NRA, and dinner with Mothers Against Drunk Drivers and wolf down dry banquet chicken like it was manna from the gods every time. He wore expensive suits, a gold Rolex, and drove a pearl-black Eldorado that shone like a starry night on wheels (rapt attention and copious coats of carnuba from the grunts in the county motor pool). He had been sheriff of San Junipero County for sixteen years, and in that time the crime rate had dropped steadily until it was the lowest, per capita, of any county in California. His endorsement of Theophilus Crowe, someone with no law enforcement experience, had come as more than somewhat of a surprise to the people of Pine Cove, especially since Theo's opponent was a retired Los Angeles policeman who'd put in a highly decorated five and twenty. What the people of Pine Cove did not know was that Sheriff Burton not only endorsed Theo, he had forced him to run in the first place.

Theophilus Crowe was a quiet man, and Sheriff John Burton had his reasons for not wanting to hear a peep out of the little North County burg of Pine Cove, so when Theo walked into his little two-room cabin, he wasn't surprised to see a red seven blinking on his answering machine. He punched the button and listened to Burton's assistant insisting that he call right away—seven times. Burton never called the cell phone.

Theo had come home to shower and ponder his meeting with Val Riordan. The fact that she had treated at least three of his ex-girlfriends bothered him. He wanted to try and figure out what the women had told her. Obviously, they'd mention that he got high occasionally. Well, more than occasionally. But like any man, it worried him that they might have said something about his sexual performance. For some reason, it didn't bother him nearly as much that Val Riordan think him a loser and a drug fiend as it did that she might think he was bad in the rack. He wanted to ponder the possibilities, think away the paranoia, but instead he dialed the sheriff's private number and was put right through.

"What in the hell is the matter with you, Crowe? You stoned?"

"No more than usual," Theo said. "What's the problem?"

"The problem is you removed evidence from a crime scene."

"I did?" Talking to the sheriff could drain all of Theo's energy instantly. He fell into a beanbag chair that expectorated Styrofoam beads from a failing seam with a sigh. "What evidence? What scene?"

"The pills, Crowe. The suicide's husband said you took the pills with you. I want them back at the scene in ten minutes. I want my men out of there in half an hour. The M.E. will do the autopsy this afternoon and this case will close by dinnertime, got it? Run-of-the-mill suicide. Obit page only. No news. You understand?"

"I was just checking on her condition with her psychiatrist. See if there were any indications she might be suicidal."

"Crowe, you must resist the urge to play investigator or pretend that you are a law enforcement officer. The woman hung herself. She was depressed and she ended it all. The husband wasn't cheating, there was no money motive, and Mommy and Daddy weren't fighting."

"They talked to the kids?"

"Of course they talked to the kids. They're detectives. They investigate things. Now get over there and get them out of North County. I'd send them over to get the pills from you, but I wouldn't want them to find your little victory garden, would *you*?"

"I'm leaving now," Theo said.

"This is the last I will hear of this," Burton said. He hung up.

Theo hung up the phone, closed his eyes, and turned into a human puddle in the beanbag chair.

Forty-one years old and he still lived like a college student. His books were stacked between bricks and boards, his bed pulled out of a sofa, his refrigerator was empty but for a slice of pizza going green, and the grounds around his cabin were overgrown with weeds and brambles. Behind the cabin, in the middle of a nest of blackberry vines, stood his victory garden: ten bushy marijuana plants, sticky with buds that smelled of skunk and spice. Not a day passed that he didn't want to plow them under and sterilize the ground they grew in. And not a day passed that he didn't work his way through the brambles and lovingly harvest the sticky green that would sustain his habit through the day.

The researchers said that marijuana was only psychologically addictive. Theo had read all the papers. They only mentioned the night sweats and mental spiders of withdrawal in passing, as if they were no more unpleasant than a tetanus shot. But Theo had tried to quit. He'd wrung out three sets of sheets in one night and paced the cabin looking for distraction until he thought his head might explode, only to give up and suck the piquant smoke from his Sneaky Pete so he could find sleep. The researchers obviously didn't get it, but Sheriff John Burton did. He understood Theo's weakness and held it over him like the proverbial sword. That Burton had his own Achilles' heel and more to lose from its discovery didn't seem to matter. Logically, Theo had him in a standoff. But emotionally, Burton had the upper hand. Theo was always the one to blink.

He snatched Sneaky Pete off his orange crate coffee table and headed out the door to return Bess Leander's pills to the scene of the crime.

Valerie

Dr. Valerie Riordan sat at her desk, looking at the icons of her life: a tiny digital stock ticker that she would surreptitiously glance down at during appointments; a gold Mont Blanc desk set, the pens jutting from the jade base like the antennae of a goldbug; a set of bookends fashioned in the likenesses of Freud and Jung, bracing leather-bound copies of *The Psychology of the Unconscious*, *The Diagnostic and Statistical Manual of Mental Disorders (DSM-IV)*, *The Interpretation of Dreams*, and *The Physician's Desk Reference*; and a plaster-cast bust of Hippocrates that dispensed Post-it notes from the base. Hippocrates, that wily Greek who turned medicine from magic to science. The author of the famous oath that Val had uttered twenty years ago on that sunny summer day in Ann Arbor when she graduated from med school: *"I will use treatment to help the sick according to my ability and judgment, but I will never use it to injure or wrong them. I will not give poison to anyone though asked to do so, nor will I suggest such a plan."*

The oath had seemed so silly, so antiquated then. What doctor, in their right mind, would give poison to a patient?

"But in purity and in holiness I will guard my life and my art."

It had seemed so obvious and easy then. Now she guarded her life and her art with a custom security system and a Glock 9 mm. stashed in the nightstand.

"I will not use the knife on sufferers from stone, but I will give place to such as are craftsmen therein."

She'd never had a problem with that part of the oath. She was loathe to use the knife. She'd gone into psychiatry because she couldn't handle the messy parts of medicine. Her father, a surgeon himself, had been only mildly disappointed. At least she was a doctor, of sorts. She'd done her internship and residency in a rehab center where movie stars and rock idols learned to be responsible by making their own beds, while Val distributed Valium like a flight attendant passing out peanuts. One wing of the Sunrise Center was druggies, the other eating disorders. She preferred the eating disorders. "You haven't lived until you've force-fed minestrone to a supermodel through a tube," she told her father.

"Into whatsoever houses I enter, I will do so to help the sick, keeping myself free from all intentional wrongdoing and harm, especially from fornication with woman or man, bond or free."

Well, abstinence from fornication hadn't been a problem, had it? She hadn't had sex since Richard left five years ago. Richard had given her the bust of Hippocrates as a joke, he said, but she'd put it on her desk just the same. She'd given him a statue of Blind Justice wearing a garter belt and fishnets the year before to display at his law office. He'd brought her here to this little village, passing up offers from corporate law firms to follow his dream of being a country lawyer whose daily docket would include disagreements over pig paternity or the odd pension dispute. He wanted to be Atticus Finch, Pudd'nhead Wilson, a Jimmy Stewart or Henry Fonda character who was paid in fresh-baked bread and baskets of avocados. Well, he'd gotten that part; Val's practice had supported them for most of their marriage. She'd be paying him alimony now if they'd actually divorced.

Country lawyer indeed. He left her to go to Sacramento to lobby the California Coastal Commission for a consortium of golf course developers. His job was to convince the commission that sea otters and elephant seals would enjoy nothing better than to watch Japanese businessmen slice Titleists into the Pacific and that what nature needed was one long fairway from Santa Barbara to San Francisco (maybe sand traps at the Pismo and Carmel dunes). He carried a pocket watch, for Christ's sake, a gold chain with a jade fob carved into the shape of an endangered brown pelican. He played his front-porch, rocking-chair-wise, country lawyer against their Botany 500 sophistication and pulled down over two hundred grand a year in the bargain. He lived with one of his clerks, an earnest doe-eyed Stanfordite with surfer girl hair and a figure that mocked gravity. Richard had introduced Val to the girl (Ashley, or Brie, or Jordan) and it had been oh-so-adult and oh-so-gracious and later, when Val called Richard to clear up a tax matter, she asked, "So how'd you screen the candidates, Richard? First one to suck-start your Lexus?"

"Maybe we should start thinking about making our separation official," Richard had said.

Val had hung up on him. If she couldn't have a happy marriage, she'd have everything else. Everything. And so had begun her revolving door policy of hustling appointments, prescribing the appropriate meds, and shopping for clothes and antiques.

Hippocrates glowered at her from the desk.

"I didn't intentionally do harm," Val said. "Not intentionally, you old buggerer. Fifteen percent of all depressives commit suicide, treated or not."

"Whatsoever in the course of practice I see or hear (or even outside my practice in social intercourse) that ought never to be published abroad, I will not divulge, but consider such things to be holy secrets."

"Holy secrets or do no harm?" Val asked, envisioning the hanging body of Bess Leander with a shudder. "Which is it?" Hippocrates sat on his Post-its, saying nothing. Was Bess Leander's death her fault? If she had talked to Bess instead of put her on antidepressants, would that have saved her? It was possible, and it was also possible that if she kept to her policy of a "pill for every problem," someone else was going to die. She couldn't risk it. If using talk therapy instead of drugs could save one life, it was worth a try.

Val grabbed the phone and hit the speed dial button that connected her to the town's only pharmacy, Pine Cove Drug and Gift.

One of the clerks answered. Val asked to speak to Winston Krauss, the pharmacist. Winston was one of her patients. He was fifty-three, unmarried, and eighty pounds overweight. His holy secret, which he shared with Val during a session, was that he had an unnatural sexual fascination with marine mammals, dolphins in particular. He'd confessed that he'd never been able to watch "Flipper" without getting an erection and that he'd watched so many Jacques Cousteau specials that a French accent made him break into a sweat. He kept an anatomically correct inflatable porpoise, which he violated nightly in his bathtub. Val had cured him of wearing a scuba mask and snorkel around the house, so gradually the red gasket ring around his face had cleared up, but he still did the dolphin nightly and confessed it to her once a month.

"Winston, Val Riordan here. I need a favor."

"Sure, Dr. Val, you need me to deliver something to Molly? I heard she went off in the Slug this morning." Gossip surpassed the speed of light in Pine Cove.

"No, Winston, you know that company that carries all the look-alike placebos? We used them in college. I need you to order look-alikes for all the antidepressants I prescribe: Prozac, Zoloft, Serzone, Effexor, the whole bunch, all the dosages. Order in quantity."

"I don't get it, Val, what for?"

Val cleared her throat. "I want you to fill all of my prescriptions with the placebos."

"You're kidding."

"I'm not kidding, Winston. As of today, I don't want a single one of my patients getting the real thing. Not one."

"Are you doing some sort of experiment? Control group or something?"

"Something like that."

"And you want me to charge them the normal price?"

"Of course. Our usual arrangement." Val got a twenty percent kickback from the pharmacy. She was going to be working a lot harder, she deserved to get paid.

Winston paused. She could hear him going through the glass door into the back of the pharmacy. Finally he said, "I can't do that, Val. That's unethical. I could lose my license, go to jail."

Val had really hoped it wouldn't come to this. "Winston, you'll do it. You'll do it or the Pine Cove *Gazette* will run a front-page story about you being a fish-fucker."

"That's illegal. You can't divulge something I told you in therapy."

"Quit telling me what's illegal, Winston. I'm married to a lawyer."

"I'd really rather not do this, Val. Can't you send them down to the Thrifty Mart in San Junipero? I could say that I can't get the pills anymore."

"That wouldn't work, would it, Winston? The people at the Thrifty Mart don't have your little problem."

"You're going to have some withdrawal reactions. How are you going to explain that?"

"Let me worry about that. I'm quadrupling my sessions. I want to see these people get better, not mask their problems."

"This is about Bess Leander's suicide, isn't it?"

"I'm not going to lose another one, Winston."

"Antidepressants don't increase the incidence of suicide or violence. Eli Lilly proved that in court."

"Yes and O.J. walked. Court is one thing, Winston, the reality of losing a patient is another. I'm taking charge of my practice. Now order the pills. I'm sure the profit margin is going to be quite a bit higher on sugar pills than it is on Prozac."

"I could go to the Florida Keys. There's a place down there where they let you swim with bottlenose dolphins."

"You can't go, Winston. You can't miss your therapy sessions. I want to see you at least once a week."

"You bitch."

"I'm trying to do the right thing. What day is good for you?"

"I'll call you back."

"Don't push me, Winston."

"I have to make this order," he said. Then, after a second, he said, "Dr. Val?"

"What?"

"Do I have to go off the Serzone?"

"We'll talk about it in therapy." She hung up and pulled a Post-it out of Hippocrates' chest.

"Now if I keep this oath, and break it not, may I enjoy honor, in my life and art, among all men for all time; but if I transgress and forswear myself, may the opposite befall me."

Does that mean dishonor for all time? she wondered. I'm just trying to do the right thing here. Finally.

She made a note to call Winston back and schedule his appointments.

four

Estelle Boyet

As September's promise wound down, a strange unrest came over the people of Pine Cove, due in no small part to the fact that many of them were going into withdrawal from their medications. It didn't happen all at once—the streets were not full of middle-class junkies rocking and sweating and begging for a fix—but slowly as the autumn days became shorter. And as far as they knew (because Val Riordan had called every one of them), they were experiencing the onset of a mild seasonal syndrome, sort of like spring fever. Call it autumn malaise.

The nature of the medications kept the symptoms spread out over the next few weeks. Prozac and some of the older antidepressants took almost a month to leave the system, so those people slipped into the fray more slowly than those on Zoloft or Paxil or Wellbutrin, which was flushed from the system in only a day or two, leaving the deprived with symptoms resembling a low-grade flu, then a scattered disorientation akin to a temporary case of attention deficit disorder, and, in some, a rebound of depression that dropped on them like a smoky curtain.

One of the first to feel the effects was Estelle Boyet, a local artist, successful and semifamous for her seascapes and idealized paintings of Pine Cove shore life. Her prescription had run out a day before Dr. Val had replaced the supply with sugar pills, so she was already in the midst of withdrawal when she took the first dose of the placebo.

Estelle was sixty, a stout, vital woman who wore brightly colored caftans and let her long gray hair fly around her shoulders as she moved through life with an energy and determination that inspired envy from women half her age. For thirty years she had been a teacher in the decaying and increasingly dangerous Los Angeles Unified School District, teaching eighth graders the difference between acrylics and oils, a brush and a pallet knife, Dali and Degas, and using her job and her marriage as a justification for never producing any art herself.

She had married right out of art school: Joe Boyet, a promising young businessman, the only man she had ever loved and only the third she had ever slept with. When Joe had died eight years ago, she had nearly lost her mind. She tried to throw herself into her teaching, hoping that by inspiring the children she might find some reason to go on herself. In the face of the escalating violence in her school, she resigned herself to wearing a bulletproof vest under her artist smocks and even brought in some paintball guns to try to gain the pupils' interest, but the latter only backfired into several incidents of drive-by abstract expressionism, and soon she received death threats for not allowing students to fashion crack pipes in ceramics class. Her students—children living in a hyperadult world where playground disputes were settled with 9 mms—eventually drove her out of teaching. Estelle lost her last reason to go on. The school psychologist referred her to a psychiatrist, who put her on antidepressants and recommended immediate retirement and relocation.

Estelle moved to Pine Cove, where she began to paint and where she fell under the wing of Dr. Valerie Riordan. No wonder then that Estelle's painting had taken a dark turn over the last few weeks. She painted the ocean. Every day. Waves and spray, rocks and serpentine strands of kelp on the beach, otters and seals and pelicans and gulls. Her canvases sold in the local galleries as fast as she could paint them. But lately the inner light at the heart of her waves, titanium white and aquamarine, had taken on a dark shadow. Every beach scene spoke of desolation and dead fish. She dreamed of leviathan shadows stalking her under the waves and she woke shivering and afraid. It was getting more difficult to get her paints and easel to the shore each day. The open ocean and the blank canvas were just too frightening.

Joe is gone, she thought. I have no career and no friends and I produce nothing but kitschy seascapes as flat and soulless as a velvet Elvis. I'm afraid of everything.

Val Riordan had called her, insisting that she come to a group therapy session for widows, but Estelle had said no. Instead, one evening, after finishing a tormented painting of a beached dolphin, she left her brushes to harden with acrylic and headed downtown—anywhere where she didn't have to look at this shit she'd been calling art. She ended up at the Head of the Slug Saloon—the first bar she'd set foot in since college.

The Slug was full of Blues and smoke and people chasing shots and running from sadness. If they'd been dogs, they would have all been in the yard eating grass and trying to yak up whatever was making them feel so lousy. Not a bone gnawed, not a ball chased—all tails went unwagged. Oh, life is a fast cat, a short leash, a flea in that place where you just can't scratch. It was dog sad in there, and Catfish Jefferson was the designated howler. The moon was in his eye and he was singing up the sum of human suffering in A-minor, while he worked that bottleneck slide on the National guitar until it sounded like a slow wind through heartstrings. He was grinning.

Of the hundred or so people in the Slug, half were

experiencing some sort of withdrawal from their medications. There was a self-pity contingent at the bar, staring into their drinks and rocking back and forth to the Delta rhythms. At the tables, the more social of the depressed were whining and slurring their problems into each other's ears and occasionally trading hugs or curses. Over by the pool table stood the agitated and the aggressive, the people looking for someone to blame. These were mostly men, and Theophilus Crowe was keeping an eye on them from his spot at the bar.

Since the death of Bess Leander, there had been a fight in the Slug almost every night. In addition, there were more pukers, more screamers, more criers, and more unwanted advances stifled with slaps. Theo had been very busy. So had Mavis Sand. Mavis was happy about it.

Estelle came through the doors in her paint-spattered overalls and Shetland sweater, her hair pulled back in a long gray braid. Just inside, she paused as the music and the smoke washed over her. Some Mexican laborers were standing there in a group, drinking Budweisers, and one of them whistled at her.

"I'm an old lady," Estelle said. "Shame on you." She pushed her way through the crowd to the bar and ordered a white wine. Mavis served it in a plastic beer cup. (She was serving everything in plastic lately. Evidently, the Blues made people want to break glass—on each other.)

"Busy?" Estelle said, although she had nothing to compare it to.

"The Blues sure packs 'em in," Mavis said.

"I don't much care for the Blues," said Estelle. "I enjoy Classical music."

"Three bucks," said Mavis. She took Estelle's money and moved to the other end of the bar.

Estelle felt as if she'd been slapped in the face.

"Don't mind Mavis," a man's voice said. "She's always cranky."

Estelle looked up, caught a shirt button, then looked up farther to find Theo's smile. She had never met the constable, but she knew who he was.

"I don't even know why I came in here. I'm not a drinker."

"Something going around," Theo said. "I think maybe we're going to have a stormy winter or something. People are coming out of the woodwork. "

They exchanged introductions and Theo complimented Estelle on her paintings, which he'd seen in the local galleries. Estelle dismissed the compliment.

"This seems like a strange place to find the constable," Estelle said.

Theo showed her the cell phone on his belt. "Base of operations," he said. "Most of the trouble has been starting in here anyway. If I'm here already, I can stop it before it escalates."

"Very conscientious of you."

"No, I'm just lazy," Theo said. "And tired. In the last three weeks I've been called to five domestic disputes, ten fights, two people who barricaded themselves in the bathroom and threatened suicide, a guy who was going house to house knocking the heads off garden gnomes with a sledgehammer, and a woman who tried to take her husband's eye out with a spoon."

"Oh my. Sounds like one day in the life of an L.A. cop."

"This isn't L.A.," Theo said. "I don't mean to complain, but I'm not really prepared for a crime wave."

"And there's nowhere left to run," Estelle said.

"Pardon?"

"People come here to run away from conflict, don't you think? Come to a small town to get out of the violence and the competition in the city. If you can't handle it here, there's nowhere else to go. You might as well give up."

"Well, that's a little cynical. I thought artists were supposed to be idealists."

"Scratch a cynic and you'll find a disappointed romantic," Estelle said.

"That's you?" Theo asked. "A disappointed romantic?"

"The only man I ever loved died."

"I'm sorry," Theo said.

"Me too." She drained her cup of wine.

"Easy on that, Estelle. It doesn't help."

"I'm not a drinker. I just had to get out of the house."

There was some shouting over by the pool table. "My presence is required," Theo said. "Excuse me." He made his way through the crowd to where two men were squaring off to fight.

Estelle signaled Mavis for a refill and turned to watch Theo try to make peace. Catfish Jefferson sang a sad song about a mean old woman doing him wrong. That's me, Estelle thought. A mean old worthless woman.

Self-medication was working by midnight. Most of the customers at the Slug had given in and started clapping and wailing along with Catfish's Blues. Quite a few had given up and gone home. By closing time, there were only five people left in the Slug and Mavis was cackling over a drawer full of money. Catfish Jefferson put down his National steel guitar and picked up the two-gallon pickle jar that held his tips. Dollar bills spilled over the top, change skated in the bottom, and here and there in the middle fives and tens struggled for air. There was even a twenty down there, and Catfish dug in after it like a kid going for a Cracker Jack prize. He carried the jar to the bar and plopped down next to Estelle, who was gloriously, eloquently crocked.

"Hey, baby," Catfish said. "You like the Blues?"

Estelle searched the air for the source of the question,

as if it might have come from a moth spiraling around one of the lights behind the bar. Her gaze finally settled on the Bluesman and she said, "You're very good. I was going to leave, but I liked the music."

"Well, you done stayed now," Catfish said. "Look at this." He shook the money jar. "I got me upward o' two hundred dollar here, and that mean old woman owe me least that much too. What you say we take a pint and my guitar and go down to the beach, have us a party?"

"I'd better get home," Estelle said. "I have to paint in the morning."

"You a painter? I never knowed me a painter. What you say we go down to the beach and watch us a sunrise?"

"Wrong coast," Estelle said. "The sun comes up over the mountains."

Catfish laughed. "See, you done saved me a heap of waiting already. Let's you and me go down to the beach."

"No, I can't."

"It 'cause I'm Black, ain't it?"

"No."

" 'Cause I'm old, right?"

"No."

" 'Cause I'm bald. You don't like old bald men, right?"

"No," Estelle said.

" 'Cause I'm a musician. You heard we irresponsible?"

"No."

" 'Cause I'm hung like a bull, right?"

"No!" Estelle said.

Catfish laughed again. "Well, you wouldn't mind spreadin that one around town just the same, would you?"

"How would I know how you're hung?"

"Well," Catfish said, pausing and grinning, "you could go to the beach with me."

"You are a nasty and persistent old man, aren't you, Mr. Jefferson?" Estelle asked.

Catfish bowed his shining head, "I truly am, miss. I truly am nasty and persistent. And I am too old to be trouble. I admits it." He held out a long, thin hand. "Let's have us a party on the beach."

Estelle felt like she'd just been bamboozled by the devil. Something smooth and vibrant under that gritty old down-home shuck. Was this the dark shadow her paintings kept finding in the surf?

She took his hand. "Let's go to the beach."

"Ha!" Catfish said.

Mavis pulled a Louisville Slugger from behind the bar and held it out to Estelle. "Here, you wanna borrow this?"

They found a niche in the rocks that sheltered them from the wind. Catfish dumped sand from his wing tips and shook his socks out before laying them out to dry.

"That was a sneaky old wave."

"I told you to take off your shoes," Estelle said. She was more amused than she felt she had a right to be. A few sips from Catfish's pint had kept the cheap white wine from going sour in her stomach. She was warm, despite the chill wind. Catfish, on the other hand, looked miserable.

"Never did like the ocean much," Catfish said. "Too many sneaky things down there. Give a man the creeps, that's what it does."

"If you don't like the ocean, then why did you ask me to come to the beach?"

"The tall man said you like to paint pictures of the beach."

"Lately, the ocean's been giving me a bit of the creeps too. My paintings have gone dark."

Catfish wiped sand from between his toes with a long finger. "You think you can paint the Blues?"

"You ever seen Van Gogh?"

Catfish looked out to sea. A three-quarter moon was pooling like mercury out there. "Van Gogh . . . Van Gogh . . . fiddle player outta St. Louis?"

"That's him," Estelle said.

Catfish snatched the pint out of her hand and grinned. "Girl, you drink a man's liquor and lie to him too. I know who Vincent Van Gogh is."

Estelle couldn't remember the last time she'd been called a girl, but she was pretty sure she hadn't liked hearing it as much as she did now. She said, "Who's lying now? Girl?"

"You know, under that big sweater and them overalls, they might be a girl. Then again, I could be wrong."

"You'll never know."

"I won't? Now that is some sad stuff there." He picked up his guitar, which had been leaning on a rock, and began playing softly, using the surf as a backbeat. He sang about wet shoes, running low on liquor, and a wind that chilled right to the bone. Estelle closed her eyes and swayed to the music. She realized that this was the first time she'd felt good in weeks.

He stopped abruptly. "I'll be damned. Look at that."

Estelle opened her eyes and looked toward the waterline where Catfish was pointing. Some fish had run up on the beach and were flopping around in the sand.

"You ever see anything like that?"

Estelle shook her head. More fish were coming out of the surf. Beyond the breakers, the water was boiling with fish jumping and thrashing. A wave rose up as if being pushed from underneath. "There's something moving out there."

Catfish picked up his shoes. "We gots to go."

Estelle didn't even think of protesting. "Yes. Now."

She thought about the huge shadows that kept appearing under the waves in her paintings. She grabbed Catfish's shoes, jumped off the rock, and started down the beach to the stairs that led up to a bluff where Catfish's station wagon waited. "Come on."

"I'm comin'." Catfish spidered down the rock and stepped after her.

At the car, both of them winded and leaning on the fenders, Catfish was digging in his pocket for the keys when they heard the roar. The roar of a thousand phlegmy lions—equal amounts of wetness, fury, and volume. Estelle felt her ribs vibrate with the noise.

"Jesus! What was that?"

"Get in the car, girl."

Estelle climbed into the station wagon. Catfish was already fumbling the key into the ignition. The car fired up and he threw it into drive, kicking up gravel as he pulled away.

"Wait, your shoes are on the roof."

"He can have them," Catfish said. "They better than the ones he ate last time."

"He? What the hell was that? You know what that was?"

"I'll tell you soon as I'm done havin this heart attack."

five

The Sea Beast

The great Sea Beast paused in his pursuit of the delicious radioactive aroma and sent a subsonic message out to a gray whale passing several miles ahead of him. Roughly translated, it said, "Hey, baby, how's about you and I eat a few plankton and do the wild thing."

The gray whale continued her relentless swim south and replied with a subsonic thrum that translated, "I know who you are. Stay away from me."

The Sea Beast swam on. During his journey he had eaten a basking shark, a few dolphins, and several hundred tuna. His focus had changed from food to sex. As he approached the California coast, the radioactive scent began to diminish to almost nothing. The leak at the power plant had been discovered and fixed. He found himself less than a mile offshore with a belly full of shark—and no memory of why he'd left his volcanic nest. But there was a buzz reaching his predator's senses from shore, the listless resolve of prey that has given up: depression. Warm-blooded food, dolphins, and whales sent off the same signal sometimes. A large school of food was just asking to be eaten, right near the edge of the sea. He stopped out past the surf line and came to the surface in the middle of a kelp bed, his massive head breaking though strands of kelp like a zombie pickup truck breaking sod as it rises from the grave.

Then he heard it. A hated sound. The sound of an enemy. It had been half a century since the Sea Beast had left the water, and land was not his natural domain, but his instinct to attack overwhelmed his sense of self-preservation. He threw back his head, shaking the great purple gills that stood out on his neck like trees, and blew the water from his vestigial lungs. Breath burned down his cavernous throat for the first time in fifty years and came out in a horrendous roar of pain and anger. Three of the protective ocular membranes slid back from his eyes like electric car windows. allowing him to see in the bitter air. He thrashed his tail, pumped his great webbed feet, and torpedoed toward the shore.

Gabe

It had been almost ten years since Gabe Fenton had dissected a dog, but now, at three o'clock in the morning, he was thinking seriously about taking a scalpel to Skinner, his three-year-old Labrador retriever, who was deep in the throes of a psychotic barking fit. Skinner had been banished to the porch that afternoon, after he had taken a roll in a dead seagull and refused to go into the surf or get near the hose to be washed off. To Skinner, dead bird was the smell of romance.

Gabe crawled out of bed and padded to the door in his boxers, scooping up a hiking boot along the way. He was a biologist, held a Ph.D. in animal behavior from Stanford, so it was with great academic credibility that he opened the door and winged the boot at his dog, following it with the behavior-reinforcing command of: "Skinner, shut the fuck up!"

Skinner paused in his barking fit long enough to duck under the flying L. L. Bean, then, true to his breeding, retrieved it from the washbasin that he used as a water dish and brought it back to the doorway where Gabe stood. Skinner set the soggy boot at the biologist's feet. Gabe closed the door in Skinner's face.

Jealous, Skinner thought. No wonder he can't get any females, smelling like fabric softener and soap. The Food Guy wouldn't be so cranky if he'd get out and sniff some butts. (Skinner always thought of Gabe as "the Food Guy.") Then, after a quick sniff to confirm that he was, indeed, the Don Juan of all dogs, Skinner resumed his barking fit. Doesn't he get it, Skinner thought, there's something dangerous coming. Danger, Food Guy, danger!

Inside, Gabe Fenton glanced at the computer screen in his living room as he returned to bed. A thousand tiny green dots were working their way, en masse, across the map of the Pine Cove area. He stopped and rubbed his eyes. It wasn't possible.

Gabe went to the computer and typed in a command. The map of the area reappeared in wider scale. Still, the dots were all moving in a line. He zoomed the map to only a few square miles, the dots were still on the move. Each green dot on the map represented a rat that Gabe had live-trapped, injected with a microchip, and released into the wild. Their location was tracked and plotted by satellite. Every rat in a ten-square-mile area was moving east, away from the coast. Rats did not behave that way.

Gabe ran the data backward, looking at the rodents' movements over the last few hours. The exodus had started abruptly, only two hours ago, and already most of the rats had moved over a mile inland. They were running full-tilt and going far beyond their normal range. Rats are sprinters, not long-distance runners. Something was up.

Gabe hit a key and a tiny green number appeared next to each of the dots. Each chip was unique, and each rat could be identified like airplanes on the screen of an air traffic controller. Rat 363 hadn't moved outside of a two-meter range for five days. Gabe had assumed that she had either given birth or was ill. Now 363 was half a mile from her normal territory.

Anomalies are both the bane and bread of researchers. Gabe was excited by the data, but at the same time it made him anxious. An anomaly like this could lead to a discovery, or make him look like a total fool. He cross-checked the data three different ways, then tapped into the weather station on the roof. Nothing was happening in the way of weather, all changes in barometric pressure, humidity, wind, and temperature were well within normal ranges. He looked out the window: a low fog was settling on the shore, totally normal. He could just make out the lighthouse a hundred yards away. It had been shut down for twenty years, used only as a weather station and as a base for biological research.

He grabbed a blanket off of his bed and wrapped it around his shoulders against the chill, then returned to his desk. The green dots were still moving. He dialed the number for JPL in Pasadena. Skinner was still barking outside.

"Skinner, shut the fuck up!" Gabe shouted just as the automated answering service put him through to the seismology lab. A woman answered. She sounded young, probably an intern. "Excuse me?" she said.

"Sorry, I was yelling at my dog. Yes, hello, this is Dr. Gabe Fenton at the research station in Pine Cove, just wondering if you have any seismic activity in my area."

"Pine Cove? Can I get a longitude and latitude?"

Gabe gave it to her. "I think I'm looking for something offshore."

"Nothing. Minor tremor centered at Parkfield yesterday at 9 A.M. Point zero-five-three. You wouldn't even be able to feel it. Have you picked something up on your instruments?"

"I don't have seismographic instruments. That's why I called you. This is a biological research and weather station."

"I'm sorry, Doctor, I didn't know. I'm new here. Did you feel something?"

"No. My rats are moving." As soon as he said it, he wished he hadn't.

"Pardon me?"

"Never mind, I was just checking. I'm having some anomalous behavior in some specimens. If you pick up anything in the next few days, could you call me?" He gave her his number.

"You think your rats are predicting an earthquake, Doctor?"

"I didn't say that."

"You should know that there's no concrete data on animals predicting seismic activity."

"I know that, but I'm trying to eliminate all the possibilities."

"Did it occur to you that your dog might be scaring them?"

"I'll factor that in," Gabe said. "Thank you for your time." He hung up, feeling stupid.

Nothing seismic or meteorological, and a call to the highway patrol confirmed that there were no chemical spills or fires. He had to confirm the data. Perhaps something was wrong with the satellite signal. The only way to find out was to take out his portable antenna and track the rats in the field. He dressed quickly and headed out to his truck.

"Skinner, you want to go for a ride?"

Skinner wagged his tail and made a beeline for the truck. About time, he thought. You need to get away from the shore, Food Guy, right now.

Inside the house, ten green dots were moving away from the others toward the shore.

The Sea Beast

The Sea Beast crawled up the beach, roaring as his legs took the full weight of his body and the undertow sucked at his haunches. The urgency of killing his enemy had diminished now and hunger was upon him in response to the effort of moving out of the ocean. An organ at the base of his brain that had disappeared from other species when man's only living ancestors were tree shrews produced an electric signal to call food. There were many prey here, that same organ sensed.

The Sea Beast came to the fifty-foot cliff that bordered the beach, reared back on his tail, and pulled himself up with his forelegs. He was a hundred feet long, nose to tail, and stood twenty-five feet tall with his broad neck extended to its full height. His rear feet were wide and webbed, his front talonlike, with a thumb that opposed three curved claws for grasping and killing prey.

On the dry grass above the beach, some of the prey he had called already waited. Raccoons, ground squirrels, a few skunks, a fox, and two cats cavorted on the grass— some copulated, others dug at fleas with blissful abandon, others just rolled on their backs as if overcome by a fit of joy. The Sea Beast swept them into his great maw with a flick of his tongue, crunching a few bones on the way down, but swallowing most whole. He belched and savored the skunky bouquet, his jaws smacking together like two wet mattresses, and a flash of neon color ran across his flanks with the pleasure.

He moved over the bluff, across the Coast Highway, and into the sleeping town. The streets were deserted, lights off in all the businesses on Cypress Street. A low fog splashed against the pseudo-Tudor half-timbered buildings and formed green coronas around the streetlights. Above it all, the red Texaco sign shone like a beacon.

ow Smiley, he my friend from way back—my part-
ee. So I says I will get the Blues to jump on him,
e got to promise not to get mad how I do it. So he
kay, and I say okay, and I sets to sic the Blues on
o we can go to Chicago and Dallas and makes us
records and get us some Cadillacs and so on like
boys Muddy Waters and John Lee Hooker and

iley, he had him a wife name of Ida May, sweet
hing. He keep her up there in Clarksville. And he
s sayin how he don't have to worry 'bout Ida May
he on the road cause she love him true and only.
e day I tell Smiley they's a man down Baton Rouge
m a prime Martin guitar he gonna sell for ten dol-
nd would Smiley go get it for me cause I got me a
f the runs and can't take the train ride.
Smiley ain't out of town half a day before I takes
ne liquor and flowers and make my visit on little
ay. She's a young thing, ain't much for drinkin li-
ut once I tells her that ol' Smiley done got hisself
over by a train, she takes to drinkin like a natural
ween the screamin and cryin and all, and I had my
lf some tears too, he being my partner and all, God
s soul). And before you know it, I'm givin' Ida
me good lovin to comfort her in her time of grief

you know when Smiley get back, he don't say a
out my sleepin with Ida May. He say he sorry he
d the man with the guitar, gives me my ten dol-
' say he got to go home 'cause Ida May so happy
him she been doing him special all day. I say,
she done me special too," and he say that okay,
g sad and me being his best friend. That boy was
to the Blues, and they just wouldn't stick to him.
borrowed a Model T Ford, drove over to Smiley's,
e run over his dog, who was tied up in the yard.

The Sea Beast changed the color of his skin to the same smoky gray as the fog and moved down the center of the street looking like a serpentine cloud. He followed a low rumbling sound coming from under the red beacon, broke out of the fog, and there he saw her.

She purred, taunting and teasing him from the front of the deserted Texaco station. That come-hither rumble. That low, sexy growl. Those silver flanks reflecting fog and the red Texaco sign called to him, begged him to mount her. The Sea Beast flashed a rainbow of color down his sides to display his magnificent maleness. He fanned the gill trees on his neck, sending bands of color and light into their branches.

The Sea Beast sent her a signal, which roughly translated into: "Hey, baby, haven't seen you around before." She sat there, purring, playing coy, but he knew she wanted him. She had short black legs, a stumpy tail, and smelled as if she may have recently eaten a trawler, but those magnificent silver flanks were too much to resist.

The Sea Beast turned himself silver as well, to make her feel a little more comfortable, then reared up on his hind legs and displayed his aroused member. No response, just that shy purring. He took it as an invitation and moved across the parking lot to mount the fuel truck.

Estelle

Estelle placed a mug of tea in front of Catfish, then sat down across the table from him with her own. Catfish sipped the tea and grimaced, then pulled the pint from his back pocket and unscrewed the cap. Estelle caught his hand before he could pour.

"You have some explaining to do first, Mr. Bluesman." Estelle was more than a little rattled. When they were only half a mile away from the beach, she had been overtaken by a sudden urge to return and had fought Catfish for control of the car. It was crazy behavior. It frightened her as much as the thing at the beach had, and when they got to her house she immediately took a Zoloft, even though she'd already had her dose for the day.

"Leave me be, woman. I said I'd tell you. I needs me some nerve medicine."

Estelle released his hand. "What was that at the beach?"

Catfish splashed some whiskey into Estelle's tea first, then into his own. He grinned, "You see my name wasn't always Catfish. I was born with the name of Meriwether Jefferson. Catfish come on me sometime later."

"Christ, Catfish, I'm sixty years old. Am I going to live long enough to hear the end of this story? What in the hell was out in the water tonight?" She was definitely not herself, swearing like this.

"You wanna know or not?"

Estelle sipped her tea. "Sorry, go ahead."

Six

Catfish's Stor

Was 'bout fifty year ago. I was hobo playin juke joints with my partner ley cause he don't never get the Bl Blues, but he never *got* the Blues, broke and hungover and he still a crazy. I say, "Smiley, you ain't n ter'n Deaf Cotton, lessin you feels

Deaf Cotton Dormeyer was t play with time to time. See, them men was blind, so they be called Blind Willie Jackson—like that. Ar them some Blues. But ol' Cotton little bit more of a burden than b ing music. We be playing "Cross ton be over on the side playin' "\ a-howlin like a ol' dog, and we st have us a Nabs and a Co-Cola, a right on playin. And he the lu hear how bad he is. And didn't tell him.

So, anyway, I says, "You a better than ol' Deaf Cotton, le on you."

And Smiley say, "You gots

ner,
but h
say
him
some
them
them.
Sr
little
alway
when
So on
got hi
lars, a
case o
So
me so
Ida M
quor,
runned
(in bet
own se
rest hi
May s
and all
An
word '
can't fi
lars, ar
to see
"Well,
her bei
greased
So I
and do

"That dog was old anyways," he say. "I had him since I was a boy. Time I get Ida May a puppy anyways."

"You ain't sad?" I say.

"Naw," he say. "That ol' dog had his time."

"You hopeless, Smiley. I gots to do some ponderin."

So I ponders. Takin me two days to come up with a way to put the Blues on ol' Smiley. But you know, even when that boy standing there over the smokin ashes of his house, Ida May in one arm and his guitar in the other, he don't do nothin but thank God they had time to get out without gettin burnt up.

Preacher once told me that they is people who rises to tragedy. He says colored folk gots to rise to tragedy like ol' Job in the Bible, iffin they gonna get they propers. So I figures that Smiley is one of them who rises to tragedy, get stronger when bad things come on him. But they more than one way to get the Blues on you. Ain't just bad things happening, sometime it good things *not* happenin—disappointment, iffin you know what I mean?

So I hears that down Biloxi way, round 'bout one of them salt marshes on the Gulf, they is a catfish big as a rowboat, but nobody can catch him. Even a white man down there will give five hundred dollars to the man bring that big ol' catfish in. Now you know people be trying to catch him, but they don't have no luck. So I tells Smiley I got me a secret recipe, and we gonna go get that catfish, get that money, and go up to Chicago and make us a record.

Now I knows they ain't no catfish big as a rowboat, and iffin there was, he'd be caught by now, but Smiley need him a disappointment iffin the Blues gonna jump on him. So I spends the whole ride down there buildin up that boy's hopes. Cadillacs and big ol' houses ridin on the back of that catfish. We ridin in that ol' dog-killin Model T Ford, two hundred feet a rope and some shark hooks in the back with my secret catfish recipe. I figure we get us some bait on the way, and sho' nuff, I accidentally run me over two chickens got too close to the road.

'For dark we down on the bayou where that ol' cat spose to live. Them days 'bout half the counties in Mississippi got signs say: NIGGER, DON'T LET THE SUN GO DOWN ON YOU IN THIS COUNTY, so we always plan to get where we goin' 'for dark.

My secret recipe a gallon jar of chicken guts I keep buried in the backyard for a year. I takes that jar and punches some holes in the lid and toss her out in the water. "A catfish smell them rotten guts, they be there lickety-split," I tells Smiley. Then we hooks up one them chickens and throw it out there and we sits back and has us a drink or two, me all the time talkin trash 'bout that five hundred dollar and Smiley grinnin like he does.

'For long Smiley doze off on the bank. I lets him sleep, thinkin he be more disappointed if he wake up and we ain't caught that catfish. Just to be sure, I starts to pull in the rope, and 'for I got it pulled in ten feet, somethin grab on. That ol' rope start burning through my hand like they's a scared horse on t'other end. I musta yelled, cause Smiley woke up and goes running off the other way. "Watch you doin?" I yells, and that old rope burnin through my hands like a snake on fire.

Well, that it, I think, and I lets go of the rope. (A Bluesman got to take care of his hands.) But when the rope come to the end, it tighten up like an E string and make a twang—throw moss and mud up into my face— and I looks round and see Smiley crankin up that Model T Ford. He done tied the rope on the bumper and now he drivin it back out the bayou, pullin whatever out there in the water as he go. And it ain't comin easy, that ol' Ford screamin and slidin and sound like it like to blow up, but up on the bank come the biggest catfish I ever seen, and that fish ain't happy. He floppin and thrashin and just bout buryin me in mud.

Smiley set the brake and look back at what we catch, when that ol' catfish make a noise I don't know can come out a fish. Sound like woman screaming. Which scares me, but not as much as the noise that come back out the bayou, which sound like the devil done come home.

"You done it now, Smiley," I says.

"Get in," he say.

Don't take more than that for me, cause somethin risin up out the bayou look like a locomotive with teeth, and it comin fast. I'm in that Model T Ford and we off, draggin that big catfish right with us and that monster thing coming behind.

'For long we got us some distance, and I tells Smiley to stop. We gets out and looks at our five-hundred-dollar catfish. He dead now, dragged to death, and not lookin too good at that, but in a full moon we can see this ain't no ordinary catfish. Sho, he got his fins and tail and all, but down on his belly he growin things look like legs.

Smiley say, "What that?"

And I say, "Don't know."

"What that back there?" he say.

"That his momma," I say. "She ain't happy one bit with us."

Seven

It has the soul-sick wail of the Blues, the cowboy tragedy of Country Western. It goes like this:

You pay your dues, do your time behind the wheel, put in long hours on boring roads, your vertebrae compress and your stomach goes sour from too much strong coffee, and finally, just when you get a good-paying job with benefits and you're seeing the light at the end of the retirement tunnel, just when you can hear the distant siren song of a bass boat and a case of Miller calling to you like a willing truck stop waitress named Darlin', a monster comes along and fucks your truck and you are plum blowed up. Al's story.

Al was drowsing in the cab of his tank truck while unleaded liquid dinosaurs pulsed through the big black pipe into the underground tanks of the Pine Cove Texaco. The station was closed, there was no one at the counter to shoot the bull with, and this was the end of his run, but for a quick jog down the coast to a motel in San Junipero. On the radio, turned low, Reba sang of hard times with the full authority of a cross-eyed redheaded millionaire.

When the truck first moved, Al thought he might have been rear-ended by some drunk tourist, then the shaking started and Al was sure he was in the middle of the bull moose earthquake of the century—the big one—the one that twisted cities and snapped overpasses like dry twigs. You thought about those things when you towed around ten thousand gallons of explosive liquid.

Al could see the tall Texaco sign out of the windshield, and it occurred to him that it should be waving like a sapling in the wind, but it wasn't. Only the truck was moving. He had to get out and stop the pump.

The truck thumped and rocked as if rammed by a rhino. He pulled the door handle and pushed. It didn't budge. Something blocked it, blocked the whole window. A tree? Had the roof over the pumps come down on him? He looked to the passenger door, and something was blocking that one too. Not metal, not a tree. It had scales. Through the windshield he saw a dark, wet stain spreading over the concrete and his bladder emptied.

"Oh shit, oh shit, oh shit, oh shit."

He reached behind his seat for the tire thumper to knock out the windshield and in the next instant Al was flaming bits and smoking pieces flying over the Pacific.

A mushroom cloud of greasy flame rose a thousand feet into the sky. The shock wave leveled trees for a block and knocked out windows for three. Half a mile away, in downtown Pine Cove, motion detector alarms were triggered and added their klaxon calls to the roar of the flames. Pine Cove was awake—and frightened.

The Sea Beast was thrown two hundred feet into the air and landed on his back in the flaming ruins of Bert's Burger Stand. Five thousand years on the planet and he had never experienced flight. He found he didn't care for it. Burning gasoline covered him from nose to tail. His gill trees were singed to stumps, jagged shards of metal protruded between the scales of his belly. Still flaming, he headed for the nearest water, the creek that ran behind the business district. As he lumbered down into the creek bed, he looked back to the place where his lover had rejected him and sent out a signal. She was gone now, but he sent the signal anyway. Roughly translated, it said, "A simple *no* would have sufficed."

Molly

The poster covered half of the trailer's living room wall: a younger Molly Michon in a black leather bikini and spiked dog collar, brandishing a wicked-looking broadsword. In the background, red mushroom clouds rose over the desert. *Warrior Babes of the Outland,* in Italian, of course; Molly's movies had only been released to overseas theaters—direct to video in the United States. Molly stood on the wire-spool coffee table and struck the same pose she had fifteen years before. The sword was tarnished, her tan was gone, the blonde hair had gone gray, and now a jagged five-inch scar ran above her right breast, but the bikini still fit and muscles still raked her arms, thighs, and abdomen.

Molly worked out. In the wee hours of the morning, in the vacant space next to her trailer, she spun the broadsword like a deadly baton. She lunged, and thrust, and leapt into the improbable back flip that had made her a star (in Thailand anyway). At two in the morning, while the village slept around her, Molly the crazy lady became, once again, Kendra, Warrior Babe of the Outland.

She stepped off the coffee table and went to her tiny kitchen, where she opened the brown plastic pill bottle and ceremoniously dropped one tablet into the garbage disposal as she had every night for a month now. Then she went out the trailer door, careful not to let it slam and wake her neighbors, and began her routine.

Stretches first—the splits in the high wet grass, then a hurdler's hamstring stretch, touching her forehead to her knee. She could feel her vertebrae pop like a string of muted firecrackers as she did her back stretches. Now, with dew streaking her legs, her hair tied back with a leather boot lace, she began her sword work. A two-handed slash, a thrust, riposte, leap over the blade, spin and slash—slowly at first, working up momentum—one-handed spin, pass to the other hand, reverse, pass the sword behind her back, speeding up as she went until the sword cut the air with a whistling whirr as she worked up to a series of backflips executed while the sword stayed in motion: one, two, three. She tossed the sword into the air, did a back flip, reached to catch it in midspin—a light sweat sheeted her body now—*reached to catch it*—the sword silhouetted against a three-quarter moon—*reached to catch it* and the sky went red. Molly looked up as the shock wave rocketed through the village. The blade slashed the back of her wrist to the bone and stuck in the ground, quivering. Molly swore and watched the orange mushroom cloud rise in the sky over Pine Cove.

She held her wrist and stared at the fire in the sky for several minutes, wondering if what she was seeing was really there, or if perhaps she'd been a little hasty about stopping her meds. A siren sounded in the distance, then she heard something moving down in the creek bed—as if huge rocks were being kicked aside. Mutants, she thought. Where there were mushroom clouds, there were mutants, the curse of Kendra's nuked-out world.

Molly snatched the sword and ran into her trailer to hide.

Theo

The shock wave from the explosion had dissipated to the level of a sonic boom by the time it reached Theo's little cabin two miles out of town. Still, he knew that something had happened. He sat up in bed to wait for the phone to ring. A minute and a half later, it did. The 911 dispatcher from San Junipero was on the line.

"Constable Crowe? You've had some sort of explosion at the Texaco station on Cypress Street in Pine Cove.

There are fires burning nearby. I've dispatched fire and ambulance, but you should get over there."

Theo struggled to sound alert. "Anyone hurt?"

"We don't know yet. The call just came in. It sounds like a fuel tank went up."

"I'm on my way."

Theo swung his long legs out of bed and pulled on his jeans. He snatched his shirt, cell phone, and beeper from the nightstand and headed out to the Volvo. He could see an orange corona from the flames in the sky toward town and billowing black smoke streaking the moonlit sky.

As soon as he started the car, the radio crackled with the voices of volunteer firemen who were racing to the site of the explosion in Pine Cove's two fire engines.

Theo keyed the mike. "Hey, guys, this is Theo Crowe. Anyone on scene yet?"

"ETA one minute, Theo" came back at him. "Ambulance is on scene."

An EMT from the ambulance came on the radio. "The Texaco is gone. So's the burger stand. Doesn't look like the fire is spreading. I don't see anyone around, but if there was anybody in those two buildings, they're toast."

"Delicate, Vance. Very professional," Theo said into the mike. "I'll be there in five."

The Volvo bucked over the rough dirt road. Theo's head banged on the roof and he slowed enough to buckle his seat belt.

Bert's Burger Stand was gone. Gone. And the minimarket at the Texaco, gone too. Theo felt an empty rumbling in his stomach as he pictured his beloved minimarket nachos going black in the flames.

Five minutes later he pulled in behind the ambulance and jumped out of the Volvo. The firefighters seemed to have the fire contained to the asphalt area of the Texaco and the burger stand. A little brush had burned on the hill behind the Texaco and had charred a few trees, but the firemen had drenched that area first to keep the fire from climbing into the residential area.

Theo shielded his face with his hands. The heat coming off the burning Texaco was searing, even at a hundred yards. A figure in fire-fighting regalia approached him out of the smoke. A few feet away he pulled up the shield on his helmet and Theo recognized Robert Masterson, the volunteer fire chief. Robert and his wife Jenny owned Brine's Bait, Tackle, and Fine Wines. He was smiling.

"Theo, you're gonna starve to death—both your food sources are gone."

Theo forced a smile. "Guess I'll have to come to your place for brie and cabernet. Anyone hurt?" Theo was shaking. He hoped Robert couldn't see it by the light of the fire and the rotating red lights of the emergency vehicles. He'd left his Sneaky Pete pipe on the nightstand.

"We can't locate the driver of the truck. If he was in it, we lost him. Still too hot to get close to it. The explosion threw the cab two hundred feet that way." Robert pointed to a burning lump of metal at the edge of the parking lot.

"What about the underground tanks? Should we evacuate or something?"

"No, they'll be fine. They're designed with a vapor lock, no oxygen can get down there, so no fire. We're going to have to let what's left of the minimart just burn out. Some cases of Slim Jims caught fire and they burn like the sun, we can't get close."

Theo squinted into the flames. "I love Slim Jims," he said forlornly.

Robert patted his shoulder. "It'll be okay. I'll order some for you, but you can't tell anyone I'm carrying them. And Theo, when this is all over, come see me at the shop. We'll talk."

"About what?"

Robert pulled off his fire helmet and wiped back his

receding brown hair. "I was a drunk for ten years. I quit. I might be able to help you."

Theo looked away. "I'm fine. Thanks." He pointed to a ten-foot-wide burned strip that started across the street and led away from the fire in a path to the creek. "What do you make of that."

"Looks like someone drove a burning vehicle out of the fire."

"I'll check it out." Theo got a flashlight from the Volvo and crossed the street. The grass was singed and there were deep ruts cut into the dirt. They were lucky this had happened after the rainy season had started. Two months earlier and they would have lost the town.

He followed the track to the creek bed, fully expecting to find a wrecked vehicle pitched over the bank, but there was nothing there. The track ended at the bank. The water wasn't deep enough to cover anything large enough to make a trail like that. He played the flashlight around the bank and stopped it on a single deep track in the mud. He blinked and shook his head to clear his vision, then looked again. It couldn't be.

"Anything over there?" Robert was coming across the grass toward him.

Theo jumped down onto the bank and kicked the mud until the print was obliterated.

"Nothing," Theo said. "Must have just been some burning fuel sprayed out this way."

"What are you doing?"

"Stomping out the last of a burning squirrel. Must have gotten caught in the flames and ran over here. Poor guy."

"You really need to come see me, Theo."

"I will, Robert. For sure I will."

 *eight*

The Sea Beast

He knew he should return to the safety of the sea, but his gill trees were singed and he didn't relish the idea of treading water until they healed. If he'd known the female was going to react so violently, he would have retracted his gills into the folds beneath his scales where they would have been safe. He made his way down the creek bed until he spotted a herd of animals sleeping above the bank. They were ugly things, pale and graceless, and he could sense parasites living in every one of them, but this was no time to be judgmental. After all, some brave beast had to be the first to eat a mastodon, and who would have thought that those furballs would turn out to be the tasty treats that they were.

He could hide among this wormy herd until his gills healed, then perhaps he'd take one of the females on a grateful hump. But not now, his heart still ached for the purring female with the silvery flanks. He needed time to heal.

The Sea Beast slithered up the bank into an open space among the herd, then curled his legs and tail under his body and assumed their shape. The change was painful and took more effort than he was used to, but after a few minutes he was finished and he quietly fell asleep.

Molly

No, this wasn't what she had planned at all. She had stopped taking her meds because they had been giving her the shakes, and she'd been willing to deal with the voices if they came back, but not this. She hadn't counted on this. She was tempted to run to her kitchen area and gulp down one of her blue pills (Stelazine—"the Smurfs of Sanity," she called them) to see if it could chase the hallucination, but she couldn't tear herself from the trailer window. It was too real—and too weird. Could there be a big, burnt beast lumbering out of the creek? And if so, had she just watched it turn into a double-wide trailer?

Hallucinations, that was one of the five symptoms of schizophrenia. Molly kept a list of all the symptoms. In fact, she'd stolen a desk drawer version of the *DSM-IV— The Diagnostic and Statistical Manual of Mental Disorders,* the book psychiatrists use to diagnose mental illness— from Valerie Riordan. According to the *DSM-IV,* you had to have two of the five symptoms. Hallucinations were one; okay, that was a possibility. But delusions, no way; she wasn't the least bit deluded, she knew she was having hallucinations. Number three was disorganized speech or incoherence. She'd give it a try.

"Hi, Molly, how the heck are you?" she asked.

"Not well, thank you. I'm worried that my speech may be disorganized," she answered.

"Well, you sound fine to me," she said, by way of being polite.

"Thanks for saying so," she replied with genuine gratitude. "I guess I'm okay."

"You're fine. Nice ass, by the way."

"Thanks, you're not too bad yourself."

"See, not disorganized at all," she said, not realizing that the conversation was over.

Symptom four was grossly disorganized or catatonic

behavior. She looked around her trailer. Most of the dishes were done, the videotapes of her movies were arranged chronologically, and the goldfish were still dead in the aquarium. Nope, nothing disorganized in this place. Schizo 1, Sanity 3.

Number five, negative symptoms, such as "affective flattening, alogia, or avolition." Well, a woman hits her forties, of course there's a little affective flattening, but she was sure enough that she didn't have the other two symptoms to not even look them up.

But then there was the footnote: "Only one criterion required if delusions are bizarre or hallucinations consist of a voice keeping up a running commentary on the person's behavior or thoughts."

So, she thought, if I have a narrator, I'm batshit. In most of the Kendra movies, there had been a narrator. It helped tie a story together that was supposed to take place in the nuked-out future when, in fact, it was being filmed in an abandoned strip mine near Barstow. And narration was easy to dub into foreign languages because you didn't have to match the lips. So the question she had to ask herself, was: "Do I have a narrator?"

"No way," said the narrator.

"Fuck," said Molly. Just when she'd settled into having a simple personality disorder, she had to learn to be psychotic all over again. Being schizo wasn't all bad. Being diagnosed schizo ten years ago had gotten her the monthly disability check from the state, but Val Riordan had assured her that since then her status had changed from schizophrenic: paranoid type, single episode, in partial remission, with prominent negative symptoms, persecutory-type delusions, and negative stressors (Molly liked to think of the negative stressors as "special sauce") to a much more healthy, postmorbid shizotypal personality disorder, bipolar type (no "special sauce"). To make the latter you had to fulfill the prerequisite of at least one psychotic event, then hit five out of nine symptoms. It was a much tougher and more subtle form of batshit. Molly's favorite symptom was: "Odd beliefs or magical thinking that influences behavior and is inconsistent with subcultural norms."

The narrator said, "So the magical thinking—that would be that you believe that in another dimension, you actually are Kendra, Warrior Babe of the Outland?"

"Fucking narrator again," Molly said. "You're not going away, are you? I don't need this symptom."

"You can't really say that your 'magical thinking' affects your behavior, can you?" the narrator asked. "I don't think you can claim that symptom."

"Oh hell no," Molly said. "I'm just out practicing with a broadsword at two in the morning, waiting for the end of civilization so I can claim my rightful identity."

"Simple physical fitness regimen. Everyone's trying to get into shape these days."

"So they can hack apart evil mutants?"

"Sure, Nautilus makes a machine for that. Mutant Master 5000. "

"That's a crock."

"Sorry, I'll shut up now."

"I'd appreciate that. I really don't need the 'voices' symptom, thanks."

"You've still got the monster-trailer hallucination outside."

"I thought you were going to shut up."

"Sorry, that's the last you'll hear from me. Really."

"Jerk."

"Bitch."

"You said . . ."

"Sorry."

So without voices all she had to deal with was the hallucination. The trailer was still sitting there, but admittedly, it just looked like a trailer. Molly could imagine trying to tell the shrink at county about it when they admitted her.

"So you saw a trailer?"

"That's right."

"And you live in a trailer park?"

"Yep."

"I see," the shrink would say. And somewhere between those two little words the judgment would be pronounced: crazy.

No, she wasn't going to go that route. She would confront her fears and go forward, just as Kendra had in *The Mutant Slayer: Warrior Babes II*. She grabbed her sword and left her trailer.

The sirens had subsided now, but she could still see an orange glow from the explosion. Not a nuclear blast, she thought, just some sort of accident. She strode across the lot and stopped about ten feet away from the trailer.

Up close, it looked—well, it looked like a damn trailer. The door was in the wrong place, on the end instead of the side, and the windows were frosty, as if they'd iced over. There was a thin patina of soot over its entire length, but it was a trailer. It didn't look like a monster at all.

She stepped forward and ventured a poke with her sword. The aluminum skin of the trailer seemed to shy away from the sword point. Molly jumped back.

A warm wave of pleasure swept through her body. For a second she forgot why she had come out here and let the wave take her. She poked the trailer again, and again the pleasure wave washed over her, this time even more intense. There was no fear, no tension, just the feeling that this was exactly where she should be—where she should always have been. She dropped her sword and let the feeling take her.

The frosty layer on the trailer's two end windows seemed to lift, revealing the slitlike pupils of two great golden eyes. Then the door began to open, not from side to side, but splitting itself in the middle and opening like a mouth. Molly turned on her heel and ran, wondering even as she went why she hadn't just stayed there by the trailer where everything felt so good.

Estelle

Estelle was wearing a leather fedora, a pair of dark sunglasses, a single lavender sock, and a subtle and satisfied smile. Sometime after her husband had died—after she'd moved to Pine Cove and started taking the antidepressants, after she'd stopped coloring her hair or giving a damn about her wardrobe—Estelle had vowed that no man would ever see her naked again. At the time, she considered it a fair trade: carnal pleasures, of which there were few, for guilt-free cookies, of which there were many. Now, having broken that vow and lying in her feather bed next to this sweaty, stringy old man, who was teasing her left nipple with his tongue (and who didn't seem to mind that said nipple was leading her breast over her arm rather than jutting skyward like the cupola on the Taj Mahal), Estelle felt like she understood, at last, the Mona Lisa's smile. Mona had been getting some, and she had her cookies too.

"You are some storyteller," Estelle said.

A spidery black hand crawled up her thigh and parked an index finger moistly on her pleasure button—just settled there—and she shuddered. "I didn't finish," Catfish said.

"You didn't? Then what was all that 'Hallelujah, Lord, I'm comin home!' followed by the barking?"

"I didn't finish the story," Catfish said, his enunciation remarkably clear, considering he didn't miss a lick.

Harmonica player, Estelle thought. She said, "I'm sorry, I don't know what came over me."

And she didn't. One minute they were sipping spiked tea and the next there was an explosion and she had her mouth locked over his, moaning into him like a saxophonist playing passion.

"You didn't see me fightin you," Catfish said. "We got time."

"We do?"

"Sho', but you gonna have to pay my way now. You done chased the Blues off me and I feels like they ain't never comin back. I'm out a job."

Estelle looked down to see Catfish grinning in the soft orange light and grinned herself. Then she realized that they hadn't lit any candles, and she didn't have any orange lights. Somewhere in the tussle between the kitchen and the bedroom, amid the tossing of clothes and groping of flesh, they had turned the lights out. The orange glow was coming through the window at the foot of the bed.

Estelle sat up. "The town is on fire."

"It is in here," Catfish said.

She pulled the sheets up to cover herself. "We need to do something."

"I got an idea a somethin we can do." He moved his spidery fingers and her attention was taken away from the window.

"Already?"

"Seem soon to me too, girl, but I'm old and this could be my last one."

"That's a cheery thought."

"I'm a Bluesman."

"Yes, you are," she said. Then she rolled over on him and stayed there, off and on, until dawn.

nine

When Mikey "the Collector" Plotznik wheeled into town and saw that the Texaco station had blown up, leaving a charred circle two hundred yards wide around it, he knew that it was going to be a great day. It was a shame about the burger stand going up too, and he'd miss their spicy fries, but hey, you don't often get to see the toasting of a major landmark like the Texaco. The fire was all out now, but several firemen were still sifting through the wreckage. The Collector waved to them as he wheeled by. They waved back, somewhat reticently, for the Collector's reputation preceded him and made them nervous.

Today would be the day, Mikey thought. The Texaco was an omen, the star in the sky over his lifelong dream. Today he'd catch Molly Michon naked, and when he did (and brought back the proof), his reputation would grow to mythic proportions. He patted the disposable camera he carried in the front pouch of his hooded sweatshirt. Oh yes, he'd have evidence to back up his story. They would believe him—and bow to him.

At this point in his life, the Collector was more interested in explosions than in naked women. He was only ten, and it would be a couple of years before his interests moved to girls. Freud never identified a stage of development known as "pyrotechnic fascination," but that was only because there wasn't an abundant supply of disposable lighters in nineteenth-century Vienna. Ten-year-old boys blow shit up. It's what they do. But today a strange new feeling had come over Mikey, a feeling he couldn't put a word to, but if he could, the word would have been "horny." As he Rollerbladed through town, tossing the *Los Angeles Times* into the shrubs and gutters of businesses along Cypress Street, he felt a tightness in his shorts that until now he had associated with having to take a raging pee in the morning. Today it signified a need to see the Crazy Lady in a state of undress.

Paperboys are the carriers of preadolescent myth. On every paper route, there is a haunted house, a kid-eating dog, an old woman who tips with twenties, and a woman who answers the door in the nude. Mikey had never actually seen any of these things, but that never stopped him from spinning wild stories for his buddies at school. Today he would get proof, he could feel it in his loins.

He skated down the driveway into the Fly Rod Trailer Court, chucked a paper into the rose bushes in front of Mr. Nunez's trailer, then made a beeline for the Crazy Lady's house. He could see a blue glow coming through her windows, a TV. She was home and awake. Yes!

He pulled up a couple of doors down and noticed that a new trailer had moved in next to the Crazy Lady. A new customer? Why not give it a try? The Crazy Lady didn't receive the paper, so his pretense for knocking on her door was to get her to subscribe. He could practice on these new people. As he skated up to the front door of the new trailer, lights came on in the two front windows. Yes! Someone was home. Strange curtains—they looked like cat's eyes.

Through a part in the curtains, Molly watched the kid come down the road into the trailer park. She liked kids, but she didn't like *this* kid. At least once a week he knocked on her door and tried to get her to subscribe to the paper, and once a week she told him to go away and never come back. Sometimes he would bring one of his little buddies along. She could hear them skulking around her trailer, trying to peek in the windows. "Swear to God, she's got a dead guy in there that she does it with. I've seen him. And she ate a kid once."

The kid was heading for the monster trailer.

In the background, a videotape was playing on her TV—*Mechanized Death: Warrior Babe VII*—and THE SCENE was coming up. Molly looked away from the window and watched THE SCENE for the thousandth time.

Kendra is standing in the back of a jeep, manning a rack of net guns as the jeep pursues the Evil Warlord across the desert. The driver turns, as he is supposed to, throwing up a fishtail of dust, but the front wheel of the jeep hits a rock and the jeep rolls. Kendra is thrown fifty feet in the air and lands in a heap. The steel bra she is wearing cuts deep into her chest and blood sprays out across the dust.

The bastards! Every time she watches THE SCENE she can't believe the bastards left it in. The accident was real, the blood was Molly's, and when she returned to the set ten days later, a security guard escorted her to the producer's trailer.

"I can pay you extra's wages as a mutant," the producer said, "but let's face it, babe, you didn't get your billing because of your acting ability. You think I'm gonna hold up filming for ten days when the whole schedule is only three weeks long? We got a new Kendra. Wrote the accident and the facial reconstruction into the script. She's a cyborg now. Now you can get in line with the mutants to pick up your bag of rags, or you can get the fuck off the set. My audience wants perfect bodies, and you were getting up there anyway. With that scar you don't sell anymore."

Molly had just turned twenty-seven years old.

She pulled herself from THE SCENE and looked out

the window again. The kid was there, right there in front of the monster trailer. She should warn him or something.

She pounded on the window and the kid looked up, not startled, but with a dreamy expression on his face. Molly gestured for him to move away. The window she was looking out of didn't open. (Trailers built in those days were designed so people would burn up in case of a fire. The manufacturers thought it would keep the lawsuits down.)

The kid just stood there, his fist poised before the door as if he were frozen in the middle of knocking.

As Molly watched, the door began to open. Not on the hinges, but vertically, like a garage door. Molly pounded furiously on the window with the hilt of her sword. The kid smiled. A huge red tongue snaked out of the door, wrapped around the kid, and slurped him in, Rollerblades, paper satchel, and all. Molly screamed. The door slammed shut.

Molly watched, stunned, not knowing what to do. A few seconds later the mouth opened and expectorated a soccer-ball-sized wad of newspaper.

Theo

The hours of Theo's day had moved like slugs crawling on razor wire. By four in the afternoon, he felt as if he'd been awake for a week and the cups of French roast he'd been drinking had turned to foaming acid in his stomach. Mercifully, there hadn't been a single call for a bar fight or domestic dispute, so he had spent the entire day at the scene of the fuel truck explosion, talking to firemen, representatives from Texaco Oil, and an arson investigator sent up from the San Junipero Fire Department. Much to his surprise, going all day without a hit from his Sneaky Pete pot pipe had not sent him into fits of anxiety as it usually did. He was a little paranoid, but he wasn't sure that that wasn't just an informed response to the world anyway.

At a quarter past four, the arson investigator crossed the charred parking lot to where Theo was leaning on the hood of his Volvo. The investigator was in his late twenties, clean-cut, and carried himself like an athlete, even in the orange toxic waste suit. He carried a plastic space helmet under his arm like a tumorous football.

"Constable Crowe, I think that's about all I can do today. It'll be dark soon, and as long as we keep the area closed off, I'm sure everything will still be here in the morning."

"What's your call so far?

"Well, we generally look for evidence of accelerants, gas, kerosene, paint thinner—and I'd say there were definitely some flammable liquids involved here." He smiled a weary smile.

"So you don't know what happened?"

"Offhand, I'd say a fuel truck blew up, but without further investigation I'd hate to make a commitment at this time." Again the smile.

Theo smiled back. "So no cause?"

"The driver probably didn't seal the hose correctly and a cloud of fumes got set off. There wasn't much wind last night, so the fumes would have just clung to the ground and built up. Anything could have set it off: the driver could have been smoking, the pilot lights at the hamburger place, a spark in the truck exhaust. Right now I'd say it was totally accidental. It was a company-owned store, and it was turning a profit, so there really isn't a financial motive for arson. Texaco will definitely be building your town a new burger stand and probably paying off some nuisance settlements from people claiming trauma, duress, and irritation."

"I have the information on the driver," Theo said. "I'll check to see if he was a smoker."

"I asked him. He's keeping quiet" came a voice from a few yards away.

Theo and the arson investigator looked up to see Vance McNally coming toward them holding up a Ziploc bag full of white and gray powder. "I've got him right here," the EMT said. "You want to interrogate him?"

"Very funny, Vance," Theo said.

"They're going to have to do the autopsy with a flour sifter," Vance said.

The investigator took the Ziploc from Vance and examined it. "You find any remains of a cigarette lighter? Anything like that?"

"Not my job," Vance said. "The fire was so hot it turned the seat springs to liquid. Even incinerated the bones, except for those little bits of calcium in there. Honestly, this might not all be our boy. We might be giving his wife a bag full of burnt-up truck parts to put in an urn on the mantel."

The investigator shrugged and handed the bag back to Vance. Then to Theo he said, "I'm going home. I'll come back tomorrow and look around some more. As soon as I give the okay, the oil company will send in a crew to drain the ground tanks."

"Thanks," Theo said. The investigator left in a county car.

Vance McNally turned the Ziploc bag of truck driver in the air. "Theo, this ever happens to me, I want you to get all my friends together, have a big party, and snort me, okay?"

"You have friends, Vance?"

"Okay, it was just an idea," Vance said. He turned and carried his bag to the waiting ambulance.

Theo sipped his coffee and noticed something moving in the charred brush beyond the Texaco. It looked as if someone was holding up a TV antenna and getting altogether too close to the yellow tape he had run around the perimeter. Jeez, was he going to have to stay here all night guarding the scene? He pried himself off the Volvo and headed for the offender.

"Hey there!" Theo called.

Gabe Fenton, the biologist, emerged from the brush, indeed holding up some kind of antenna, followed by his Labrador retriever, Skinner. The dog ran to meet Theo and greeted him with two muddy paw prints on the chest.

Theo rubbed Skinner's ears to hold him at bay, the classic slobbering Labrador control move. "Gabe, what in the hell are you doing down here?"

The biologist was covered with burrs and foxtails, his face striped with soot from the charred brush. He looked exhausted, yet there was a note of excitement bordering on ecstasy in his voice. "You won't believe this, Theo. My rats moved en masse this morning."

Theo tried, but couldn't match Gabe's enthusiasm. "That's swell, Gabe. Texaco blew up last night."

Gabe Fenton looked around at the surrounding area as if seeing the destruction for the first time. "What time?"

"About four in the morning."

"Hmmm, maybe they sensed it."

"They?"

"The rats. Around 2 A.M. they all started moving west. I can't figure out what caused it. Here, look at the screen." Gabe had a laptop computer strapped into a harness around his waist. He turned it so Theo could see the screen. "Each of these dots represents an animal I have implanted with a tracking chip. Here's their location at 1 A.M." He clicked a key and the screen drew a topographical map of the area. Green dots were scattered pretty much evenly along the creek bed and the business district of Pine Cove.

Gabe hit another key. "Now here they are at two." All but a few of the dots had moved into the ranchland east of Pine Cove.

"Uh-huh," Theo said. Gabe was a nice guy. Spent too much time with vermin, but he was a nice guy. Gabe needs to talk to humans occasionally, Theo thought.

"Well, don't you see? They all moved at once, except for these ten over here that moved to the shore."

"Uh-huh," Theo said. "Gabe, the Texaco blew up. A guy was killed. I was talking to firemen in space suits all day. Every paper in the county has called me. The battery is almost out on my cell phone. I haven't eaten since yesterday and I only slept an hour last night. Help me find the significance in rat migration, okay?"

Gabe looked crestfallen. "Well, I don't know the significance yet. I'm tracking the ten that didn't move east, hoping the anomalies will give a clue to the behavior of the larger group. Strange thing is, four of the ten disappeared off my screen a little after two. Even if they were killed, the chips should still transmit. I need to find them."

"And I wish you the best of luck, but this area may still be dangerous. You can't be here, buddy."

"Maybe there were fumes," Gabe said. "But that doesn't explain why they all moved in the same direction. Some even came through this area from the shore."

Theo couldn't bear to express to Gabe how little he cared. "You had any dinner, Gabe?"

"No, I've been doing this since last night."

"Pizza, Gabe. We need pizza and beer. I'll buy."

"But I need to . . ."

"You're a single guy, Gabe. You need pizza every eighteen hours or you can't function properly. And I have a question to ask you about footprints, but I want you to watch me drink a few beers before I ask so I can claim diminished capacity. Come, Gabe, let me take you to the land of pizza and beer. " Theo gestured to his Volvo. "You can stick the antenna out the sunroof."

"I guess I could take a break."

Theo opened the passenger door and Skinner leapt into the car, leaving sooty paw prints on the seat. "Your dog needs pizza. It's the humane thing to do."

"Okay," Gabe said.

"I want to show you something over by the creek bed."

"What."

"A footprint. Or what's left of one."

Ten minutes later they sat over frosty mugs of beer at Pizza in the Pines, Pine Cove's only pizza parlor. They'd taken a window table so Gabe could keep an eye on Skinner, who was bouncing up and down outside, giving them an ever-changing view of the street, then the street with dog face (ears akimbo), then the street, then the street with dog face again. Other than to order a beer, Gabe Fenton hadn't said a word since they'd gone to the creek bed.

"Will he just keep doing that?" Theo asked.

"Until we take him a slice of pizza, yes."

"Amazing."

Gabe shrugged. "He's a dog."

"Always the biologist."

"One needs to keep the mind limber."

"Well, what do you think?"

"I think that you obliterated most of what you thought was a footprint."

"Gabe, it was a footprint. A talon or something."

"There are a thousand explanations for a depression in the mud like that, Theo, but one of them is not an animal track."

"Why not?"

"Well, for one, there hasn't been anything that large on this continent for about sixty million years, and for another, animals tend to leave more than one track, unless it's a creature especially adapted for hopping." Gabe grinned.

The flying dog head pogoed by the windowsill.

"There were a lot of people and vehicles around there, the other tracks might have been wiped out."

"Theo, don't let your imagination run away with you. You've had a long day and . . ."

"And I'm a pothead."

"I wasn't going to say that."

"I know, I'm saying it. Tell me about your rats. What will you do when you find them?"

"Well, first I'm going to keep searching for the stimulus of their behavior, then I'll catch a few of the group that migrated and compare their brain chemistry to those that headed toward the shore."

"Does that hurt them?"

"You have to blend up their brains and run the liquid in a centrifuge."

"I guess so then."

The waitress brought their pizza and Gabe was severing cables of cheese from his first slice when Theo's cell phone rang. The constable listened for a second, then stood and dug into his pocket for money. "I've got to go, Gabe."

"What's up?"

"The Plotznik kid is missing. No one's seen him since he left on his paper route this morning."

"Probably hiding. That kid is evil. He rigged up something with his remote control car that affected the chips in my rats once. I spent three weeks trying to figure out why they were running figure eights in the parking lot outside the grocery story before I found him lurking in the weeds with the controller. "

"I know," Theo said. "Mikey told me that if he wired ten of your rats together, he could pick up the Discovery Channel. I still have to find him. He has parents."

"Skinner is a pretty good tracker. Want to take him?"

"Thanks, but I doubt that the kid had a pizza in his pocket."

Theo folded his phone, snagged a slice of pizza for the road, and headed out the door.

ten

Val Riordan leaned against her office door, trying to catch her breath and maintain her temper. Nothing in her clinical experience compared to the sessions she held on the day after the Texaco exploded. She had seen twenty patients in ten hours, and every one of them had wanted to talk about sex. And not abstract sex either, not issues or attitudes about sex, just squishy, thumping sex itself. It was unnerving.

She'd anticipated a spike in libido among her patients (it was a common symptom of withdrawal from antidepressants), but the books said not more than five to fifteen percent would have a reaction—about the same number that experienced a loss of libido upon taking the drugs. But today she'd hit one hundred percent. It was as if she were running a kennel for hopeless horndogs rather than a psychiatric practice.

After the last patient, she'd come out of her office to find her new receptionist, Chloe, furiously masturbating, her feet hooked into the edge of the desk, her steno chair squeaking like a tortured squirrel. Val had excused herself, turned on her heel, walked back into her office, and shut the door.

Chloe, twenty-one, had maroon hair, an entire wardrobe rendered in black, and a sapphire nose ring. Val had begun treating the girl in her teens for bulimia, then hired her when the volume of appointments skyrocketed after

the placebo went into effect. Chloe worked in exchange
for therapy; Val had thought it would be a good financial
move. Frankly, she'd liked her better when she just threw
up a lot.

Val was still trying to figure out exactly what to do
when there was a soft knock on the door.

"Yes?"

"Sorry," Chloe said through the door.

"Uh, Chloe, that is not appropriate office behavior."

"Well, your last appointment had left. I thought that
you would be working on your notes or something for a
while. I'm really sorry."

"That's it? My last appointment leaves, so let the wild
rumpus begin?"

"Am I fired?"

Val thought for a second. There were twenty more
patients to see tomorrow and twenty the day after that.
If the weirdness didn't kill her, the workload would. She
couldn't afford to lose Chloe now. "No, you're not fired.
But please, no more of that in the office."

"Do you have time to talk? I know my next session
isn't until next week, but I really need to talk to you."

"Wouldn't you prefer to go home and, uh, think
about things?"

"You mean finish? No, I'm finished for now. That's
what I want to talk to you about. That wasn't the first
time today."

Val gulped. It was highly unprofessional to talk to a
patient through a door. She steeled herself and opened it.
"Come in." She returned to her desk without looking at
the girl. Chloe took a seat across from her.

"So this wasn't the first time today?" Val was the psy-
chotherapist now, not the boss. If she'd been the boss,
she would have come over the desk and strangled the
little slut.

"No, I can't seem to get enough. I, well, it started

something like buffing the muffin while I'm at work, yes, Dr. Riordan, I'm a little worried. Can't you adjust my medication or something?"

There it was. In the past, that would have been the answer. Increase the Prozac to eighty milligrams, about four times the dose for the average depressed patient, and let the side effect of reduced libido do the work. Val had used the method to treat a nymphomaniac when she was an intern and it had worked marvelously. But what now? Duct tape oven mitts to her receptionist's hands? Although her typing probably wouldn't suffer much, it might make the patients nervous.

Val said. "Chloe, masturbation is a natural thing. Everyone does it. But obviously there are appropriate times and places. Perhaps you should just cut back. Allow yourself to masturbate as a reward for controlling your urges."

Chloe's face went slack. "Cut *down*? I'm worried about driving home safely. I have a stick shift. I need both hands to drive, but I don't think I'm going to have them. Do you have a patch you can prescribe, like they do for smoking?"

"A patch?" Val suppressed a laugh. She imagined a twitching, moaning line of people around the block at the pharmacy, there to pick up their prescriptions for the orgasm patch. It would make heroin look like Gummi Bears. "No, there's no patch, Chloe. You're just going to have to try to control yourself. I have a feeling that this is a side effect of your medication. It should pass in a day or two. I want to hear more about this dream of yours. We'll talk tomorrow, okay? "

Chloe stood, obviously not satisfied with the help her therapist was offering, which was none. "I'll try." She left the office, closing the door behind her.

Val let her head fall to the desk. Jesus, Joseph, and Mary, why didn't I go into pathology? she thought. It would be so peaceful sitting around, boiling up beakers

about two in the morning, and I went straight
until time to get ready for work. Then once or twic
each patient was in session."

Val's jaw dropped. Sixteen hours of intermitten
turbation? The other patients she had seen had cite
in the morning as when their sexual adventures
started too. She said, "And how do you feel about th

"I feel okay. My wrist hurts a little. Do you thi
could have carpal tunnel?"

"Chloe, if you think that you're going to file a wc
men's compensation claim for this . . ."

"No no no, I just want to stop."

"Did something happen to set this off? Something
two in the morning? A dream perhaps?" Her other pa
tients had described various sexual dreams. Winstor
Krauss, the pharmacist with the sexual obsession for marine mammals, confessed to dreaming of having sex with
a blue whale, riding it through the depths like Ahab with
a hard-on. Upon awakening, he'd abused his inflatable
Flipper until it would no longer hold air.

Chloe shifted uncomfortably in her chair. Her long
maroon hair hid her face. "I dreamed I was having sex
with a tank truck, and it blew up."

"A tank truck?"

"I came."

"Sexual dreams are completely normal, Chloe." Right,
a tank truck? That's normal. "Tell me, was there fire in
your dream?" Pyromaniacs derived sexual pleasure from
setting and watching fires. That's how they caught them,
look in the crowd for a grinning guy with a woody and
gas stains on his shoes.

"No, no fire. I woke up at the explosion. Val, what's
wrong with me? All I want to do is, you know, do it."

"And you feel that you might do something
impulsive?"

Chloe put on her cynical Goth-girl face. "If you mean

of urine and culturing bugs. No wackos. No stress. Okay, occasionally you'd be exposed to some deadly anthrax spores, but at least other people's sex lives stay in the bedroom and the tabloids where they belong.

Her appointment with Martin and Lisbeth Luder rose in her head. They were in their seventies, had been in counseling because they hadn't had a decent conversation since 1958, and today they had come in and dumped a half hour of explicit sexual narrative on her, an account of perversions they'd indulged in the night before, starting at around 2 A.M. The visual conjured in Val's mind—all that parched, wrinkled flesh in furious friction—culminated in flames, as if some giant cosmic Boy Scout had decided to rub two old people together to make a fire. The worst of it, the absolute worst of it, is that she'd found herself getting turned on while listening. She'd had to change her panties between appointments four times today.

She considered pouring herself a hefty tumbler of brandy and settling down in front of the television, but that wasn't going to do it. Batteries; she needed four C-cell batteries and she needed them now. Then it was time to dig through her lingerie drawers and find a long-forgotten friend—and hope that it still worked.

Molly

Long past dark and Molly was still staring though the gap in the curtains at the trailer that ate the kid. The problem with being nuts, she thought, is that you don't always feel as if you're nuts. Sometimes, in fact, you feel perfectly sane, and there just happens to be a trailer-shaped dragon crouching in the lot next door. Not that she was ready to go out and proclaim that fact to anyone, because no matter how sane you feel, some stuff just sounds too crazy. So she watched, still wearing her Warrior Babe outfit, hoping someone else would come along and notice. Around eight, someone did.

She saw Theophilus Crowe going from door to door in the park. He came into view two trailers down at the Morales home, spoke briefly with Mr. Morales at the door, then headed for the dragon trailer.

Molly was torn. She liked Theo. Yes, he'd taken her to County once or twice, but he'd always been kind to her—warned her about the guy in the day room who cheated at Parcheesi by eating the marbles. And he never spoke to her like she was a crazy woman. Theo was a fan.

As Theo was raising his black Mag lite to tap on the dragon trailer's door, Molly saw the two windows on the end slowly open, revealing the cat's-eye pupils. Theo obviously didn't see them. He was looking at his shoes.

She threw up the aluminum sash and shouted, "They're not home!"

The constable turned toward Molly. "Just a second," she said.

She bolted out the door of her trailer and stopped by the street where Theo could see her. "They aren't home. Come here a second," she repeated.

Theo tucked his Mag lite into his belt. "Molly, how are you?"

"Fine, fine, fine. I need to talk to you, okay? Over here, okay?" She didn't want to tell him why. What if the eyes weren't there? What if it was just a trailer? She'd be on her way to County in a heartbeat.

"They're not home then?" Theo said, pointing over his shoulder to the dragon trailer. He was staring at her now, at the same time trying not to stare. He had a goofy grin on his face, the same sort Molly had seen on the kid right before he got slurped.

"Nope, gone all day."

"What's with the sword?

Oh shit! She forgot she'd grabbed the sword on the way out. "I was just making some stir-fry. Chopping up some veggies."

"That ought to do it."

"Broccoli stems," she said, as if that explained everything. He was looking at the leather bikini, and she watched his eyes stop on the scar above her breast, then look away. She covered the scar with her hand. "One of my old Kendra costumes. Everything else is in the dryer."

"Sure. Hey, you don't get the *Times*, do you?"

"Nope. Why?"

"The kid that delivers it, Mikey Plotznik, left for his route this morning and no one has seen him since. Looks like the last paper he delivered was a few doors down. You didn't happen to see him, did you?"

"About ten, blond kid, Rollerblades? Kinda evil?"

"That's him."

"Nope, haven't seen him." She watched the eyes of the dragon trailer close behind Theo and took a deep breath.

"You seem a little tense, Molly. You okay?"

"Fine, fine, just wanted to get back to my stir-fry. You hungry? "

"Did Val Riordan get hold of you?"

"Yep, she called. I'm not nuts."

"Of course not. I'd like you to keep an eye out for this kid, Molly. One of his buddies fessed up that Mikey had a little bit of an obsession with you."

"Me? No kidding?"

"He might be creeping around your trailer."

"Really?"

"If you see him, give me a call, would you? His folks are worried about him."

"I'll do that."

"Thanks. And ask your neighbors when they get home, would you?"

"You betcha." Molly realized he was stalling. Just staring at her with that goofy grin on his face. "They just moved in. I don't know them very well, but I'll ask."

"Thanks." He said, still just standing there, like a twelve-year-old ready to make an assault on the wallflowers at his first dance.

"I'd better go, Theo. I have broccoli in the dryer." No, she had wanted to say she had to get back to dinner, or to her laundry, not both.

"Okay. See ya."

She ran into her trailer, slammed the door, and leaned against it. Through the window she could see the dragon trailer open an eye and close it quickly. She could have sworn it was winking at her.

Theo

A niggling voice in Theo's head told him that finding the Crazy Lady attractive—extremely attractive—was an indicator that he was less than sane himself. On the other hand, he didn't feel that bad about it. He didn't feel bad about anything, not since he'd walked into the trailer park anyway. He had to deal with an explosion, a lost kid, the recent increase in general nuttiness in town—a virtual shit storm of responsibility—but he didn't feel all that bad. And in that moment outside of Molly's trailer, reflecting and waiting for the tide of lust to ebb, he realized that he hadn't smoked any pot all day. Strange. Normally this long without nursing from his Sneaky Pete and his skin would be crawling.

He was heading back to his Volvo to resume the search for the lost boy when his cell phone rang. Sheriff John Burton didn't say hello.

"Get to a land line," Burton said.

"I'm in the middle of trying to find a lost kid," Theo replied.

"A land line now, Crowe. My private line. You have five minutes."

Theo drove to a pay phone outside the Head of the Slug Saloon and checked his watch. When fifteen minutes had passed, he dialed Burton's number.

"I said five minutes."

"Yes, you did." Theo smiled to himself in spite of Burton's tone, which was on the verge of screaming.

"No one goes on the ranch, Crowe. The lost kid is not on the ranch, do you hear me?"

"It's standard procedure to search all the ranchland. Emergency services has the area gridded out. We have to cover the whole grid. I was going to call in some deputies to help us. The volunteer fire guys are exhausted from the explosion this morning."

"No. None of my guys. Don't call the Highway Patrol or the CCC either. And no aircraft. If the grid on the ranch has to be checked off, then check it off. No one goes on that land, is that clear?"

"And what if the kid actually is on the ranch. You're talking about a thousand acres of pasture and forest that won't be searched."

"Oh bullshit, the kid is probably in a tree house somewhere with a stack of *Playboys*. He's only been missing for what, twelve hours?"

"What if he's not?"

There was silence on the line for a moment. Theo waited, watching three new couples leave the Head of the Slug in less than a minute. New couples: in Pine Cove everyone knew who everyone else was dating, and these were people who didn't go together. Not that unusual a phenomenon perhaps on a Friday night at 2 A.M., but this was Wednesday, and it was barely eight o'clock. Maybe he wasn't the only one feeling a wave of horniness. The couples were groping each other as if trying to get all the foreplay out of the way before they reached the car.

Burton came back on the line. "I'll see that the ranchland is searched and call you if they find the kid. But I want to be the first to know if *you* find him."

"That it?"

"Find that little fucker, Crowe." Burton hung up.

Theo got into his Volvo and drove to his cabin at the edge of the ranch. There were at least twenty citizen volunteers searching for Mikey Plotznik. The effort could spare him long enough to catch a shower and change his smoke-saturated clothes. As he parked the Volvo, an expensive, tricked-out red pickup truck pulled into the ranch entrance and rolled slowly by. As they passed, a Hispanic man sitting in the bed laughed and saluted Theo with the barrel of an AK-47 assault rifle.

Theo looked away and walked to the dark cabin, wishing that there was someone there waiting for him.

 e|even

Catfish

Catfish awoke to find a paint-spattered woman padding about the house in nothing but a pair of wool socks, in which she had stuck several sable brushes that delivered ochre, olive, and titanium white strokes to her calves whenever she moved. Canvases were propped on easels, chairs, counters, and windowsills—seascapes every one. Estelle moved from canvas to canvas, palette in hand, furiously painting details in the waves and beaches.

"Y'all woke up inspired," Catfish said.

It was past dusk, they had slept away the daylight. Estelle painted by the light of fifty candles and the orange glow that washed from the open doors of the wood stove. Color correctness be damned, these paintings should be viewed by fire.

Estelle stopped painting and raised her brush arm to cover her breasts. "They weren't finished. I knew something was missing when I painted them, but I didn't know what until now."

Catfish cinched his pants around his waist and walked shirtless among the paintings. The waves writhed with tail and scale and teeth and talon. Predator eyes shone out of the canvases, brighter, it seemed, than the candles that lit them.

"You done painted that old girl in all of 'em?"

"It's not a girl. It's male."

"How you know that?"

"I know." Estelle turned and went back to her painting. "I feel it."

"How you know it look like that?"

"It does, doesn't it? It looks like this?"

Catfish scratched the stubble on his chin and pondered the paintings. "Close. But it ain't a boy. That ol' monster the same one come after me an Smiley for catchin its little one."

Estelle stopped painting and turned to him. "You have to play tonight?"

"In a little while."

"Coffee?"

He stepped up to her, took the brush and palette from her, and kissed her on the forehead. "That sho' would be sweet."

She padded to the bedroom and came back wearing a tattered kimono. "Tell me, Catfish. What happened?"

He was sitting at the table. "I think we done broke a record. I'm sore."

Estelle smiled in spite of herself, but pressed on. "What happened back then, in the bayou? Did you call that thing up out of the water somehow?"

"What you thinkin, woman? I can do that, you think I be playin clubs for drinks and part the door?"

"Tell me how you felt back then, when that thing came out of the swamp."

"Scared."

"Besides that."

"Wasn't nothing besides that. You heard it. Scared is all there is."

"You weren't scared after we got back here last night."

"No."

"Neither was I. What did you feel back then? Before and after the thing came after you."

"Not like I'm feelin now."

"And how is that?"

"I'm feelin real good to be here talkin to you."

"No kidding. Me too. How about back then?"

"Stop doggin me, girl. I'll tell you. But I gots to go play in an hour and I don't know that I can."

"Why not?"

"The Blues ain't on me. You done chased 'em off."

"I can throw you out in the cold without a shirt if you think it will help."

Catfish squirmed in his chair. "Maybe some coffee."

Catfish's Story

After we gets some distance from whatever chasin us, we stop the Model T Ford and me and Smiley put that big ol' catfish thing in the backseat—his tail hangin out one side an' his head out t'other. Now this ain't at all what I expected, and Smiley ain't got the Blues on him, but I'm gettin me a grand case myself. Then I realizes we got us five hundred dollar coming, and them ol' Blues done melt right away.

I say, "Smiley, I believes we should have us some celebratin, startin with some liquor and endin up with some fine Delta pussy. What you say?"

Ol' Smiley, like usual, don't wanna piss on the parade, but bein who he is, he point out we aint got no money and Ida May don't approve of no pussy more'en a hundred yard from the house. But he feelin it too, I can tell, and before long we headed down a back road to find a bootlegger I know down there name of Elmore that sells to colored folk.

That ol' white boy ain't got but two teeth, but he grindin 'em when we pulls up, all mad and wavin his shotgun like we come to bust up his still. I say, "Hey, Elmore, how your lovely wife and sister?"

He say she fine, but lessin we shows some money quick, he gonna shoot him some niggers and get back to her before she cool off.

"We a little short," I say. "But we have us five hundred dollar come morning iffin you kind enough to give us a jug on credit." An' then I shows him the catfish.

That boy liked to shit his pants, and I was hopin he would, just to cover the smell comin off him natural, but instead he say, "I ain't waitin 'til mornin'. You want a jug, you give me a hunk o' that catfish right now. A big hunk."

Smiley and I thinks it over, and before long we got us a half-gallon of corn mash and ol' Elmore got hisself enough catfish to feed his wives and children and them-thats both for a week or more.

Up the road a spell and this old whore name of Okra givin us the same speech about money, plus she sayin we need to take us a bath before she let us anywhere near her girls. And I comes back with the five-hundred-dollar story. She say five hundred dollar tomorrow and we can come in tomorrow, but if we want some pussy tonight, she want a hunk of that old catfish in the back. Them hos can eat some catfish too, I'm tellin you. I thought Smiley finally gettin the Blues on him when I hears him sayin how he give up a hundred dollar worth of catfish just for a bath. But that his choice. He wait in the car 'til I'm done and we head off to find a place to sleep 'til morning when we can cash in the fish.

We pulls down a side road into some bushes, and we commencin to get us some sleep after a drink or two, when who come out the woods but a whole bunch of boys wearin them white sheets and pointy hoods, sayin, "Nigger, I guess you didn't read the sign."

And they tie us up to that ol' catfish and make us drag it back in the woods to a big ol' fire they got goin. That sho' a chill, I gots to tell you. To this day I can't walk by sheets hangin on a line without my backbone freeze up. I knows we sho' gonna die now, sayin my prayers and all best I can, while them boys kickin me in the mouth an' such while eatin catfish pieces what they roasted on sticks.

Then I feels it and the kickin stops. I see ol' Smiley lyin in the dirt, coverin his head with his arms, one ol' bloody eye lookin' over at me. He feel it too.

Them Klansmen staring into the woods like they long-lost momma gonna come out, big ol' grins on they faces, half of 'em rubbin they dicks through they pants. And she come out, all right. Big as a train, a howl like to make your ears bust and bleed. She take two of them in the first bite.

I don't have to write Smiley no letter. Before we can say somethin, we up and runnin, still tied up to what left of that catfish carcass, running back for the road. We finds us a knife in the car and we gets loose lickety-split— Smiley crankin that ol' Model T and me behind the wheel workin the choke. Hollerin and screamin comin out the woods sounding like music now, them Klansmen gettin all eat up.

Then it get quiet, just the sound of our breath and Smiley crankin the Model T. I'm yellin for him to hurry, I can hear that thing crashin though the woods. And finally, the Model T cranks over, but I can hardly hear it, 'cause that old dragon thing done broken out the woods and lets go a roar. I tells Smiley to get in, but he run back to the back of the car.

"What you doing?" I say.

"Five hundred dollar," he say.

And I see he throwing the catfish in the backseat. That stinky thing ain't nothin but a head now, so Smiley throw it in by hisself. Then he makes to jump on the running board and I looks over and he just snatched out the air. Gone. And them jaws coming down for the second time when I pull that ol' Model T in gear and take off.

Smiley gone. Gone.

Next day I find that white man say he pay five hundred dollar for the catfish, and he look at that big fish head and jus laugh at me. I say I lose the best friend I ever had, he better give me my goddamn money. But he laugh and tell me go away. So I hit him.

Took that old fish head to court with me, but it don't make no difference. That judge give me six months in jail—hittin a white man and all. He tell the bailiff, "Take Catfish away."

They call me Catfish since. I don't tell the story no more, but the name still there. Had the Blues on me ever since, but they ain't no makin amends. By the time I get out, Ida May die of grief, and I ain't got a friend alive. Been on the road since.

That thing on the beach, make that sound, she lookin for me.

Catfish

"It's a male," Estelle said. She didn't know what else to say.

"How you know?"

"I know." She took his hand. "I'm sorry about your friend."

"I just wanted him to get the Blues on him so we can make us a record."

They sat there at the table for a while, holding hands.

Catfish let his coffee go cold in the cup. Estelle ran the story around in her head, both relieved and fearful that the shadows in her paintings now had a shape. Somehow, as fantastic as it was, Catfish's story seemed familiar.

She said, "Catfish, did you ever read *The Old Man and the Sea* by Ernest Hemingway?"

"He that boy write about bullfights and fishing? I met him once, down Florida way. Why?'

"You met him?"

"Yeah, that sumbitch didn't believe that story neither. Said he like to fish, but he don't believe me. Why you ask?"

"Never mind," Estelle said. "If this thing eats people, don't you think we should report it?"

"I been tellin folks about that monster for some fifty years, ain't no one believed me yet. Said I was the biggest liar ever come outta the Delta. I'd have me a big house and a stack of records if not for that. You call the law and tell them 'bout this, they gonna call you the crazy woman of Pine Cove."

"We already have one of those."

"Well, ain't no one gonna get eat but me, and if I lose this gig 'cause they thinkin I'm crazy, I have to be movin on then. You understand?"

Estelle took Catfish's cup from the table and placed it in the sink. "You'd better get ready to go play."

 twelve

Molly

To distract herself from the dragon next door, Molly had put on her sweats and started to clean her trailer. She got as far as filling three black trash bags with junk food jetsam and was getting ready to vacuum up the collection of sow bug corpses that dotted her carpet when she made the mistake of Windexing the television. *Outland Steel: Kendra's Revenge* was playing on the VCR and when the droplets of Windex hit the screen, they magnified the phosphorescent dots, making the picture look like an impressionist painting: Seurat's *Sunday Afternoon on the Island of Le Grande Warrior Babe* perhaps.

Molly froze the frame on the gratuitous shower scene. (There was always a shower scene in the first five minutes of her films, despite the fact that Kendra lived on a planet almost completely devoid of water. To address this problem, one young director had gotten the bright idea of using "anti-radioactive foam" in the shower scene and Molly had spent five hours with whipped Ivory Snow suds being blown on to her by an offscreen Shop-Vac. She ended up playing the rest of the film in a Bedouin burnoose to cover the rash that developed all over her body.)

"Art film," Molly said, sitting on the floor in front of the TV, dowsing it with Windex for the fiftieth time. "I could have been a model in Paris in those days."

"Not a chance," said the narrator. He was still around. "Too skinny. They liked fat chicks back then."

"I'm not talking to you."

"You've used half a bottle of Windex for this little trip to Paris."

"Seems like cheap travel to me," Molly said. Even so, she got up and took two glasses from the top of the TV. She was taking them to the kitchen when the doorbell rang.

She opened the door with the rims of the glasses pinched in one hand. Outside, two women in dresses and heels and lots of hair spray were standing on her steps. They were both in their early thirties, blonde, and wore stiff smiles of either insincerity or drug use, Molly couldn't be sure which.

"Avon?" Molly asked.

"No," the blonde in front said with a titter. "I'm Marge Whitfield, this is Katie Marshall, we're from the Coalition for a Moral Society. We'd like to talk to you about our campaign to reinstate school prayer. I hope we haven't caught you at a bad time." Katie was in pink. Marge in pastel blue.

"I'm Molly Michon. I was just cleaning up a little." Molly held up the two glasses. "Come on in."

The two women stepped in and stood in the doorway as Molly took the glasses to the sink. "You know, it's interesting," Molly said, "but if you put Diet Coke in one glass, and regular Coke in another, and let them sit for, oh, say six months, then come back, there will be all sorts of green stuff growing on the regular Coke, but the Diet Coke will be as good as new."

Molly returned to the living room. "Can I get you two something to drink?"

"No thank you," Marge droned in robot response. She and Katie were staring at the paused image of a wet and naked Molly on the television screen. Molly breezed by them and flipped off the television. "Sorry, an art film I made in Paris when I was younger. Won't you sit down?"

The women sat down next to each other on Molly's tattered couch, their knees pinched together so tight they could have crushed diamonds to powder.

"I love your air freshener," Katie said, trying to pull out of her terror. "It smells so clean."

"Thanks, it's Windex."

"What a cute idea," Marge said.

This was good, Molly thought. Normal people. If I can hold myself together for normal people like these, I'll be okay. This is good practice. She sat down on the floor in front of them. "So your name is Marge. You don't hear that outside of detergent commercials anymore. Did your parents watch a lot of TV?"

Marge tittered. "It's short for Margaret, of course. My grandmother's name."

Katie jumped in. "Molly, we're very concerned that our children's education is totally without any spiritual instruction. The Coalition is collecting signatures for reinstatement of prayer in school."

"Okay," Molly said. "You're new in town, aren't you?"

"Why, yes, we've both moved here from Los Angeles with our husbands. A small town is just a better place to raise children, as I'm sure you know."

"Right," Molly said. They had no idea who she was. "That's why I brought my little Stevie here." Stevie was Molly's goldfish who had died during one of her stays in County. Now he lived in a Ziploc in her freezer and regarded her with a frosty gaze every time she retrieved some ice.

"And how old is Stevie?"

"Uh, seven or eight. I forget sometimes, it was a long labor."

"He's a year behind my Tiffany," Marge said.

"Well, he's a little slow."

"And your husband is . . . ?"

"Dead."

"I'm so sorry," Katie said.

"No need, you probably didn't kill him."

"Anyway," Katie said, "we'd really like to have your signature to send to the state senate. Single mothers are an important part of our campaign. And we're also collecting donations for the campaign to have the Constitution amended." She put on an embarrassed smile. "God's work needs funding too."

"I live in a trailer," Molly said.

"We understand," Marge said. "Finances are difficult for a single mother. But your signature is just as important to God's work."

"But I live in a trailer. God hates trailers."

"Beg pardon?"

"He burns them up, freezes them out, tears them up with tornadoes. God hates trailers. Are you sure I wouldn't be hurting your cause?"

Katie giggled. "Oh, Mrs. Michon, don't be silly. Just last week I read where a woman's trailer was picked up by a tornado and dropped almost a mile away and she survived. She said that she was praying the whole time and that God had saved her. You see?"

"Then who sent the tornado in the first place?"

The two pastel women squirmed on the couch. The blue one spoke first. "We'd love to have you at our Bible study group, where we could discuss that, but we have to be getting along. Would you mind signing the petition?" She pulled a clipboard out of her oversized purse and handed it over to Molly with a pen.

"So if this works, kids will be able to pray in school?"

"Why, yes." Marge brightened.

"So the Muslim kids can turn to Mecca seven times a day or whatever and it won't count against their grades?"

The blue and pink pastel ladies looked at each other. "Well, America is a Christian nation, Mrs. Michon."

Molly didn't want them to think she was a pushover. She was a smart woman. "But kids of other faiths can pray too, right?"

"I suppose so," Katie said. "To themselves."

"Oh good," Molly said as she signed the petition, "because I know that Stevie could move up to the Red Jets reading group if he could sacrifice a chicken to Vigoth the Worm God, but the teacher won't let him." Why did I say that? Why did I say that? What if they ask where Stevie is?

"Mrs. Michon!"

"What? He'd do it at recess," Molly said. "It's not like it would cut into study time."

"We are working on behalf of the One True God, Mrs. Michon. The Coalition is not an interfaith organization. I'm sure that if you had felt the power of His spirit, you wouldn't talk that way."

"Oh, I've felt it. "

"You have?"

"Of course. You can feel it too. Right now."

"What do you mean?"

Molly handed the clipboard back to Katie and stood up. "Come next door with me. It'll only take a second. I know you'll feel it."

Theo

Theo's hopes of finding Mikey Plotznik rose as he drove through the residential areas of Pine Cove. Nearly every neighborhood had two or three people out searching with flashlights and cell phones. Theo stopped and took reports from each search party, then made suggestions as if he had the slightest idea what he was doing. Who was he kidding? He couldn't even find his car keys half the time.

Most of Pine Cove's neighborhoods were without sidewalks or streetlights. The canopy of pine trees absorbed the moonlight and darkness drank up Theo's headlights like an ocean of ink. He plugged his handheld spotlight in the lighter socket and swept it across the houses and into the vacant lots, spotting nothing but a pair of mule deer eating someone's rosebuds. As he drove by the beach park—a grass playground the size of a football field, surrounded by cypress trees and blocked from the Pacific wind by an eight-foot redwood fence—he spotted a flash of white moving on one of the picnic tables. He pulled into the parking strip beside the park and pointed the Volvo's headlights, as well as the spotlight, at the table.

A couple was going at it right there on the table. The flash of white had been the man's bare ass. Two faces turned into the light, eyes as wide as the two deer Theo had surprised earlier. Normally, Theo would have driven on. He was used to finding people "in the act" in cars behind the Head of the Slug, or parked along the more rugged strips of coastline. He wasn't the sex police, after all. But tonight he was irritated by the scene. It had been almost a whole day since he'd had a hit from his Sneaky Pete. Maybe it's a symptom of withdrawal, he thought.

He turned off the Volvo and got out, taking his flashlight with him. The couple scrambled into their clothes as he approached, but didn't try to escape. There was nowhere for them to go except over the fence, where a narrow beach was bordered on both sides by cliffs and washed by treacherous, freezing rip tides.

When he was halfway across the park, Theo recognized the fornicators and stopped. The woman, a girl really, was Betsy Butler, a waitress down at H.P.'s Cafe. She was struggling to pull down her skirt. The man, balding and slack-chested, was the newly widowed Joseph Leander. Theo flashed on the image of Bess Leander hanging from a peg in the spotless dining room.

"A little discretion's in order here, you think, Joe?" Theo shouted as he walked toward them.

"Uh, it's Joseph, Constable."

Theo felt his scalp go hot with anger. He wasn't an angry man by nature, but nature hadn't been working the last few days. "No, it's Joseph when you're doing business or when you're grieving over your dead wife. When you're boning a girl half your age on a picnic table in a public park, it's Joe."

"I—we—things have been so difficult. I don't know what came over us—I mean, me. I mean . . ."

"I don't suppose you've seen a kid around here tonight? A boy, about ten?"

The girl shook her head. She was covering her face with one hand and staring into the grass at her feet. Joseph Leander's gaze darted around the park as if a magic escape hatch would open up in the dark if he could only spot it. "No, I haven't seen a boy."

Technically, Theo knew he could arrest them both on the spot for indecent exposure, but he didn't want to take the time to process them into County Justice. "Go home, Joe. Alone. Your daughters shouldn't be by themselves right now. Betsy, do you have a ride?"

Without uncovering her face, she said, "I only live two blocks away."

"Go home. Now." Theo turned and walked back to the Volvo. No one had ever accused Theo of being clever (except for the time at a college party when he fashioned an emergency bong out of a two-liter Coke bottle and a Bic pen), but he was feeling somewhat less than clever for not having investigated Bess Leander's death more carefully. It was one thing to be hired because you're thought to be a fool, it's quite another to live up to the reputation.

Tomorrow, he thought. First find the kid.

Molly

Molly stood in the mud with the two pastel Christian ladies looking at the dragon trailer.

"Can you feel it?"

"Why, whatever do you mean?" Marge said. "That's just a dirty old trailer—excuse me—mobile home." Until a second ago, she had only been concerned with her powder-blue high heels sinking into the wet turf. Now she and her partner were staring at the dragon trailer, wide-eyed.

They *could* feel it, Molly could tell. She could feel it too: a low-grade sense of contentment, something vaguely sexual, not quite joy, but close. "You're feeling it?"

The two women looked to each other, trying to deny that they were feeling anything. Their eyes were glazed over as if they'd been drugged, and they fidgeted as if suppressing giggles. Katie, the pink one, said, "Maybe we should visit these people." She took a tentative step toward the dragon trailer.

Molly stepped in front of her. "There's no one there. It's just a feeling. You two should probably go fill out your petition."

"It's late," said powder blue. "Maybe one more visit, then we have to go."

"No!" Molly blocked their path. This wasn't as fun as she thought it would be. She had wanted to freak them out a little, not harm them. She had the distinct feeling that if they got any closer to the dragon trailer, school prayer would be losing two well-groomed votes. "You two need to get home." She took each by a shoulder and led them back to the street, then pushed them toward the entrance of the trailer park. They looked longingly over their shoulders at the dragon trailer.

"I feel the spirit moving in me, Katie," Marge said.

Molly gave them another push. "Right, that's a good thing. Off you go." And she was supposed to be the crazy one.

"Go, go, go," Molly said. "I have to get Stevie's dinner ready."

"We're sorry we missed meeting your little boy," Katie said. "Where is he?"

"Homework. See ya. Bye."

Molly watched the women walk out of the park and climb into a new Chrysler minivan, then she turned back to the dragon trailer. For some reason, she was no longer afraid.

"You're hungry, aren't you, Stevie?"

The dragon trailer shifted shape, angles melting to curves, windows going back to eyes, but the glow wasn't as intense as it had been in the early dawn. Molly saw the burned gill trees, the soot and blistered flesh between the scales. Soft blue lines of color flashed across the dragon's flanks and faded. Molly felt her heart sink in sympathy. This thing, whatever it was, was hurting.

Molly took a few steps closer. "I have a feeling you're too old to be a Stevie. And the original Stevie might be offended. How about Steve? You look like a Steve." Molly liked the name Steve. Her agent at CAA had been named Steve. Steve was a good name for a reptile. (As opposed to Stevie, which was more of a frozen goldfish name.)

She felt a wave of warmth run through her amid the sadness. The monster liked his name.

"You shouldn't have eaten that kid."

Steve said nothing. Molly took another step forward, still on guard. "You have to go away. I can't help you.

I'm crazy, you know? I have the papers from the state to prove it."

The Sea Beast rolled over on his back like a submissive puppy and gave Molly a pathetically helpless look, no easy task for an animal capable of swallowing a Volkswagen.

"No," Molly said.

The Sea Beast whimpered, no louder than a newborn kitten.

"Oh, this is just swell," Molly said. "Imagine the meds Dr. Val is going to put me on when I tell her about this. The vegetable and the lizard, that's what they'll call us. I hope you're happy."

Peer Pressure

"But I don't want to go among mad people," Alice remarked.

"Oh, you can't help that," said the cat. "We're all mad here. I'm mad. You're mad."

"How do you know I'm mad?" said Alice.

"You must be," said the cat, "or you wouldn't have come here."

—LEWIS CARROL,
Alice's Adventures in Wonderland

 **thirteen**

Breakfast

Somehow, through the night, the residents of Pine Cove, especially those who had been withdrawing from antidepressants, found a satisfied calm had fallen over them. It wasn't that their anxiety was gone, but rather that it ran off their backs like warm rain off a naked toddler who has just discovered the splash and magic of mud. There was joy and sex and danger in the air—and a euphoric need to share.

Morning found many of them herding at the local restaurants for breakfast. Gathering together like wildebeests in the presence of a pride of lions, knowing instinctively that only one of them is going to fall to the fang: the one that is caught alone.

Jenny Masterson had been waiting tables at H.P.'s Cafe for twelve years, and she couldn't remember a day out of the tourist season when it had been so busy. She moved between her tables like a dancer, pouring coffee and decaf, taking orders and delivering food, catching the odd request for more butter or salsa, and snatching up a dirty plate or glass on her way back to the window. No movement wasted, no customer ignored. She was good—really good—and sometimes that bugged the hell out of her.

Jenny was just forty, slender and fair-skinned with

killer legs and long auburn hair that she wore pinned up when she worked. With her husband Robert, she owned Brine's Bait, Tackle, and Fine Wines, but after three months of trying to work with the man she loved and after the birth of her daughter Amanda, who was five, she returned to waitressing to save her marriage and her sanity. Somewhere between college and today, she had become a bull moose waitress, and she never ceased to wonder how in the hell that had happened. How had she become the repository for local information bordering on gossip, and how had she become so damn good at picking up her customers' conversations, and following them as she moved around the restaurant?

Today the restaurant was full of talk about Mikey Plotznik, who had disappeared along his paper route the day before. There was talk of the search and speculation on the kid's fate. At a few of her two-tops were seated couples who seemed intent on reliving their sexual adventures from the night before and—if the pawing and fawning were any indication—were going to resume again after breakfast. Jenny tried to tune them out. There was a table of her old-guy coffee drinkers, who were trading misinformation on politics and lawn care; at the counter a couple of construction workers intent on putting in a rare Saturday's work read the paper over bacon and eggs; and over in the corner, Val Riordan, the local shrink, was scribbling notes on a legal pad at a table all by herself. That was unusual. Dr. Val didn't normally make appearances in Pine Cove during the day. Stranger than that, Estelle Boyet, the seascape painter, was having her tea with a Black gentleman who looked as if he would jump out of his skin at the slightest touch.

Jenny heard some commotion coming from the register and turned to see her busgirl arguing with Molly Michon, the Crazy Lady. Jenny made a beeline for the counter.

"Molly, you're not supposed to be in here," Jenny said calmly but firmly. Molly had been eighty-sixed for life after she had attacked H.P.'s espresso machine.

"I just need to cash this check. I need to get some money to buy medicine for a sick friend."

The busgirl, a freshman at Pine Cove High, bolted into the kitchen, tossing "I told her" over her shoulder as she went.

Jenny looked at the check. It was from the Social Security Administration and it was above the amount she was allowed to accept. "I'm sorry, Molly, I can't do it."

"I have photo ID." Molly pulled a videotape out of her enormous handbag and plopped it on the counter. There was a picture of a half-naked woman tied between two stakes on the cover. The titles were in Italian.

"That's not it, Molly. I'm not allowed to cash a check for that much. Look, I don't want any trouble, but if Howard sees you in here, he'll call the police."

"The police are here" came a man's voice.

Jenny looked up to see Theophilus Crowe towering behind Molly. "Hi, Theo." Jenny liked Theo. He reminded her of Robert before he had quit drinking—semitragic but good-natured.

"Can I help here?"

"I really need to get some money," Molly said. "For medicine."

Jenny shot a look to the corner, where Val Riordan looked up from her notes with an expression of dread on her face. The psychiatrist obviously didn't want to be brought into this.

Theo took the check gently from Molly and looked at it, then said to Jenny, "It's a government check, Jenny. I'm sure it's good. Just this once? Medicine." He winked at Jenny from behind Molly's back.

"Howard will kill me when he sees it. Every time he

looks at the espresso machine, he mutters something about spawn of evil."

"I'll back you up. Tell him it was in the interest of public safety."

"Oh, okay. You're lucky we're busy today and I have the cash to spare." Jenny handed Molly a pen. "Just endorse it."

Molly signed the check with a flourish and handed it over. Jenny counted out the bills on the counter. "Thanks," Molly said. Then to Theo, "Thanks. Hey, you want a collector's edition of *Warrior Babes*?" She held the videotape out to him.

"Uh, no thanks, Molly. I can't accept gratuities."

Jenny craned her neck to look at the cover of the tape.

"It's in Italian, but you can figure it out," Molly said.

Theo shook his head and smiled.

"Okay," Molly said. "Gotta go." She turned and walked out of the restaurant, leaving Theo staring at her back.

"I guess she really was in movies," Jenny said. "Did you see the picture on the cover?"

"Nope," Theo said.

"Amazing. Did she look like that?"

Theo shrugged. "Thanks for taking her check, Jenny. I'll find a seat. Just some coffee and an English muffin."

"Any luck finding the Plotznik kid?"

Theo shook his head as he walked away.

Gabe

Skinner barked once to warn the Food Guy that he was about to collide with the crazy woman, but it came a little too late and, as usual, the dense but good-hearted Food

Guy didn't get the message. Skinner had finally talked the Food Guy into stopping work and going to get something to eat. Catching rats and hiking around in the mud was fun, but eating was important.

Gabe, covered with mud to the knees and burrs to the shoulder, was head down, digging in his backpack for his wallet as he approached H.P.'s Cafe. Coming out, Molly was counting her money, not looking at all where she was going. She heard Skinner bark just as they conked heads.

"Ouch, excuse me," Gabe said, rubbing his head. "I wasn't watching where I was going."

Skinner took the opportunity to sniff Molly's crotch. "Nice dog," Molly said. "Did he produce B movies in his last life?"

"Sorry." Gabe grabbed Skinner by the collar and pulled him away.

Molly folded her money and stuffed it into the waistband of her tights. "Hey, you're the biologist, huh?"

"That's me."

"How many grams of protein in a sow bug?"

"What?"

"A sow bug. You know, roly-polies, pill bugs—gray, lotsa legs, designed to curl up and die?"

"Yes, I know what a sow bug is."

"How many grams of protein in one?"

"I have no idea."

"Could you find out?"

"I suppose I could."

"Good," Molly said. "I'll call you."

"Okay."

"Bye." Molly ruffled Skinner's ears as she walked off.

Gabe stood there for a second, distracted from his research for the first time in thirty-six hours. "What the hell?"

Skinner wagged his tail to say, "Let's eat."

Dr. Val

Val Riordan watched the lanky constable coming through the restaurant toward her. She wasn't ready to be official, that's why she'd taken herself out to breakfast in the first place—that and she didn't want to face her assistant Chloe and her newfound nymphomania. She was months, no, years behind on her professional journals, and she'd packed a briefcase full of them in hope of skimming a few over coffee before her appointments began. She tried to hide behind a copy of *Pusher: The American Journal of Clinical Psychopharmacological Practice*, but the constable just kept coming.

"Dr. Riordan, do you have a minute?"

"I suppose." She gestured to the chair across from her.

Theo sat down and dove right in. "Are you sure that Bess Leander never said anything about problems with her marriage? Fights? Joseph coming home late? Anything?"

"I told you before. I can't talk about it."

Theo took a dollar out of his pocket and slid it across the table. "Take this."

"Why?"

"I want you to be my therapist. I want the same patient confidentiality that you're giving Bess Leander. Even though that privilege isn't supposed to extend beyond the grave. I'm hiring you as my therapist."

"For a dollar? I'm not a lawyer, Constable Crowe. I don't have to accept you as a patient. And payment has nothing to do with it." Val was willing him to go away. She had tried to bend people to her will since she was a child. She'd spoken to her therapist about it during her residency. Go away.

"Fine, take me as a patient. Please."

"I'm not taking any new patients."

"One session, thirty seconds long. I'm your patient. I promise you'll want to hear what I have to say in session."

"Theo, have you ever addressed, well, your substance abuse problem?" It was a snotty and unprofessional thing to say, but Crowe wasn't exactly being professional either.

"Does that mean I'm your patient?"

"Sure, okay, thirty seconds."

"Last night I saw Joseph Leander engaging in sexual relations with a young woman in the park." Theo folded his hands and sat back. "Your thoughts?"

Jenny couldn't believe she'd heard it right. She hadn't meant to, she was just delivering an English muffin when the gossip bomb hit her unprepared. Bess Leander, not even cold in the grave, and her straitlaced Presbyterian husband was doing it with some bimbo in the park? She paused as if checking her tables, waited for a second, then slid the muffin in front of Theo.

"Can I bring you anything else?"

"Not right now," Theo said.

Jenny looked at Val Riordan and decided that whatever she needed right now was not on the menu. Val was sitting there wide-eyed, as if someone had slapped her with a dead mackerel. Jenny backed away from the table. She couldn't wait for Betsy to come in to relieve her for the lunch shift. Betsy always waited on Joseph Leander when he came in the cafe and made comments about him being the only guy with two children who had never been laid. She'd be blown away.

Betsy, of course, already knew.

Gabe

Gabe tied Skinner up outside and entered the cafe to find all the tables occupied. He spotted Theophilus Crowe sitting at a four-top with a woman that he didn't know. Gabe debated inviting himself to their table, then decided it would be better to approach Theo under the pretense of a rat news update and hope for an invitation.

Gabe pulled his laptop out of his shoulder bag as he approached the table.

"Theo, you won't believe what I found out last night."

Theo looked up. "Hi, Gabe. Do you know Val Riordan? She's our local psychiatrist."

Gabe offered his hand to the woman and she took it without looking away from his muddy boots. "Sorry," Gabe said. "I've been in the field all day. Nice to meet you."

"Gabe's a biologist. He has a lab up at the weather station."

Gabe was feeling uncomfortable now. The woman hadn't said a word. She was attractive in a made-up sort of way, but she seemed a little out of things, stunned perhaps. "I'm sorry to interrupt. We can talk later, Theo."

"No, sit down. You don't mind, do you, Val? We can finish our session later. I think I still have twenty seconds on the books."

"That's fine," Val said, seeming to come out of her haze.

"Maybe you'll be interested in this," Gabe said. He slipped into an empty chair and pushed his laptop in front of Val. "Look at this." Like many scientists, Gabe was oblivious to the fact that no one gave a rat's ass about research unless it could be expressed in terms of dollars.

"Green dots?" Val said.

"No, those are rats."

"Funny, they look like green dots."

"This is a topographical map of Pine Cove. These are my tagged rats. See the divergence? These ten that didn't move the other night when the others did?"

Val looked to Theo for an explanation.

"Gabe tracks rats with microchips in them," Theo said.

"It's only one of the things I do. Mostly, I count dead things on the beach."

"Fascinating work," Val said with no attempt to hide her contempt.

"Yeah, it's great," Gabe said. Then to Theo, "Anyway, these ten rats didn't move with the others."

"Right, you told me this. You thought they might be dead."

"They weren't, at least the six of them that I found weren't. It wasn't death that stopped them, it was sex."

"What?"

"I live-trapped twenty of the group of rats that moved, but when I went to find the group that hadn't, I didn't have to trap them. There were three pairs, all engaged in coitus."

"So what made the others move?"

"I don't know."

"But the other ones were, uh, mating?"

"I watched one pair for an hour. They did it a hundred and seventeen times."

"In an hour? Rats can do that?"

"They can, but they don't."

"But you said they did."

"It's an anomaly. But all three pairs were doing it. One of the females had died and the male was still going at her when I found them."

Theo's face was becoming strained with the effort of trying to figure out what in the hell Gabe was trying to tell him, and why he was telling him in the first place. "What does that mean?"

"I have no idea," Gabe said. "I don't know why there

was a mass evacuation of the large group, and I don't know why the smaller group stayed in one place copulating."

"Well, thanks for sharing."

"Food and sex," Gabe said.

"Maybe you should eat something, Gabe." Theo signaled for the waitress.

"What do you mean, food and sex?" Val asked.

"All behavior is related to obtaining food and sex," Gabe said.

"How Freudian."

"No, Darwinian, actually."

Val leaned forward and Gabe caught a whiff of her perfume. She actually seemed interested now. "How can you say that? Behavior is much more complex than that."

"You think so?"

"I know so. And whatever this is, this radio rat study of yours proves it." She swiveled the screen of the laptop so they all could see it. "You have six rats that were engaged in sex, but if I have this straight, you have, well, a lot of rats that just took off for no reason at all. Right?"

"There was a reason, I just don't know it yet."

"But it wasn't food and it obviously wasn't sex."

"I don't know yet. I suppose they could have been exposed to television violence."

Theo was sitting back and watching now, enjoying two people with three decades of education between them puffing up like schoolyard bullies.

"I'm a psychiatrist, not a psychologist. Our discipline has moved more toward physiological causes for behavior over the last thirty years, or hadn't you heard?" Val Riordan was actually grinning now.

"I'm aware of that. I'm having the brain chemistry worked up on animals from both groups to see if there's a neurochemical explanation."

"How do you do that again?" Theo asked.

"You grind up their brains and analyze the chemicals," Gabe said.

"That's got to hurt," Theo said.

Val Riordan laughed. "I only wish I could diagnose my patients that way. Some of them anyway."

Val

Val Riordan couldn't remember the last time she'd enjoyed herself, but she suspected it was when she'd attended the Neiman-Marcus sale in San Francisco two years ago. Food and sex indeed. This guy was so naive. But still, she hadn't seen anyone so passionate about pure research since med school, and it was nice to think about psychiatry in terms other than financial. She found herself wondering how Gabe Fenton would look in a suit, after a shower and a shave, after he'd been boiled to kill the parasites. Not bad, she thought.

Gabe said, "I can't seem to identify any outside stimulus for this behavior, but I have to eliminate the possibility that it's something chemical or environmental. If it's affecting the rats, it might be affecting other species too. I've seen some evidence of that."

Val thought about the wave of horniness that seemed to have washed over all of her patients in the last two days. "Could it be in the water, do you think? Something that might affect us?"

"Could be. If it's chemical, it would take longer to affect a mammal as large as a human. You two haven't seen anything unusual in the last few days, have you?"

Theo nearly spit his coffee out. "This town's a bughouse."

"I'm not allowed to talk about my patients specifically," Val said. She was shaken. Of course there was some weird behavior. She'd caused it, hadn't she, by taking fifteen hundred people off of their medication at once? She had to get out of here. "But in general, Theo is right."

"I am?" Theo said.

"He is?" Gabe said.

Jenny had returned to the table to fill their coffees. "Sorry I overheard, but I'd have to agree with Theo too."

They all looked at her, then at each other. Val checked her watch. "I've got to get to an appointment. Gabe, I'd like to hear the results of the brain chemistry test."

"You would?"

"Yes."

Val put some money on the table and Theo picked it up and handed it back to her, along with the dollar he'd put there earlier for her fee. "I need to talk to you about that other matter, Val."

"Call me. I don't know if I can help though. Bye."

Val left the cafe actually looking forward to seeing her patients, if for no other reason than to imagine grinding up each of their brains. Anything to address the responsibility of driving an entire town crazy. But perhaps by driving them a little crazy, she could save some of them from self-destruction: not a bad reason for going to work.

Gabe

"I've got to go too," Theo said, standing up. "Gabe, should I have the county test the water or something? I have to go into San Junipero to the county building today anyway."

"Not yet. I can do a general toxins and heavy metals test. I do them all the time for the frog population studies."

"You wanna walk out with me?"

"I have to order something to go for Skinner."

"Didn't you say that you had ten rats that diverged from the pack?"

"Yes, but I could only find six."

"What happened to the other four?"

"I don't know. They just disappeared. Funny, these chips are nearly indestructible too. Even if the animals are dead, I should be able to pick them up with the satellites."

"Out of range maybe?"

"Not a chance, the coverage is over two hundred miles. More if I look for them."

"Then where did they go?"

"They last showed up down by the creek. Near the Fly Rod Trailer Court."

"You're kidding. That's where the Plotznik kid was last seen."

"You want to see the map?"

"No, I believe you. I've got to go." Theo turned to leave.

Gabe caught him by the shoulder. "Theo, is, uh . . ."

"What?"

"Is Val Riordan single?"

"Divorced."

"Do you think she likes me?"

Theo shook his head. "Gabe, I understand. I spend too much time alone too."

"What? I was just asking."

"I'll see you."

"Hey, Theo, you look, uh, well, more alert today."

"Not stoned, you mean?"

"Sorry, I didn't mean . . ."

"It's okay, Gabe. Thanks, I think."

"Hang tough."

Jenny

As Jenny passed Estelle Boyet's table, she heard the old Black gentleman say, "We don't need to tell nobody nothin'. Been fifty years since I seen that thing. It probably done gone back to the sea."

"Still," Estelle said, " there's a little boy missing. What if the two are connected?"

"Ain't nobody ever called you a crazy nigger, did they?"

"Not that I can remember."

"Well, they have me. For some twenty years after I talked about that thing the last time. I ain't sayin' nothin' to no one. It's our secret, girl."

"I like it when you call me girl," Estelle said.

Jenny went off to the kitchen, trying to put the morning together in her mind, pieces of conversations as surreal as a Dali jigsaw puzzle. There was definitely something going on in Pine Cove.

fourteen

Molly

Pine Cove was a decorative town—built for show—only one degree more functional than a Disneyland attraction and decidedly lacking in businesses and services that catered to residents rather than tourists. The business district included ten art galleries, five wine-tasting rooms, twenty restaurants, eleven gift and card shops, and one hardware store. The position of hardware clerk in Pine Cove was highly coveted by the town's retired male population, for nowhere else could a man posture well past his prime, pontificate, and generally indulge in the arrogant self-important chest-pounding of an alpha male without having a woman intercede to remind him that he was patently full of shit.

Crossing the threshold of Pine Cove Hardware and breaking the beam that rang the bell was tantamount to setting off a testosterone alarm, and if they'd had their way, the clerks would have constructed a device to atomize the corners with urine every time the bell tolled. Or at least that's the way it seemed to Molly when she entered that Saturday morning.

The clerks, three men, broke from their heated argument on the finer points of installing a wax toilet seal ring to stare, snicker, and make snide comments under their breath about the woman who had entered their domain.

Molly breezed past the counter, focusing on an aisle display of gopher poison to avoid eye contact. Raucous laughter erupted from the clerks when she turned down the aisle for roofing supplies.

The clerks, Frank, Bert, and Les—all semiretired, balding, paunchy, and generally interchangeable, except that Frank wore a belt to hold up his double knits, while the other two sported suspenders fashioned to look like yellow measuring tape—planned to make Molly beg. Oh, they'd let her wander around for a while, let her try to comprehend the arcane function of the gizmos, geegaws, and widgets binned and bubble-wrapped around the store. Then she would have to come back to the counter and submit. It was Frank's turn to do the condescending, and he would do his best to drop-kick her ego before finally leading the little lady to the appropriate product, where he would continue to question her into full humiliation. "Well, is it a sheet metal screw or a wood screw? Three-eighths or seven-sixteenths? Do you have a hex head screwdriver? Well, then, you'll need one, won't you? Are you sure you wouldn't rather just call someone to do this for you?" Tears and/or sniffles from the customer would signal victory and confirm superior status for the male race.

Frank, Bert, and Les watched Molly on the security monitor, exchanged some comments about her breasts, laughed nervously after five minutes passed without her surrender, and tried to look busy when she emerged from the aisle carrying a five-gallon can of roof-patching tar, a roll of fiberglass fabric, and a long-handled squeegee.

Molly stood at the counter, shifting her weight from foot to foot. Bert and Les squinted into a catalog set on a rotating stand while concentrating on sucking in their guts. Frank manned the register and pretended he was doing something complex on the keyboard, when, in fact, he was just making it beep.

Molly cleared her throat.

Frank looked up as if he'd just noticed she was there. "Find everything you need?"

"I think so," Molly said, taking both hands to lift the heavy can of tar onto the counter.

"You need some resin for that fiberglass fabric?" Les said.

"And some hardener?" Bert said. Frank snickered.

"Some what?" Molly said.

"You can't patch a trailer roof with that stuff, miss. You live down at the Fly Rod, don't you?" They all knew who she was and where she lived. She was often the subject of hardware store gossip and speculation, even though she'd never set foot in there before today.

"I'm not going to patch a roof."

"Well, you can't use that on a driveway. You need asphalt sealer, and it should be applied with a brush, not a squeegee."

"How much do I owe you?" Molly said.

"You should wear a respirator when you work with fiberglass. You have one at home, right?" Bert asked.

"Yeah, right next to the elves and the gnomes," Les said.

Molly didn't flinch.

"He's right," Frank said. "Those fibers get down in your lungs and they could do you a world of harm, especially with those lungs."

The clerks all laughed at the joke.

"I've got a respirator out in the truck," Les said. "I could come by after work and give you a hand with your little project."

"That would be great," Molly said. "What time?"

Les balked. "Well, I, um . . ."

"I'll pick up some beer." Molly smiled. "You guys should come along too. I could really use the help."

"Oh, I think Les can handle it, can't you, Les?" Frank

said as he hit the total key. "That comes to thirty-seven sixty-five with tax."

Molly counted her money out on the counter. "So I'll see you tonight?"

Les swallowed hard and forced a smile. "You bet," he said.

"Thanks then," Molly said brightly. Then she picked up her supplies and headed for the door.

As she broke the doorbell beam, Frank whispered "Crazy slut" under his breath.

Molly stopped, turned slowly, and winked.

Once she was outside, the clerks made miserable old white guy attempts at trading high-fives while patting Les on the back. It was a hardware store fantasy fulfilled— much better than just humiliating a woman, Les would get to humiliate her and get her naked as well. For some reason they'd all been feeling a little randy lately, thinking about sex almost as often as power tools.

"My wife is going to kill me," Les said.

"What she don't know won't hurt her," the other two said in unison.

Theo

Theo actually felt his stomach lurch when he went into his victory garden and clipped a handful of sticky buds from his pot plants. They weren't for himself this time, but the reminder of how much this little patch of plants ruled his life made him ill. And how was it that he hadn't felt the need to fire up his Sneaky Pete for three days? A twenty-year drug habit suddenly ends? No withdrawal, no side effects, no cravings? The freedom was almost nauseating. It was as if the Weirdness Fairy had landed in his life with a thump, popped him on the head with a rubber chicken, bit him on the shin, then went off to inflict herself on the rest of Pine Cove.

He stuffed the marijuana into a plastic bag, tucked it into his jacket pocket, and climbed into the Volvo for the forty-mile drive to San Junipero. He was going to have to enter the bowels of the county justice building and face the Spider to find out what he wanted to know. The pot was grease for the Spider. He would stop by a convenience store on the way down and pick up a bag full of snacks to augment the bribe. The Spider was difficult, arrogant, and downright creepy, but he was a cheap date.

Through the safety-glass window, Theo could see the Spider sitting in the middle of his web: five computer screens with data scrolling across them illuminated the Spider with an ominous blue glow. The only other light in the room came from tiny red and green power indicator lights that shone through the darkness like crippled stars. Without looking away from his screens, the Spider buzzed Theo in.

"Crowe," the Spider said, not looking up.

"Lieutenant," Theo said.

"Call me Nailgun," the Spider said.

His name was Irving Nailsworth and his official position in the San Junipero Sheriff's Department was chief technical officer. He was five-foot-five inches tall, weighed three hundred and thirty pounds, and had taken to wearing a black beret when he perched in his web. Early on, Nailsworth had seen that nerds would rule the world, and he had staked out his own little information fiefdom in the basement of the county jail. Nothing happened without the Spider knowing about it. He monitored and controlled all the information that moved about the county, and before anyone recognized what sort of power that afforded, he had made himself indispensable to the system. He had never arrested a suspect, touched a firearm, or set foot in a patrol car, yet he was the third-highest-ranking officer on the force.

Besides a taste for raw data, the Spider had weaknesses for junk food, Internet porn, and high-quality marijuana. The latter was Theo's key to the Spider's lair. He put the plastic Baggie on the keyboard in front of Nailsworth. Still without looking at Theo, the Spider opened the bag and sniffed, pinched a bud between his fingers, then folded the bag up and stuffed it into his shirt pocket.

"Nice," he said. "What do you need?" He peeled the marshmallow cap off a Hostess Sno Ball, shoved it into his mouth, then threw the cake into a wastebasket at his feet.

Theo set the bag of snacks down next to the wastebasket. "I need the autopsy report on Bess Leander."

The Nailgun nodded, no easy task for a man with no discernible neck. "And?"

Theo wasn't sure what questions to ask. Nailsworth seldom volunteered information, you had to ask the right question. It was like talking to a rotund Sphinx. "I was wondering if you could come up with something that might help me find Mikey Plotznik." Theo knew he didn't have to explain. The Spider would know all about the missing kid.

The Spider reached into the bag at his feet and pulled out a Twinkie. "Let me pull up the autopsy." His fat fingers flew over the keyboard. "You need a printout?"

"That would be nice."

"It doesn't show you as the investigating officer."

"That's why I came to you. The M.E.'s office wouldn't let me see the report."

"Says here cause of death was cardiac arrest due to asphyxiation. Suicide."

"Yes, she hung herself."

"I don't think so."

"I saw the body."

"I know. Hanging in the dining room."

"So what do you mean, you don't think so?

"The ligature marks on her neck were postmortem, according to this. Neck wasn't broken, so she didn't drop suddenly."

Theo squinted at the screen, trying to make sense of the data. "There were heel marks on the wall. She had to have hung herself. She was depressed, taking Zoloft for it."

"Not according to the toxicology."

"What?"

"They ran the toxicology for antidepressants because you put it on the report, but there was nothing."

"It says suicide right there."

"Yes, it does, but the date doesn't corroborate the timing. Looks like she had a heart attack. Then she hung herself afterward."

"So she was murdered?"

"You wanted to see the report. It says cardiac arrest. But ultimately, cardiac arrest is what kills everyone. Catch a bullet in the head, get hit by a car, eat some poison. The heart tends to stop."

"Eat some poison?"

"Just an example, Crowe. It's not my field. If I were you, I'd check and see if she had a history of heart problems."

"You said it wasn't your field."

"It's not." The Spider hit a key and a laser printer whirred in the darkness somewhere.

"I don't have much on the kid. I could give you the subscription list for his paper route."

Theo realized that he had gotten all he was going to get on Bess Leander. "I have that. How about giving me any known baby-rapers in the area?"

"That's easy." The Spider's fingers danced over the keyboard. "You think the kid was snatched?"

"I don't know shit," Theo said.

The Spider said, "No known pedophiles in Pine Cove. You want the whole county?"

"Why not?"

The laser printer whirred and the Spider pointed through the dark at the noise. "Everything you want is back there. That's all I can do for you."

"Thanks, Nailgun, I appreciate it." Theo felt a chronic case of the creeps going up his spine. He took a step into the dark and found the papers sitting in the tray of the laser printer. Then he stepped to the door. "You wanna buzz me out?"

The Spider swiveled in his chair and looked at Theo for the first time. Theo could see his piggy eyes shining out of deep craters.

"You still live in that cabin by the Beer Bar Ranch?"

"Yep," Theo said. "Eight years now."

"Never been on the ranch, though, have you?"

"No." Theo cringed. Could the Spider know about Sheriff Burton's hold over him?

"Good," the Spider said. "Stay out of there. And Theo?"

"Yeah?"

"Sheriff Burton has been checking with me on everything that comes out of Pine Cove. After the Leander death and the truck blowing up, he got very jumpy. If you decide to pursue the Leander thing, stay low-key."

Theo was amazed. The Spider had actually volunteered information. "Why?" was all he could say.

"I like the herb you bring me." The Spider patted his shirt pocket.

Theo smiled. "You won't tell Burton you gave me the autopsy report?"

"Why would I?" said the Spider.

"Take care, " Theo said. The Spider turned back to his screens and buzzed the door.

Molly

Molly wasn't so sure that life as Pine Cove's Crazy Lady wasn't harder than being a Warrior Babe of the Outland. Things were pretty clear for a Warrior Babe: you ran around half-naked looking for food and fuel and occasionally kicked the snot out of some mutants. There was no subterfuge or rumor. You didn't have to guess whether or not the Sand Pirates approved of your behavior. If they approved, they staked you out and tortured you. If they didn't, they called you a bitch, then they staked you out and tortured you. They might release starving radioactive cockroaches on you or burn you with hot pokers, they might even gang-rape you (in foreign-release directors' cuts only), but you always knew where you stood with Sand Pirates. And they never tittered. Molly had had all the tittering she could handle for the day. At the pharmacy, they had tittered.

Four elderly women worked the counter at Pine Cove Drug and Gift, while above them, behind his glass window, Winston Krauss, the dolphin-molesting pharmacist, lorded over them like a rooster over a barnyard full of hens. It didn't seem to matter to Winston that his four hens couldn't make change or answer the simplest question, nor that they would retreat to the back room when anyone younger than thirty entered the pharmacy, lest they have to sell something embarrassing like condoms. What mattered to Winston was that his hens worked for minimum wage and treated him like a god. He was behind glass; tittering didn't bother him.

The hens started tittering when Molly hit the door and broke titter only when she came to the counter with an entire case of economy-sized Neosporin ointment.

"Are you sure, dear?" they kept asking, refusing to take Molly's money. "Perhaps we should ask Winston. This seems like an awful lot."

Winston had disappeared among the shelves of faux-antidepressants when Molly entered the store. He wondered if he should have ordered some faux-antipsychotics as well. Val Riordan hadn't said.

"Look," Molly finally said, "I'm nuts. You know it, I know it, Winston knows it. But in America it is your right to be nuts. I get a check from the state every month because I'm nuts. The state gives me money so I can buy whatever I need to continue being nuts, and right now I need this case of ointment. So ring it up so I can go be nuts somewhere else. Okay?"

The hens huddled and tittered.

"Or do I need to buy a case of those huge fluorescent orange prelubricated condoms with the deely-bobbers on the tip and blow them up in your card section." You never have to get this tough with Sand Pirates, Molly thought.

The hens broke their huddle and looked up in terror.

"I hear they're like thousands of tiny fingers, urging you to let go," Molly added.

Between the four of them it only took ten minutes more to ring up Molly's order and figure her change within the nearest dollar.

As Molly was leaving, she turned and said, "In the Outland, you would have all been made into jerky a long time ago."

 *fifteen*

Steve

Getting blown up had put the Sea Beast in a deep blue funk. Sometimes when he felt this way, he would swim to the edge of a coral reef and lie there in the sand while neon cleaner fish nipped at the parasites and algae on his scales. His flanks flashed a truce of color to let the little fish know that they were safe as they darted in and out of his mouth, grabbing bits of food and grunge like tiny dental hygienists. In turn, they emanated an electromagnetic message that translated roughly to: "I won't be a minute, sorry to bother you, please don't eat me."

He was getting a similar message from the warmblood that was ministering to his burns, and he flashed the truce of color along his sides to confirm that he understood. He couldn't pick up the intentions of all warmbloods, but this one was wired differently. He could sense that she meant him no harm and was even going to bring him food. He understood that when she made the "Steve" sound, she was talking to him.

"Steve," Molly said, "stop making those colors. Do you want the neighbors to see? It's broad daylight."

She was on a stepladder with a paintbrush. To the casual observer, she was painting her neighbor's trailer. In fact, she was applying great gobs of Neosporin ointment to the Sea Beast's back. "You'll heal faster with this stuff on you, and it doesn't sting."

After she had covered the charred parts of the trailer with ointment, she draped fiberglass fabric on as bandages and began ladling roof-patching tar over the fabric. Several of her neighbors looked out their windows, dismissed her actions as more eccentricities of a crazy woman, then went back to their afternoon game shows.

Molly was spreading the roofing tar over the fiberglass bandages with a squeegee when she heard a vehicle pull up in front of her trailer. Les, the hardware guy, got out of the truck, adjusted his suspenders, and headed toward her, looking a little nervous, but resolved. A light dew of sweat shone on his bald head, despite the autumn chill in the air.

"Little lady, what *are* you doing? I thought you were going to wait for me to help you."

Molly came down from her ladder and stood with the squeegee at port arms while it dripped black goo. "I wanted to get going on this before dark. Thanks for coming." She smiled sweetly—a leftover movie star smile.

Les escaped the smile to hardware land. "I can't even tell what you're trying to do here, but whatever it is, it looks like you mucked it up pretty bad already."

"No, come here and look at this."

Les moved cautiously to Molly's side and looked up at the trailer. "What the hell is this thing made of anyway? Up close it looks like plastic or something."

"Maybe you should look at it from the inside," Molly said. "The damage is more obvious in there."

The hardware clerk leered. Molly felt him trying to stare through her sweatshirt. "Well, if that's what you think. Let's go inside and have a look." He started toward the door of the trailer.

Molly grabbed his shoulder. "Wait a second. Where are the keys to your truck?"

"I leave 'em in it. Why? This town is safe."

"No reason, just wondering." Molly dazzled him with another smile. "Why don't you go on in? I'll be in as soon as I get some of this tar off of my hands."

"Sure thing, missy," Les said. He toddled toward the front door like a man badly in need of a rest room.

Molly backed away toward Les's truck. When the hardware clerk laid a hand on the door handle, Molly called, "Steve! Lunch!"

"My name isn't Steve," Les said.

"No," Molly said, "you're the other one."

"Les, you mean?"

"No, lunch." Molly gave him one last smile.

Steve recognized the sound of his name and felt the thought around the word "lunch."

Les felt something wet wrap around his legs and opened his mouth to scream just as the tip of the serpent's tongue wrapped his face, cutting off his air. The last thing he saw was the bare breasts of the fallen scream queen, Molly Michon, as she lifted her sweatshirt to give him a farewell flash before he was slurped into the waiting maw of the Sea Beast.

Molly heard the bones crunch and cringed. Boy, sometimes it just pays to be a nutcase, she thought. That sort of thing might bother a sane person.

One of the windows in the front of the dragon trailer closed slowly and opened, a function of the Sea Beast pushing his meal down his throat, but Molly took it for a wink.

Estelle

Dr. Val's office had always represented a little island of sanity to Estelle, a sophisticated status quo, always clean, calm, orderly, and well appointed. Like many artists, Estelle lived in an atmosphere of chaotic funk, taken by observers to be artistic charm, but in fact no more than a civilized way of dealing with the relative poverty and uncertainty of cannibalizing one's imagination for money. If you had to spill your guts to someone, it was nice to do it in a place that wasn't spattered with paint and covered with canvases that beckoned to be finished. Dr. Val's office was an escape, a pause, a comfort. But not today.

After being sent in to the inner office, before she even sat down in one of the leather guest chairs, Estelle said, "Your assistant is wearing oven mitts, did you know that?"

Valerie Riordan, for once with a few hairs out of place, rubbed her temples, looked at her desk blotter, and said, "I know. She has a skin condition."

"But they're taped on with duct tape."

"It's a very bad skin condition. How are you today?"

Estelle looked back toward the door. "Poor thing. She seemed out of breath when I came in. Has she seen a doctor?"

"Chloe will be fine, Estelle. Her typing skills may even improve."

Estelle sensed that Dr. Val was not having a good day and decided to let the assistant in oven mitts pass. "Thanks for seeing me on such short notice. I know it's been a while since we've had a session, but I really felt I need to talk to someone. My life has gotten a little weird lately."

"There's a lot of that going around," Dr. Val said, doodling on a legal pad as she spoke. "What's up?"

"I've met a man."

Dr. Val looked up for the first time. "You have?"

"He's a musician. A Bluesman. He's been playing at the Slug. I met him there. We've been, well, he's been staying at my place for the last couple of days."

"And how do you feel about that?"

"I like it. I like him. I haven't been with a man since my husband died. I thought I would feel like, well, like I was betraying him. But I don't. I feel great. He's funny, and he has this sense of, I don't know, wisdom. Like he's seen it all, but he hasn't become cynical. He seems sort of bemused by the hardships in life. Not at all like most people."

"But what about you?"

"I think I love him."

"Does he love you?"

"I think so. But he says he's going to leave. That's what's bothering me. I finally got used to being alone, and now that I found someone, he's going to leave me because he's afraid of a sea monster."

Valerie Riordan dropped her pen and slumped in her chair—a very unprofessional move, Estelle thought.

"Excuse me?" Val said.

"A sea monster. We were at the beach the other night, and something came up out of the water. Something big. We ran for the car, and later Catfish told me that he was once chased by a sea monster down in the Delta and that it had come back to get him. He says he doesn't want other people to get hurt, but I think he's just afraid. He thinks the monster will come back as long as he's on the coast. He's trying to get a gig in Iowa, as far from the coast as he can get. Do you think he's just afraid to commit? I read a lot about that in the women's magazines."

"A sea monster? Is that a metaphor for something? Some Blues term that I'm not getting?"

"No, I think it's a reptile, at least the way he describes it. I didn't get a good look at it. It ate his best friend when he was a young man. I think he's running away from the guilt. What do you think?"

"Estelle, there's no such thing as sea monsters."

"Catfish said that no one would believe me."

"Catfish?"

"That's his name. My Bluesman. He's very sweet. He has a sense of gallantry that you don't see much anymore. I don't think it's an act. He's too old for that. I didn't think I would ever feel this way again. These are girl feelings, not woman feelings. I want to spend the rest of my life with him. I want to have his grandchildren."

"Grandchildren?"

"Sure, he's had his days with the booze and the hos, but I think he's ready to settle down."

"The booze and the hos?"

Dr. Val seemed to have gone into some sort of fugue state, working on a stunned psychiatrist autopilot where all she could do was parrot what Estelle said back in the form of a question. Estelle needed more input than this.

"Do you think I should tell the authorities?"

"About the booze and the hos?"

"The sea monster. That Plotznik boy is missing, you know?"

Dr. Val made a show of straightening her blouse and assuming a controlled, staid, professional posture. "Estelle, I think we may need to adjust your medication."

"I haven't been taking it. But I feel fine. Catfish says that if Prozac had been invented a hundred years ago there wouldn't have been any Blues at all. Just a lot of happy people with no soul. I tend to agree with him. The antidepressants served their purpose for me after Joe died, but I'm not sure I need them now. I even feel like I could get some painting done—if I can find some time away from sex."

Dr. Val winced. "I was thinking of something besides antidepressants, Estelle. You obviously are dealing with some serious changes right now. I'm not sure how to proceed. Do you think that Mr., uh, Catfish would mind coming to a session with you?"

"That might be tough. He doesn't like your mojo."

"My mojo?"

"Not your mojo in particular. Just psychiatrist's mojo in general. He spent a little time in a mental hospital in Mississippi after the monster ate his friend. He didn't care for the staff's mojo." Estelle realized that her vocabulary, even her way of thinking, had changed over the last few days, the result of immersion in Catfish's Blues world.

The doctor was rubbing her temples again. "Estelle, let's make another appointment for tomorrow or the next day. Tell Chloe to add it on at the end of the day if I'm booked up. And try to bring your gentleman along with you. In the meantime, assure him that my practice is mojo-free, would you?"

Estelle stood. "Can that little girl write with those oven mitts on?"

"She'll manage."

"So what should I do? I don't want him to go. But I feel like I've lost a part of myself by falling in love. I'm happy, but I don't know who I am anymore. I'm worried." Estelle realized that she was starting to whine and looked at her shoes, ashamed.

"That's our time, Estelle. Let's save this for our next appointment."

"Right. Should I tell the constable about the sea monster?"

"Let's hold off on that for now. These things have a way of taking care of themselves."

"Thanks, Dr. Val. I'll see you tomorrow."

"Good-bye, Estelle."

Estelle left the office and stopped at Chloe's desk outside. The girl was gone, but there were animal noises coming from the bathroom just down the hall. Perhaps she had caught one of the oven mitts on her nose ring. Poor thing. Estelle went to the bathroom door and knocked lightly.

"Are you okay in there, dear? Do you need some help?"

The answer came back in high moan. "I'm fine. Really fine. Thanks. Oh my God!"

"You're sure?"

"No, that's all right!"

"I'm supposed to make an appointment for tomorrow or the next day. The doctor said to pencil it in late if you have to." Estelle could hear thumping noises coming from the bathroom, and it sounded as if the medicine cabinet had dumped.

"Oh wow! Wow! Oh wow!"

The scheduling must really have been tight. "I'm sorry. I won't bother you anymore. Call me to confirm, would you, dear?"

Estelle left Valerie Riordan's house even more unsettled than she had come in, thinking that it had been quite some time, half a day anyway, since she had had her skinny Bluesman between the sheets.

Dr. Val

Val had a break between appointments, time in which to reflect on her suspicion that by taking everyone in Pine Cove off antidepressants, she had turned the town into a squirrel's nest. Estelle Boyet had always been a tad eccentric, it was part of her artist persona, but Val had never seen this as unhealthy. On the contrary, the self-image of an eccentric artist seemed to help Estelle get over losing her husband. But now the woman was raving about sea monsters, and worse, she was getting involved in a relationship with a man that could only be construed as self-destructive.

Could people—rational adult people—still fall in love

like that? Could they still feel like that? Val wanted to feel like that. For the first time since her divorce, it occurred to her that she actually wanted to be involved again with a man. No, not just involved, in love. She pulled her Rolodex from the desk drawer and thumbed through it until she found the number of her psychiatrist in San Junipero. She had been in analysis all through med school and residency, it was an integral part of the training of any psychiatrist, but she hadn't seen her therapist in over five years. Maybe it was time. What sort of cynicism had come over her, that she was interpreting the desire to fall in love as a condition requiring treatment? Maybe her cynicism was the problem. Of course she couldn't tell him about what she had done to her patients, but perhaps . . .

A red light blinked on the tiny LED panel on her phone and the incoming call, screened by Chloe, who had obviously taken a short break from her self-abuse, scrolled across the screen. Constable Crowe, line one. Speaking of squirrels.

She picked up the phone. "Dr. Riordan."

"Hi, Dr. Riordan, this is Theo Crowe. I just called to tell you that you were right."

"Thank you for calling, Constable. Have a nice day."

"You were right about Bess Leander not taking the antidepressants. I just got a look at the toxicology report. There was no Zoloft in her system."

Val stopped breathing.

"Doctor, are you there?"

All her worries about the drugs, this whole perverse plan, all the extra sessions, the long hours, the guilt, the friggin' guilt, and Bess Leander hadn't been taking her medication at all. Val felt sick to her stomach.

"Doctor?" Theo said.

Val forced herself to take a deep breath. "Why? I mean, when? It's been over a month. When did you find this out?"

"Just today. I wasn't given access to the autopsy report. No one was. I'm sorry it took so long."

"Well, thank you for letting me know, Constable. I appreciate it." She prepared to ring off.

"Dr. Riordan, don't you have to get a medical history on your patients before you prescribe anything?"

"Yes. Why?"

"Do you know if Bess Leander had any heart problems?"

"No, physically she was a very healthy woman, as far as I know. Why?"

"No reason," Theo said. "Oh yeah, I never got your thoughts on the information I shared at breakfast. About Joseph Leander. I was still wondering if you had any thoughts?"

The whole world had flip-flopped. Val had stonewalled up to now on Bess Leander because she had assumed that her own negligence had had something to do with Bess's death. What now, though? Really, she didn't know much about Bess at all. She said, "What exactly do you want from me, Constable?"

"I just need to know, did she suspect her husband of having an affair? Or give you any indication that she might be afraid of him?"

"Are you saying what I think you are saying? You don't think Bess Leander committed suicide?"

"I'm not saying that. I'm just asking."

Val searched her memory. What *had* Bess Leander said about her husband? "I remember her saying that she felt he was uninvolved in their family life and that she had laid down the law to him."

"Laid down the law? In what way?"

"She told him that because he refused to put the toilet seat down, he was going to have to sit down to pee from now on."

"That's it?"

"That's all I can remember. Joseph Leander is a sales-man. He was gone a lot. I think Bess felt that he was somewhat of an intrusion on her and the girls' lives. It wasn't a healthy relationship." As if there is such a thing, Val thought. "Are you investigating Joseph Leander?"

"I'd rather not say," Theo said. "Do you think I should be?"

"You're the policeman, Mr. Crowe."

"I am? Oh, right, I am. Anyway, thanks, Doctor. By the way, my friend Gabe thought you were, uh, interest-ing, I mean, charming. I mean, he enjoyed talking with you."

"He did?"

"Don't tell him I said so."

"Of course. Good-bye, Constable." Val hung up and sat back in her chair. She had unnecessarily put an entire town in emotional chaos, committed a basketful of federal crimes as well as breaking nearly every ethical standard in her field, and one of her patients had possibly been murdered, but she felt, well, sort of excited. Charming, she thought. He found me charming. I wonder if he really said "charming" or if Theo was just making that up— the pothead.

Charming.

She smiled and buzzed Chloe to send in her next appointment.

 Sixteen

Mavis

The phone behind the bar rang and Mavis yanked it out of its cradle. "Mount Olympus, Goddess of Sex speaking," she said, and there was a mechanical ratcheting noise as she cocked a hip while she listened. "No, I haven't seen him—like I would even tell you if he was here. Hell, woman, I have a sacred trust here—I can't rat out every husband who comes in for a snort after work. How would I know? Honey, you want to keep this kind of thing from happening? Two words: long, nasty blowjobs. Yeah, well, if you were doing them instead of counting words, then maybe you wouldn't lose your husband. Oh, all right, hold on."

Mavis held her receiver to breast and shouted, "Hey! Anyone seen Les from the hardware store?" A few heads shook and a fusillade of "nopes" fired through the bar.

"Nope, he's not here. Yeah, if I see him, I'll be sure and tell him that there was a screeching harpy looking for him. Oh yeah, well, I've been done doggie-style by the Better Business Bureau and they liked it, so say hi for me."

Mavis slammed down the phone. She felt like the Tin Man left out in the rain. Her metal parts felt rusty and she was sure that her plastic parts were going to mush. Ten o'clock on a Saturday, live entertainment on the stage, and she still hadn't sold enough liquor to cover the cost of her Blues singer. Oh, the bar was full, but people were nursing their drinks, making them last, making goo-goo eyes at each other and slipping out, couple by couple, without dropping a sawbuck. What in the hell had come over this town? The Blues singer was supposed to drive them to drink, but the entire population seemed to be absolutely giddy with love. They were talking instead of drinking. Wimps. Mavis spit into the bar sink in disgust and there was a pinging sound from a tiny spring that had dislodged somewhere inside of her.

Wusses. Mavis threw back a shot of Bushmills and glared at the couples sitting at the bar, then glared at Catfish, who was finishing up a set on the stage, his National steel guitar whining as he sang about losing his soul at the crossroads.

Catfish told the story of the great Robert Johnson, the haunting Bluesman who had met the devil at the crossroads and bargained his soul for supernatural ability, but was pursued throughout his life by a hellhound that had caught his scent at the gates of hell and finally took him home when a jealous husband slipped poison into Johnson's liquor.

"Truth be," Catfish said into the microphone, "I done stood at midnight at every crossroad in the Delta lookin' to sell my soul, but wasn't nobody buyin'. Now that there is the Blues. But I gots me my own brand of hellhound, surely I do."

"That's sweet, fish boy," Mavis shouted from behind the bar. "Come over here, I gotta talk to you."

" 'Scuse me, folks, they's a call from hell right now," Catfish said to the crowd with a grin. But no one was listening. He put his guitar in the stand and ambled over to Mavis.

"You're not loud enough," Mavis said.

"Turn up your hearing aid, woman. I ain't got no

pickup in that National. They's only so high you can go into a mike or she feed back."

"People are talking, not drinking. Play louder. And no love songs."

"I gots me a Fender Stratocaster and a Marshall amp in the car, but I don't like playin 'lectric."

"Go get them. Plug in. Play loud. I don't need you if you don't sell liquor."

"This gonna be my last night anyway."

"Get the guitar," Mavis said.

Molly

Molly slammed the truck into the Dumpster behind the Head of the Slug Saloon. Glass from the headlights tinkled to the tarmac and the fan raked across the radiator with a grating shriek. It had been a few years since Molly had done any driving, and Les had left out a few parts from the do-it-yourself brake kit he'd installed. Molly turned off the engine and set the parking brake, then wiped the steering wheel and shift knob with the sleeve of her sweatshirt to remove any fingerprints. She climbed out of the truck and tossed the keys into the mashed Dumpster. There was no music coming from the back door of the Slug, only the smell of stale beer and the low murmur of conversation. She scampered out of the alley and started the four-block walk home.

A low fog drifted over Cypress Street and Molly was grateful for the cover. There were only a few lights on in the park's trailers, and she hurried past them to where her own windows flickered with the lonely blue of the unwatched television. She looked past her house to the space where Steve lay healing and noticed a figure outlined in the fog. As she drew closer, she could see that it was not one person, but two, standing not twenty feet from the dragon trailer. Her heart sank. She expected the beams of police flashlights to swing through the fog any second, but the figures were just standing there. She crept around the edge of her trailer, pressed so close that she could feel the cold coming off the aluminum skin through her sweatshirt.

A woman's voice cut the fog, "Lord, we have heeded your call and come unto you. Forgive us our casual attire, as our dry cleaner did close for the weekend and we are left sorely without outfits with matching accessories."

It was the school prayer ladies, Katie and Marge, although Molly wouldn't be able to tell which was which. They were wearing identical pink jogging suits with matching Nikes. As she watched, the two women moved closer to Steve, and Molly could see a rippling across the dragon trailer.

"As our Lord Jesus did give His life for our sins, so we come unto Thee, O Lord, to giveth of ourselves."

The end of the dragon trailer lost its angles to curves, and Molly could see Steve's broad head extending, changing, the door going from a vertical rectangle to a wide horizontal maw. The women seemed unaffected by the change and continued to move slowly forward, silhouetted now by Steve's jaws, which were opening like a toothed cavern.

Molly ran around her trailer and up the steps, reached in and grabbed her broadsword which was leaned against the wall just inside the door, and dashed back around the trailer and toward the Sea Beast.

Marge and Katie were almost inside of Steve's open mouth. Molly could see his enormous tongue snaking out the side of his mouth, reaching behind the church ladies to drag them in.

"No!" Molly leapt from a full run, slamming between Marge and Katie like a fullback leaping through blockers to the goal line, and smacked Steve on the nose with the flat of her sword. She landed in his mouth and rolled clear to the ground just as his jaws snapped shut behind her. She came up on one knee, holding the sword pointed at Steve's nose.

"No!" she said. "Bad dragon." Steve turned his head quizzically, as if wondering what she was so upset about.

"Change back," Molly said, raising the sword as if to whack his nose again. Steve's head and neck pulled back into the shape of a double-wide trailer.

Molly looked back at the church ladies, who seemed very concerned with having been knocked into the mud in their pink jogging suits, but oblivious to the fact that they had almost been eaten. "Are you two okay?"

"We felt the call," one of them said, either Marge or Katie, while the other one nodded in agreement. "We had to come to give ourselves unto the Lord." Their eyes were glazed over and they stared right past her to the trailer as they spoke.

"You guys have to go home now. Aren't your husbands worried about you or something?"

"We heard the call."

Molly helped them to their feet and pointed them away from Steve, who made a faint whining noise as she pushed the church ladies away toward the street.

Molly stopped them at the edge of the street and spoke to them from behind. "Go home. Don't come back here. Okay?"

"We wanted to bring the children to feel the spirit too, but it was so late, and we have church tomorrow."

Molly smacked the speaker across the butt with the flat of her sword, a good two-handed stroke that sent her stumbling into the street. "Go home!"

Molly was winding up to smack the other one when she turned and held up her hand as if refusing a refill on coffee. "No thank you."

"Then you're going and you're not coming back, right?"

The woman didn't seem sure. Molly turned her grip on the sword so the edge was poised to strike. "Right?"

"Yes," the woman said. Her friend nodded in agreement as she rubbed her bottom.

"Now go," Molly said. As the women walked away, she called after them, "And stop dressing alike. That's fucking weird."

She watched them until they disappeared into the fog, then went back to where Steve was waiting in trailer form. "Well?" She threw out her hip, frowned, and tapped her foot as if waiting for his explanation.

His windows narrowed, ashamed.

"They'll be back, you know. Then what?"

He whimpered, the sound coming from deep inside, where the kitchen would be if he were really a trailer.

"If you're still hungry, you have to let me know. I can help. We can find you something. Although there is only one hardware store in town. You're going to have to diversify your diet."

Suddenly an electric guitar screamed out of the fog, wailing like a tortured ghost of Chicago Blues. The dragon trailer became the dragon again, his white skin went black, then flashed brilliant streaks of red anger. The bandages Molly had spent all day applying shredded with the abrupt shape change. His gill trees hung with tatters of fiberglass fabric as if toilet-papered by mischievous boys. The Sea Beast threw back his head and roared, rattling the windows through the trailer park. Molly fell in the mud as she backed up, then rolled and came up on her feet with the broadsword poised to thrust into the Sea Beast's throat.

"Steve, I think you need to take a timeout, young man."

Theo

Such a short period of time to have so many new experiences. In just the last few days, he had coordinated his first major missing person search, including talking to worried parents and the milk carton company, whose people wanted to know if Theo could get a picture of Mikey Plotznik where he wasn't making a contorted, goofy face at the camera. (If they found a better picture, Mikey would end up with great exposure on the two percent or nonfat cartons, but if they had to go with what they had, he was going on the side of the buttermilk and would only be seen by old folks and people making ranch dressing.) Theo had also had to deal with his first major fire, the hallucination of giant animal tracks, and opening a real live murder investigation, all without the benefit of his lifelong chemical crutch. Not that he couldn't nurse at his favorite pipe, he'd just lost the desire to do so.

Now he had to decide how to go about investigating Bess Leander's murder. Should he pull someone in for interrogation? Pull them in where? His cabin? He didn't have an office. Somehow he couldn't imagine holding an effective interrogation with the suspect in a beanbag chair under a hot lava lamp. "Talk, scumbag! Don't make me turn the black light on that Jimi Hendrix poster and light some incense. You don't want that."

And amid all the other activity, he felt a nagging compulsion to go back to the Fly Rod Trailer Court and talk to Molly Michon. Crazy thoughts.

Finally he decided to drop by Joseph Leander's house, hoping he might catch the salesman off guard. As he pulled into the driveway, he noticed that weeds had grown up around the garden gnomes and there was a patina of dust on the Dutch hex sign over the front door. The garage door was open and Joseph's minivan was parked inside.

Theo paused at the front door before knocking and made sure that his ponytail was tucked into his collar and his collar was straight. For some reason, he felt as if he should be wearing a gun. He had one, a Smith & Wesson .357 revolver, but it was on the top shelf of his closet, next to his bong collection.

He rang the bell, then waited. A minute passed before Joseph Leander opened the door. He was wearing paint-spattered corduroys and an old cardigan sweater that looked like it had been pulled out of the trash a dozen times. Obviously not the sort of attire that Bess Leander would have allowed in her home.

"Constable Crowe." Leander was not smiling. "What can I do for you?"

"If you have a minute, I'd like to talk to you. May I come in?"

"I suppose," Leander said. He stepped away from the door and Theo ducked in. "I just made some coffee. Would you like some?"

"No thanks. I'm on duty." Cops are supposed to say that, Theo thought.

"It's *coffee*."

"Oh, right, sure. Milk and sugar please."

The living room had bare pine plank floors and rag rugs. An antique pew bench took the place of a sofa, two Shaker chairs and a galvanized milk can with a padded cushion on the top provided the other seating. Three antique butter churns stood in the corners of the room. But for a new thirty-six-inch Sony by the fireplace, it could have been the living room of a seventeenth-century family (a family with very high cholesterol from all that butter).

Joseph Leander returned to the living room and handed Theo a hand-thrown stoneware mug. The coffee was the color of butterscotch and tasted of cinnamon. "Thanks," Theo said. "New TV?" He nodded to the Sony.

Leander sat across from Theo on the milk can. "Yes,

I got it for the girls. PBS and so forth. Bess never approved of television."

"And so you killed her!"

Leander sprayed a mouthful of coffee on the rug. *"What?"*

Theo took a sip of his coffee while Leander stared at him, wide-eyed. Maybe he'd been a bit too abrupt. Fall back, regroup. "So did you get cable? Reception is horrible in Pine Cove without cable. It's the hills, I think."

Leander blinked furiously and did a triple-take on Theo. "What are you talking about?"

"I saw the coroner's report on your wife, Joseph. She didn't die from hanging."

"You're insane. You were there." Leander stood and took the mug out of Theo's hands. "I won't listen to this. You can go now, Constable." Leander stepped back and waited.

Theo stood. He wasn't very good at confrontation, he was a peace officer. This was too hard. He pushed himself. "Was it the affair with Betsy? Did Bess catch you?"

Veins were beginning to show on Leander's bald pate. "I just started seeing Betsy. I loved my wife and I resent you doing this to her memory. You're not supposed to do this. You're not even a real cop. Now get out of my house. "

"Your wife was a good woman. A little weird, but good."

Leander set the coffee mugs down on a butter churn, went to the front door, and pulled it open. "Go." He waved Theo toward the door.

"I'm going, Joseph. But I'll be back." Theo stepped outside.

Leander's face had gone completely red. "No, you won't."

"Oh, I think I will," Theo said, feeling very much like a second grader in a playground argument.

"Don't fuck with me, Crowe," Leander spat. "You have no idea what you're doing." He slammed the door in Theo's face.

"Do too," Theo said.

 $Seventeen$

Molly

Molly had always wondered about American women's fascination with bad boys. There seemed to be some sort of logic-defying attraction to the guy who rode a motorcycle and had a tattoo, a gun in the glove compartment, or a snifter of cocaine on the coffee table. In her acting days, she'd even been involved with a couple of them herself, but this was the first one who actually, well, ate people. Women always felt that they could reform a guy. How else could you explain the numerous proposals of marriage received by captured serial killers? That one was a bit too much even for Molly, and she took comfort in the fact that no matter how crazy she had gotten, she'd never been tempted to marry a guy who made a habit of strangling his dates.

American mothers programmed their daughters to believe that they could make everything better. Why else was she leading a hundred-foot monster down a creek bed in broad daylight?

Fortunately, the creek bed was lined in most places by a heavy growth of willow trees, and as Steve moved over the rocks, his great body changed color and texture to match his surroundings until he looked like nothing more than a trick of the light, like heat rising off blacktop.

Molly made him stay under cover as they approached the Cypress Street bridge, then waited until there was no traffic and signaled him to go. Steve slithered under the bridge like a snake down its hole, his back knocking off great hunks of concrete, and he passed through.

In less than an hour they were out of town, into the ranchland that ran along the coast to the north, and Molly led Steve up through the trees to the edge of a pasture. "There you go, big guy," Molly said, pointing to a herd of Holsteins that were grazing a hundred yards away. "Breakfast."

Steve crouched at the edge of the forest like a cat ready to pounce. His tail twitched, splintering a cypress sapling in the process. Molly sat down beside him and cleaned mud from her sneakers with a stick as the cows slowly made their way toward them.

"This is it?" she asked. "You just sit here and they come over to be eaten? A girl could lose respect for you as a hunter watching this, you know that?"

Theo

Theo found himself trying to figure out why, exactly, he was driving to Molly Michon's place, when his cell phone rang. Before he answered, he reminded himself not to sound stoned, when it occurred to him that he actually wasn't stoned, and that was even more frightening.

"Crowe here," he said.

"Crowe, this is Nailsworth, down at County. Are you nuts?"

Theo stalled while he tried to remember who Nailsworth was. "Is this a survey?"

"What did you do with that data I gave you?" Nailsworth said. Theo suddenly remembered that Nailsworth was the Spider's real name. A second call was beeping on Theo's line.

"Nothing. I mean, I conducted an interview. Can you hold? I've got another call."

"No, I can't hold. I know you've got another call. You didn't hear anything from me, do you hear? I gave you nothing, understand?"

" 'Kay," Theo said.

The Spider hung up and Theo connected to the other call.

"Crowe, are you fucking nuts!"

"Is this a survey?" Theo said, pretty sure that it wasn't a survey, but also pretty sure that Sheriff Burton wouldn't be happy with a truthful answer to the question, which was: "Yes, I probably am nuts."

"I thought I told you to stay away from Leander. That case is closed and filed."

Theo thought for a second. It hadn't been five minutes since he'd left Joseph Leander's house. How could Burton know already? No one got through to the sheriff that quickly.

"Some suspicious evidence popped up," Theo said, trying to figure out how he was going to cover for the Spider if Burton pressed. "I just stopped by to see if there was anything to it."

"You fucking pothead. If I tell you to let something lie, you let it lie, do you understand me? I'm not talking about your job now, Crowe, I'm talking about life as you know it. I hear another word out of North County and you are going to be getting your dance card punched by every AIDs-ridden convict in Soledad. Leave Leander alone."

"But . . ."

"Say 'Yes, sir,' you bag of shit."

"Yes, sir, you bag of shit," Theo said.

"You are finished, Crowe, you—"

"Sorry, Sheriff. Battery's going." Theo disconnected and headed back to his cabin, shaking as he drove.

Molly

In *Flesh Eaters of the Outland*, Kendra was forced to watch while a new breed of mutants sprayed hapless villagers with a flesh-dissolving enzyme, then lapped up puddles of human protein with disgusting dubbed sucking sounds that the foley artists had obtained at Sea World, recording baby walruses being fed handfuls of shellfish. The special effects guys simulated the carnage with large quantities of rubber cement, paraffin body parts that conveniently melted under the Mexican desert sun, and transmission fluid instead of the usual Karo syrup fake blood. (The sugary stage blood tended to attract blowflies and the director didn't want to get notice from the ASPCA for abuse.) Overall, the effect was so real that Molly insisted that all of Kendra's reaction shots be done after the cleanup to avoid her gagging and going green on camera. Between the carrion scene and some salmonella tacos served up by the Nogales-based caterer, as well as repeated propositions by an Arab coproducer with halitosis that made her eyes water, Molly was sick for three days. But none of it, even the fetid falafel breath, produced the nausea she was experiencing upon watching Steve yack up four fully masticated, partially digested Holsteins.

Molly added the contents of her own stomach (three Pop Tarts and a Diet Coke) to the four pulverized piles of beefy goo that Steve had expelled onto the pasture.

"Lactose intolerant?" She wiped her mouth on her sleeve and glared at the Sea Beast. "You have no problem gulping down a paperboy and the closet perv from the hardware store, but you can't eat dairy cows?"

Steve rolled onto his back and tried to look apologetic—streaks of purple played across his flanks, purple being his embarrassment color. Viscous tears the size of softballs welled up in the corner of his giant cat's eyes.

"So I suppose you're still hungry?"

Steve rolled back onto his feet and the earth rumbled beneath him.

"Maybe we can find you a horse or something," Molly said. "Stay close to the tree line." Using her broadsword as a walking stick, she led him over the hill. As they moved, his colors changed to match the surroundings, making it appear that Molly was being followed by a mirage.

Theo

For some reason, the words of Karl Marx kept running through Theo's mind as he dug the machete out of the tool shed behind his cabin. *"Religion is the opiate of the masses."* It follows, then, that "opium is the religion of the addict," Theo thought. Which is why he was feeling the gut-wrenching remorse of the excommunicated as he took the machete to the first of the thick, fibrous stems in his marijuana patch. The bushy green weeds fell like martyred saints with each swing of the machete, and his hands picked up a film of sticky resin as he threw each plant onto a pile in the corner of the yard.

In five minutes his shirt was soaked with sweat and the pot patch looked like a miniature version of a clear-cut forest. Devastation. Stumps. He emptied a can of kerosene over the waste-high pile of cannabis, then pulled out his lighter and set the flame to a piece of paper. "Throw off the chains of your oppressors," Marx had said. These plants, the habit that went with them, were Theo's chains: the boot that Sheriff John Burton had kept pressed to his neck these last eight years, the threat that kept him from acting freely, from doing the right thing,

He threw the burning paper, and the flames of revolution whooshed over the pile. There was no elation, no rush of freedom as he backed away from the pyre. Instead of the triumph of revolution, he felt a sense of sickening loss, loneliness, and guilt: Judas at the base of the Cross. No wonder communism had failed.

He went into the cabin, retrieved the box from the shelf in the closet, and was beating his bong collection into shrapnel with a ballpeen hammer when he heard automatic weapons fire coming from the ranch.

Ignacio and Miguel

Ignacio was lying in the shade just outside the metal shed, smoking a cigarette, while Miguel labored away inside, cooking the chemicals down into methamphetamine crystals. Beakers the size of basketballs boiled over electric burners, the fumes routed through glass tubes to a vent in the wall.

Miguel was short and wiry, just thirty years old, but the lines in his face and the grim expression he always wore made him look fifty. Ignacio was only twenty, fat and full of machismo, taken with his own success and toughness, and convinced that he was on his way to being the new godfather of the Mexican Mafia. They had crossed the border together six months ago, smuggled in by a coyote to do exactly what they were doing. And what a sweet deal it had turned out to be. Because the lab was protected by the big sheriff, they were never raided, they never had to move on a moment's notice like the other labs in California, or bolt across the border until things cooled off. Only six months, and Miguel had sent home enough money for his wife to buy a ranch in Michoacán, and Ignacio was driving a flashy Dodge four-wheel drive and wearing five-hundred-dollar alligator-skin Tony Lama boots. All of this for only eight hours of work a day, for they were only one of three crews that kept the lab running twenty-four hours a day. And there was no danger of being stopped on the road while transporting drugs, because the big sheriff had a gringo in a little van come every few days to drop off supplies and take the drugs away.

"Put out that cigarette, *cabrone!*" Miguel shouted. "Do you want to blow us up?"

Ignacio scoffed and flicked his cigarette into the pasture. "You worry too much, Miguel." Ignacio was tired of Miguel's whining. He missed his family, he worried about getting caught, he didn't know if the mix was right. When the older man wasn't working, he was brooding, and no amount of money or consoling seemed to satisfy him.

Miguel appeared at the doorway and stood over Ignacio. "Do you feel that?"

"What?" Ignacio reached for the AK-47 that was leaning against the shed. "What?"

Miguel was staring across the pasture, but seemed to be seeing nothing. "I don't know."

"It is nothing. You worry too much."

Miguel started walking across the pasture toward the tree line. "I have to go over there. Watch my stove."

Ignacio stood up and hitched his silver-studded belt up under his belly. "I don't how to watch the stove. I'm the guard. You stay and watch the stove."

Miguel strode over the hill without looking back. Ignacio sat back down and pulled another cigarette from the pocket of his leather vest. "Loco," he mumbled under his breath as he lit up. He smoked for several minutes, dreaming and scheming about a time when he would run the whole operation, but by the time he finished the cigarette he was starting to worry about his partner. He stood to get a better look, but couldn't see anything beyond the top of the hill over which Miguel had disappeared.

"Miguel?" he called. But there was no answer.

He glanced inside the shed to see that everything was in order, and as far as he could tell, it was. Then he picked up his assault rifle and started across the pasture. Before he got three steps, he saw a white woman coming over the hill. She had the face and body of a hot senorita, but the wild gray-blonde hair of an old woman, and he wondered for the thousandth time what in the hell was wrong with American women. Were they all crazy? He lowered the assault rifle, but smiled as he did it, hoping to warn the woman off without making her suspicious.

"You stop," he said in English. "No trespass." He heard the cell phone ringing back in the shed and glanced back for a second.

The woman kept coming. "We met your friend," Molly said.

"Who is we?" Ignacio asked.

His answer came over the hill behind the woman, first looking like two burned scrub oak trees, then the giant cat's eyes. "Holy Mary, Mother of God," Ignacio said as he wrestled with the bolt on the assault rifle.

Theo

Eight years of living at the edge of the ranch and never once had Theo so much as taken a walk down the dirt road. He had been under orders not to. But now what? He'd seen the trucks going in and out over the years, occasionally heard men shouting, but somehow he'd managed to ignore it all, and there had never been gunfire. Going onto the ranch to investigate automatic weapons fire seemed an especially stupid way to exercise his new-found freedom, but not investigating, well, that said something about him he wasn't willing to face. Was he, in fact, a coward?

The sound of a man screaming in the distance made the decision for him. It wasn't the sound of someone blowing off steam, it was a throat-stripping scream of pure terror. Theo kicked the shards of his bong collection off the front steps and went back to the closet to get his pistol.

The Smith & Wesson was wrapped in an oily cloth on the top shelf of his closet next to a box of shells. He unwrapped it, snapped open the cylinder, and dropped in six cartridges, fighting the shake that was moving from his hands to his entire body. He dumped another six shells into his shirt pocket and headed out to the Volvo.

He started the Volvo, then grabbed the radio mike to call for some backup. A lot of good that would do. Response time from the Sheriff's Department could run as long as thirty minutes in Pine Cove, which was one of the reasons there was a town constable in the first place. And what would he say? He was still under orders not to go onto the ranch.

He dropped the mike on the seat next to his gun, put the Volvo in gear, and was starting to back out when a Dodge minivan pulled in beside him. Joseph Leander waved and smiled at him from the driver's seat.

Theo put the Volvo in park. Leander climbed out of his van and leaned into the passenger window and looked at the .357 lying on the seat. "I need to talk to you," he said.

"You weren't much for talking an hour ago."

"I am now."

"Later. I'm just going to check something out on the ranch."

"That's perfect," Leander said, shoving a small automatic pistol through the window into Theo's face. "We'll go together."

 # eighteen

Dr. Val

The bust of Hippocrates stared up at Val Riordan from the desk. *"First, do no harm . . ."*

"Yeah, bite me," said the psychiatrist, throwing her Versace scarf over the Greek's face.

Val was having a bad day. The call from Constable Crowe, revealing that her treatment, or lack of it, had not caused Bess Leander's suicide, had thrown Val into a quandary. She'd zombied her way through her morning appointments, answering questions with questions, pretending to take notes, and not catching a word that anyone said to her.

Five years ago there had been a flood of stories in the media about the dangers of Prozac and similar antidepressants, but those stories had been set off by sensational lawsuits against the drug companies, and the follow-ups, the fact that not one jury found antidepressants to cause destructive behavior, had been buried in the back pages. One powerful religious group (whose prophet was a hack science fiction writer and whose followers included masses of deluded movie stars and supermodels) had fielded a media attack against antidepressants, recommending instead that the depressed should just cheer up, buck up, and send in some gas money to keep the Mother Ship running. The various professional journals had reported no studies that proved that antidepressants increased the incidence of suicidal or violent behavior. Val had read the religious propaganda (it had the endorsement of the rich and famous), but she hadn't read the professional journals. Yes, automatically treating her patients with antidepressants had been wrong, but her attempt to atone by taking them all off the drugs was just as wrong. Now she had to deal with the fact that she might be hurting them.

Val hit the speed dial button to the pharmacy. Winston Krauss answered, but his voice was muted, as if he had an incredibly bad cold.

"Pine Cobe Drug and Gibt."

"Winston, you sound horrible."

"I hab on my mask and snorkle."

"Oh, Winston." Val rubbed her eyes, causing her contacts to slide back in her head somewhere. "Not at the store."

"I'm in the back room." His voice became clear on the last word of the sentence. "There, I took it off. I'm glad you called, I've been wanting to talk to you about killer whales."

"Pardon?"

"I'm attracted to Orcas. I've been watching a Jacques Cousteau tape about them . . ."

"Winston, can we cover this in session . . . ?"

"I'm worried. I was especially turned on by the male one. Does that make me a homosexual?"

Jeez, it didn't worry him that he was a wannabe whale-humper, as long as he wasn't a *gay* wannabe whale-humper. As a psychiatrist, she'd tried to drop terms like "full-blown batshit" from her vocabulary, even in thought, yet with Winston, she couldn't keep the term from rising. Lately, Val felt as if she was running the batshit concession on the cave floor. It had to stop. "Winston, I'm putting everyone back on their SSRIs. Get rid of the placebos. I'm going to put everyone on Paxil to get their levels up as quickly as possible. Make sure to warn the ones who were on Prozac that they absolutely can't miss a day like they used to. I'll move those who need it later."

"You want me to take everyone off of the placebos? Do you know how much money we are making?"

"Start today. I'm going to call my patients. I want you to give them credit for the unused placebos they still have."

"I won't do it. I almost have enough saved to spend a month at the Cetacean Research Center on Grand Bahama. You can't take that away from me."

"Winston, I won't compromise my patients' mental health so you can go on vacation and fuck Flipper."

"I said I won't do it. You were the one who started this. What about your patients' mental health then?"

"I was wrong. I'm not going to put everyone back on antidepressants either, so you're going to lose some revenue there too. Some of them didn't need the drugs in the first place."

"No."

Val was shocked at the conviction in Winston's voice. His self-esteem problem no longer seemed an issue. What a crappy time for him to be making progress. "So you want the town to know about your little problem?"

"You won't do that. You have more to lose than I do, Valerie. If you blow the whistle on me, then I'll tell the whole story to the papers. I'll get immunity and you'll go to jail."

"You bastard. I'll send my patients down to the Thrifty Mart in San Junipero. Then you won't even have the legitimate sales."

"No, you won't. Things are going to stay just the way they are, Dr. Val." Winston hung up.

Valerie Riordan stared at the receiver for a second before replacing it in its cradle. How? How in the hell had she given control of her life over to someone like Winston Krauss? More important, how was she going to get it back without going to jail?

Theo

Joseph Leander had the automatic stuck against Theo's ribs. He'd thrown Theo's gun into the backseat. Leander was wearing a tweed jacket and wool dress slacks and a film of sweat was forming on his forehead. The Volvo bounced over a rut in the dirt road and Theo felt the barrel of the automatic dig into his ribs. He was trying to remember what you were supposed to do in such a situation, but all he could remember from the cop shows that he'd watched was never to give up your gun.

"Joseph, could you pull that gun out of my ribs, or put the safety on, or something? This is a pretty bumpy road. I'd hate to lose a lung because I didn't get new shocks." That sounded sufficiently glib, he thought. Professionally calm. Now if he could just avoid wetting himself.

"You couldn't leave it alone, could you? It would have just passed into history and no one would have noticed, but you had to dig things up."

"So you did kill her?"

"Let's say I helped her make a decision that she'd been waffling about."

"She was the mother of your children."

"Right, and she treated me with about as much respect as a turkey baster."

"Wow, you lost me there, partner."

"They use them for artificial insemination, Crowe, you fucking stoner. One squirt and you throw them away."

"You got tired of being a turkey baster, so you hung your wife?"

"Her herb garden killed her. Foxglove tea. Contains huge amount of digitalis. Stops the heart and it's almost undetectable unless you're looking for it. Ironic, isn't it? I would have never known about any of that crap if she hadn't blathered on about it constantly."

Theo was not at all happy that Leander was telling him this. It meant that he was going to have to make some sort of move to save himself or he was dead. Ram a tree maybe? He checked Leander's seat belt; it was buckled. What kind of criminal kidnaps someone and remembers to buckle his seat belt? Stall for now. "There were heel marks on the wall."

"Nice touches, I thought. I don't know, she may have still been alive when I hung her up there."

They were coming out of the forest that surrounded the ranch into an open pasture. Theo could see a metal shed next to a double-wide house trailer a couple of hundred yards ahead. A bright red Dodge truck was parked by the shed.

"Hmmm," Leander said. "They got a new trailer for the boys. Pull up to the shed and park."

Theo felt panic rise in his throat like acid and fought it down. Keep them talking and they won't shoot. Hadn't he heard that somewhere? "So you killed your wife for a big-screen TV and a tumble with Betsy? Divorce never occurred to you?"

Leander laughed and Theo felt a chill run through his body. "You really are dense, aren't you, Crowe? See that shed up there? Well, I hauled twenty-eight million dollars' worth of methamphetamine out of that shed last year. Granted, I only get a piece of that, but it's a nice piece. I move it all. I'm a salesman, a family man, innocuous and unnoticeable. Who'd suspect me? Mr. Milquetoast."

"Your wife?"

"Bess found out about it. Funny thing is, she was following me because she suspected an affair, but she never found out a thing about Betsy and me. She was going to turn me in. I had no choice."

Theo pulled up next to the shed and turned off the Volvo. "You have a choice now, Joseph. You don't have to do this."

"I'm not doing anything but going back to my life until there's enough money in my offshore accounts to take off. Don't get me wrong, Crowe. I didn't enjoy killing Bess. I'm not a killer. Hell, I've never even taken any drugs. This isn't crime, it's just a well-paid delivery route."

"So you're not going to shoot me?" Theo really, really wanted to believe that.

"Not if you do what I tell you to do. Get out of the car. Leave the keys. Slide over and come out on my side."

Theo did as he was told and Leander kept the pistol trained on him the whole time. Where did Leander learn to do that? He'd hadn't had a television that long. Guy must have taken a mail-order course or something.

"Miguel! Ignacio! Come out here!" Leander gestured with the pistol for Theo to move toward the shack. "Go inside."

Theo ducked to get through the door and immediately saw rack upon rack of lab glass, glass tubing, and plastic barrels of chemicals. A single metal chair sat in front of half a dozen electric burners that were filling the shed with a brutal heat.

"Sit down," Leander commanded.

As Theo sat, he felt the handcuffs being yanked out of his back pocket.

"Put your hands behind you." Theo did as he was told and Leander threaded the handcuffs through two metal bars at the back of the chair and snapped them over Theo's wrists.

"I've got to go find these guys," Leander said. "Probably taking a siesta. What was Burton thinking when he put a house trailer down here? I'll be back in a second."

"Then what?"

"Then Ignacio will shoot you, I'm guessing."

Molly

This was a first: a guy that actually did what you asked him to do. When she heard a car coming down the ranch road, she asked Steve to make himself look like a trailer and he had done it. Sure, she had to make a little box diagram in the air with her hands, and he missed the first time, trying to make himself look like the tin shed next to him, a miserable failure that resulted in only his head changing and making him look like a dragon wearing an aluminum bag over his head, but after a few seconds he got it. What a guy. Okay, his tail, which had always hung down into the creek bed before, was showing, but maybe no one would notice.

"What a guy," she said, patting him on his air-conditioning unit. Or at least it was an air-conditioning unit now. No telling what body part it had been before he changed into a trailer.

She's patting my unit, Steve thought. A low growl of pleasure rolled out of his front door.

Molly ran and hid behind the shed, peeking out to watch the white Volvo pull up and stop. She almost stepped out to say hi to Theo, then saw the other man in the car holding a gun on him. She listened as the bald guy led Theo into the shed and made some threats. She wanted to jump out and say, "No, Ignacio won't be shooting anyone, Mr. Bald Guy. He's busy being digested right now," but the guy did have a gun. How the hell did Theo let himself be taken prisoner by someone who looked like an assistant principal?

When it was evident that the bald guy was coming out, she ran to the dragon trailer, caught the edge of the air-conditioning unit, and swung herself up onto the roof.

The bald guy was going around to the front door. She ran over Steve's back and looked down over the edge.

"Miguel! Ignacio!" the bald guy yelled. "Get out here!" He seemed uncertain about going into the trailer.

"I saw them go in there," Molly said.

The bald guy stepped back, looking like he was going to go into a fit searching for where the voice had come from.

"You're an assistant principal, aren't you?" Molly said.

The bald guy finally spotted her and tried to hide the gun behind his back. "You're that crazy woman," he said. "What are you doing here?"

Molly scooched up to the edge of the dragon trailer. "'Scuse me? Pardon me? Beg your pardon? I'm the what?"

He ignored her question. "What are you doing here?"

"Excuse me. Excuse me, excuse me," she almost sang. "There is an as-yet-unapologized-for aspersion on the floor. You'll have to handle that before we move on."

"I'm not apologizing for anything. What are you doing here? Where are Ignacio and Miguel?"

"You're not apologizing?"

"No. Get down from there." He showed her the gun.

"'Kay," Molly said, patting Steve on the head/roof. "Steve, eat this impolite motherfucker."

She'd seen it before, but it was especially exciting to be sitting on Steve's head when he changed shape and his tongue leapt out below her to wrap around the assistant principal. After the initial slurp, the inevitable crunch (which had bothered her before) was sort of satisfying.

She couldn't figure out if it was because the assistant principal had pointed a gun at her friend and called her a crazy woman, or if she was just getting used to it.

"That was just swell," she said. She ran across Steve's back, slid down to the top of the air-conditioning unit, then jumped to the ground.

Steve growled and the angles of his trailer form melted into the curves and sinew of his dragon shape. He rolled over on his side and Molly watched as the scales on his belly parted and seven feet of dragon penis emerged as thick and stiff as a telephone pole. Luminescent colors flashed up the length of the organ.

"Wow, that *is* impressive," Molly said, taking a few steps backward.

Steve sent her a message similar to the one he had sent to the fuel truck. It worked better on Molly. Her knees went wobbly, a warm tingling ran up her thighs, and she could feel the pulse rising in her temples.

She looked into Steve's eyes (well, one of them anyway), stepped up to his face and gently touched him on the lips (or what would have been lips, if he'd had them), and let the sweetly acrid smell of his breath (a mix of Old Spice, manly Mexicans, and barfed cow) wash over her.

"You know," she said, "I never kissed a guy with assistant principal on his breath."

 *nineteen*

All You Need to Know About That

Intimacies, what happens between two people in private (or one person and a Sea Beast in a pasture), are not the business of anyone but the parties involved. Still, for the sake of the voyeur in us all, a tidbit or two to satisfy curiosity . . .

Molly tried, made a valiant effort in fact, but even for a woman of such fine physical conditioning, the task was too great. She did, however, manage to locate near the shed a gas-powered weed-whacker (which the late drug chefs used to clear flammables from the area) and with firm but gentle application of that rude machine, and a little coaxing, was able to bring Steve to that state the French inscrutably call "the little death."

And soon after, what at first seemed an insurmountable obstacle, the size difference, was turned to advantage, allowing Molly to join Steve in that place of peace and pleasure. How? Imagine a slow slide down a long, slippery bannister of a tongue, each taste bud a tease and tingle in just the right place, and you can understand how Molly ended up a satisfied puddle snuggled in that spot between his neck and shoulder that women so love. (Except in Steve's case, it didn't make his arm go to sleep.)

Yes, there was a bit of the awkwardness that comes with the unfamiliarity and exploration of new lovers, and

Theo's Volvo was soundly smashed before Steve realized that rolling around on the ground was an inappropriate way to display his enthusiasm, but a boxy Swedish automobile is a small price to pay for passion in the great scheme of things.

And that is all you need to know about that.

 # twenty

Theo

Over the years, Theo had learned to forgive himself for having inappropriate thoughts at inappropriate times (imagining the widow naked at the funeral, rooting for a high death toll in Third World earthquakes, wondering whether white slavers provided in-house financing), but it worried him more than somewhat that, while handcuffed to a chair, waiting for his executioner, he was thinking about getting laid instead of escaping or making amends with his creator. Sure, he'd tried to get away, managing to do little more than tip the chair over and give himself a bug's-eye view of the dirt floor, but shortly after that, when the voices outside had stopped, he was overtaken with thoughts of women he'd had and women he hadn't, including an erotic mental montage of the erstwhile actress and resident Crazy Lady, Molly Michon.

So it was embarrassment as much as relief that he felt when, after the sound of a weed-whacker and the crashing of metal, Molly popped her head into the shed.

"Hi, Theo," she said.

"Molly, what are you doing here?"

"Out for a walk." She didn't come in, just craned her head around the corner.

"You've got to get away from here, Molly. There's some very dangerous guys around here."

"Not a problem. You don't want any help then?"

"Yes, go get help. But get away from here. There's guys with guns."

"I mean, you don't want me to uncuff you or anything?"

"There's no time."

"There's plenty of time. Where are the keys?"

"On my key ring. In the ignition of my car."

"Okay. Be right back."

And she was gone. Theo heard some pounding and what sounded like safety glass being shattered. In a second Molly was back in the doorway. She tossed the keys on the floor near his head. "Can you get to those?"

"Can you unlock me?"

"Uh, I'd rather not right now. But you'll be able to get to those eventually, won't you?"

"Molly!"

"Yes or no?"

"Sure, but . . ."

"Okay. See ya, Theo. Sorry about your car."

And again she was gone.

As he scrambled in the dirt to get to the keys, he was still troubled about the unwarranted wave of horniness that had overtaken him. Could it have been set off by the handcuffs? Maybe he'd been into bondage all these years and never even knew it. Although when he'd been arrested right before Sheriff Burton had blackmailed him into becoming constable, he'd spent almost two hours in handcuffs and he didn't remember it being an especially erotic experience. Maybe it was the death threat. Was he turned on by the thought of being shot? Man, I am a sick individual, he thought.

In ten minutes he was free of both the handcuffs and the dogging thoughts of sex and death. Molly, Joseph Leander, and the house trailer were gone, and he stood before the ruins of his Volvo with an entirely new set of questions nagging him. The roof of the station wagon was now mashed down to level with the hood, three of the four tires were blown, and on the ground, all around the car, were the tracks of what had to be a very, very large animal.

There were two trails that had matted down the grass leading away from the shed and over the hill. One, obviously, was the track of a person. The other was wider than the dirt road that led into the ranch.

Theo dug into the Volvo for his gun and cell phone, having no idea what to do with either of them. There was no one to call—and certainly no one he wanted to shoot. Except maybe Sheriff John Burton. He searched the area, found Joseph Leander's gun, and tucked it into the waistband of his jeans. The keys were still in the red four-wheeler, and after a minute of measuring the ethics of "borrowing" the truck against having been kidnapped, handcuffed, and almost killed, he climbed into the truck and took off across the pasture, following the double trail.

Gabe

Gabe and the rancher stood over the pulverized remains of the Holstein, waving flies away from their faces, while Skinner crouched a few yards away, his ears back, growling at the mess.

The rancher pushed his Stetson back on his head and shuddered. "My people have been running dairy and beef cattle on this land for sixty years, and I ain't never heard or seen anything like it, Gabe."

His name was Jim Beer. He was fifty-five, going on seventy, leathery from too much sun and stress, and there was a note of the sad lonely under everything he said. He was tall and thin, but stood with the broken-backed slouch of a beaten man. His wife had left him years ago, driving off in her Mercedes to live in San Francisco and taking with her a note worth half the value of Jim Beer's thousand acres. His only son, who was to have taken the ranch over, was twenty-eight now and was busy getting thrown out of colleges and into rehabs all over the country. He lived alone in a fourteen-room house that rattled with emptiness and seemed to suck up the laughter of the ranch hands, who Jim fed in his enormous kitchen every morning. Jim was the last of his breed, and he would forever trace the beginning of his downfall to an affair he'd had with the witch who once lived in Theo's cabin at the edge of the ranch. Cursed he was, or so he believed. If the witch hadn't run off ten years ago with the owner of the general store, he would have been sure the mutilated cattle was her doing.

Gabe shook his head. "I have no idea, Jim. I can take some samples and have some test run, but I don't even know what we are looking at here."

"You think it was kids? Vandals?"

"Kids tip cows over, Jim. These look like they've been dropped from thirty thousand feet." Gabe knew what appeared to have happened, but he wasn't willing to admit it. There wasn't a creature alive that could have done this. There had to be another explanation.

"So you're saying aliens?"

"No, I am definitely not saying aliens. I'm not saying aliens."

"Something was here. Look at the tracks. Satanic cult?"

"Damn it, Jim, unless you want to be on the cover of *Crackpot Weekly*, don't talk that way. I can't tell you what did this, but I can tell you what didn't. This was not aliens, or Satanists, or Bigfoot on a binge. I can take some samples and run some tests and then maybe, maybe, I can tell you what did this, but in the meantime, you should call the state ag guys and get them out here."

"I can't do that, Gabe."

"Why not?"

"I can't have strangers running around on my land. I don't want this gettin' out. That's why I called you."

"What's that?" Gabe held up a finger to hold his place in the conversation, then looked to the hills: the sound of an engine. In a second a red four-wheel-drive pickup appeared on the hill headed toward them.

"You'd better go," Jim Beer said.

"Why?"

"You'd just better. Nobody's supposed to be on this side of the ranch but me. You need to go."

"This is your land?"

"Let's jump in your truck, son. We need to go."

Gabe squinted to get a better look at the truck, then waved. "That's Theo Crowe," he said. "What's he doing in that thing?"

"Oh shit," Jim Beer said.

Theo pulled the truck up next to Gabe's, skidded to a stop, and crawled out. To Gabe, the constable looked pissed off, but he couldn't be sure, having never seen the expression on Theo before. "Afternoon, Gabe, Jim."

Jim Beer looked at his boots. "Constable."

Gabe noticed that Theo had two pistols stuck in his jeans and was half-covered with dust. "Hi, Theo. Nice truck. Jim called me out to take a look . . ."

"I know what that is," Theo said, tossing his head toward the mashed cow. "At least I think I do." He strode up to Jim Beer, who seemed to be trying to sink into a hole in his own chest.

"Jim, you got a crank lab back there turning out enough product to hype all of Los Angeles. You wanna tell me about it?"

The life seemed to drain out of Jim Beer and he fell

to the ground in a splay-legged sit. Gabe caught his arm to keep him from cracking his tailbone. Beer didn't look up. "My wife took a note for half the ranch when she left. She called it in. Where else was I going to get three million dollars?"

Gabe looked from Jim to Theo as if to say, "What the hell?"

"I'll explain later, Gabe. I have something I have to show you anyway." Theo pushed Jim Beer's Stetson back so he could see the rancher's face. "So Burton gave you the money so he could use your land for the lab."

"Sheriff Burton?" Gabe asked, totally confused now.

"Shut up, Gabe," Theo snapped.

"Not all of the money. Payments. Hell, what could I do? My grandfather started this ranch. I couldn't sell off half of it."

"So you went into drug dealing?"

"I ain't never even seen this lab you're talking about. Neither have my hands. That part of the ranch is off-limits. Burton said he had you in the cabin to keep anyone from coming in the back gate. I just run my cattle and mind my own business. I never even asked Burton what he was doing out there."

"Three million dollars! What the hell did you think he was doing? Raising rabbits?"

Jim Beer didn't answer, he just stared at the ground between his legs. Gabe held his shoulder to steady him and looked to Theo. "Maybe finish this later, Theo?"

Theo turned and walked in a tight circle, waving his hands in the air as if chasing away annoying spirits.

"You okay?" Gabe asked.

"What the fuck do I do now? What do I do? What am I supposed to do?"

"Calm down?" Gabe ventured.

"Fuck that! I got murders, drug manufacturing, some fucking giant animal of some kind, a whole town that's gone nuts, my car is mashed, and I have a crush on a crazy woman—I don't have the training for this! *No one* has the fucking training for this!"

"So calming down isn't an option right now?" Gabe said. "I understand."

Theo interrupted his anxiety Tilt-A-Whirl and wheeled on Gabe. "And I haven't smoked any pot in a week, Gabe."

"Congratulations."

"It's made me insane. It's ruined my life."

"Come on, Theo, you never had a life." Gabe immediately realized that perhaps he had chosen the wrong tack in consoling his friend.

"Yeah, there's that." Theo strode to the red truck and punched the fender. "Ouch! Goddamn it!" He turned to Gabe again. "And I think I just broke my hand."

"Mad cow disease worries me," Jim Beer said from his stupor of defeat.

"Shut up, Jim," Gabe said. "Theo has a gun."

"Guns!" Theo shouted.

"I stand corrected," said Gabe. "You mentioned a giant animal?"

Theo massaged his temples as if trying to squeeze out a coherent thought. After a few minutes, he walked to where Jim Beer was sitting and kneeled down in front of him. "Jim, I need you to pull it together for a second."

The rancher looked at Theo. Tears had traced the creases in his cheeks.

"Jim, this never happened, okay? You haven't seen me and you haven't heard anything from this side of the ranch, okay? If Burton calls you, everything is standard operating procedure. You know nothing, you understand?"

"No, I don't understand. Am I going to jail?"

"I don't know that, Jim, but I do know that Burton finding out about this will only make it worse for everyone. I need some time to figure some things out. If you help, I'll do my best to protect you, I promise."

"Okay." Beer nodded. "I'll do what you say."

"Good, take Gabe's truck home. We'll pick it up in an hour or so."

Skinner watched all this with heightened interest, tentatively wagging his tail between Theo's tirades, hoping in his heart of hearts that he would get a ride in that big red truck. Even dogs harbor secret agendas.

"Theo, these can't be real," Gabe said, running his hand over a footprint nearly three feet across. "This is some sort of hoax. Although the depth of the claw impressions and the scuffing would indicate that whoever did this really knows something about how animals move."

Theo was fairly calm now, as if he had settled into the whole unreality of the situation. "And they know something about crushing a Volvo too. They're real, Gabe. I've seen a track like this before."

"Where?"

"By the creek, the night the fuel truck blew up. I didn't want to believe it then either."

Gabe looked up from the track. "That's the night I had the mass exodus with my rats."

"Yep."

"There's no way, Theo. That couldn't be what happened. A creature that could leave tracks like this would dwarf a T. Rex. There hasn't been anything this size on the planet for sixty million years."

"Not anything we know about. Look, Gabe, I followed the trail through the grass to the mutilated cows. I thought that was where they went, but evidently that's where they just came from."

"They? You think there's more than one?"

"So you accept that this thing is real?"

"No, Theo. I'm just asking what you think."

"I think that this thing was with Molly Michon."

Gabe laughed. "Theo, I think the withdrawal has you addled."

"I'm not joking. Molly was here right after I heard my car getting crunched. She gave me the keys to the handcuffs. When I came out, she was gone, and so were Joseph Leander and whoever he came here to see. "

"So what do you think happened to them?"

"The same thing that happened to those cows. Or something like it. The same thing that I think happened to the Plotznik kid. The last time anyone saw him was at the Fly Rod Trailer Court. That's where Molly lives."

Gabe stood and looked around at the pattern of tracks. "You haven't been into town today, have you, Theo?"

"No, I've been busy."

"Les from the hardware store is missing. They found his truck behind the Head of the Slug, but there's no sign of him."

"We've got to go to Molly's, Gabe."

"We? Theo, I'm a biologist, not a cop. I say we try and track whatever this is. Skinner's a pretty good tracker. I'd bet we find an explanation that doesn't involve some sort of giant creature."

"I'm not a cop anymore either. And what if we track this thing and you're wrong, Gabe? Do you want to meet up with whatever did that to my car? Those cows?"

"Well, yes, I do."

"We can do that later. It shouldn't be too hard. Whatever it is, it's pulling a house trailer."

"What?"

"There was a trailer here when Leander took me into the shed. When I came out, it was gone."

Gabe checked his watch. "Have you eaten today? I'm not questioning you, but maybe you're having a hypoglycemic reaction or something. Let's go get some dinner and when your head clears, we can go by Molly Michon's."

"Right, I'm hallucinating from a bad case of the munchies."

Gabe grabbed his shoulder. "Theo, please. I have a date."

Theo nodded. "Molly's first. Then I'll go to dinner."

"Deal," Gabe said, still staring at the tracks. "I want to come back here with some casting materials. Even if this is a hoax, I want a record of it."

Theo started for the truck and pulled up when he heard the sound of a cell phone ringing inside the shed. He walked into the shed, located the cell phone, and looked at the display for the number that was ringing in. It was Burton's private number. He drew his .357 Magnum and blew the phone into a thousand pieces. He walked out of the shed to find Gabe hiding behind the fender of the red truck and Skinner cowering in the bed.

"What in the hell do you mean, you have a date?"

 twenty-one

Gabe and Theo

"This is where I found the aberrant rats," Gabe said as they pulled into the Fly Rod Trailer Court.

"That's nice," Theo said, not really paying attention.

"Did I tell you I got the brain chemistry back from Stanford? It's interesting, but I'm not sure that it explains the behavior."

"Not now, Gabe, please." Theo slammed on the brakes and the truck rocked to a stop. "What the hell?" There were no lights on in Molly Michon's trailer. In the empty lot next door, a dozen well-dressed adults stood in a circle, holding candles.

"Prayer meeting?" Gabe ventured. "It's Sunday night."

"There was a trailer there last time I was here," Theo said. "Just like the one on the ranch."

"I know. This is the lot where I found the rats with the low serotonin levels."

Theo shut off the truck, set the parking brake, and climbed out. Then he looked back at Gabe. "You found your rats right here?"

"The six that I could find. But this is where the other ones that were last tracked disappeared as well. I can show you the graphic later."

"That would be good."

Theo pulled his flannel shirt over the guns in his waistband and approached the circle. Skinner jumped out of the truck and ran ahead. Gabe reluctantly followed. They did, indeed, seem to be praying. Their heads were bowed and a woman in a powder-blue dress and pillbox hat was leading the group. "Bless us, Lord, for we have felt the stirrings of your power within us and heeded your call to come to this holy place on the eve of . . ."

Skinner drove his nose into the woman's crotch, and she yipped like a bee-stung poodle. Everyone in the group looked up.

"Excuse me," Theo said. "I don't mean to interrupt, but what are you all doing here?" Several of the men looked irritated and stepped up behind the powder-blue woman to give support.

The woman held Skinner's nose away from her dress while trying to keep the candle flame away from her hair spray. "Constable Crowe? Is that right?"

"Yes, ma'am," Theo said. The woman was younger than he was by at least five years and pretty in a Texas Big Hair sort of way, but her dress and manner of speaking made him feel as if he'd just been busted by his first-grade teacher for eating paste.

"We've been called here, Constable," the woman explained. She reached behind her, grabbed the shoulder of a woman who looked like her clone in pink, and pulled her forward. Skinner stamped the pink woman's dress with the Wet-Nose Inspection Seal. "Margie and I felt it first, but when we started talking about it after services this afternoon, all these other people said that they had felt drawn to this place as well. The Holy Spirit has moved us here."

"Ask them if they've seen any rats." Gabe said.

"Call your dog," Theo tossed over his shoulder.

Gabe called Skinner and the Labrador looked around.

They smell fine to me, Food Guy. I say fuck 'em, Skinner thought. But he got no response except a minor scolding.

"The Holy Spirit called you here?" Theo said.

Everyone in the group nodded earnestly.

"Did any of you happen to see the woman who lives in that trailer next door?"

The pink lady chimed in, "Oh yes, she was the one to call our attention to this place two nights ago. We wondered about that at first, being as how she is and all, but then Katie pointed out"—she gestured to her friend—"that our Lord Jesus spent time with Mary Magdalene, and she, as I'm sure you know, was—well—she was . . ."

"A whore," Theo offered.

"Well. Yes. And so we thought, who are we to judge?"

"Very charitable of you," Theo said. "But have you seen Molly Michon tonight?"

"No, not tonight."

Theo felt his energy reserves drain even more. "Look, folks, you shouldn't be here. I'm not sure it's safe. Some people have gone missing . . ."

"Oh, that poor boy," Margie said.

"Yes and maybe some others. I have to ask you all to take your meeting somewhere else, please."

The group looked disappointed. One of the men, a portly bald fellow in his fifties, puffed himself up and stepped forward. "Constable, we have the right to worship when and where we please."

"I'm just thinking of your safety," Theo said.

"This country was founded on the basis of religious freedom, and . . ."

Theo stepped up to the man and loomed over him with all of his six-foot-six frame, "Then start praying that I don't throw you in jail with the biggest, horniest sodomite the county jail has to offer, which is what I'm going to do if you all don't go home right now."

"Smooth," Gabe said.

Make him roll over and pee on himself, Skinner thought.

The bald man made a harumph sound and turned to the group. "Let's meet at the church to discuss the removal of our local law enforcement official."

"Yeah, get in line," Theo said. He watched as the group dispersed to their cars and drove away.

When the last one pulled out, Gabe said, "Theories?"

Theo shook his head. "Everyone in this town is nuts. I'm going to check Molly's trailer, but I doubt she's there. Do you want me to take you home to shower and change clothes before your date?"

Gabe looked down at his stained work pants and safari shirt. "Do you think I should?"

"Gabe, you're the only guy I know that makes me look suave."

"You're coming along, right?"

"Casanova," Theo said. "Compared to you, I feel like Casanova."

"What?" Gabe said. "It's fried chicken night at H.P.'s."

Steve

Steve lay under a stand of cypress trees, his new lover snuggled up to his right foreleg, snoring softly. He let his tongue slide out and the tip just brushed her bare back. She moaned and nuzzled closer to his leg. She tasted pretty good. But he had eaten all those other warmbloods and he wasn't really hungry.

When he had been a female, some fifty years ago, and going back another five thousand, he had become accustomed to eating his lovers after mating. That's just how it was done. But as a male, he wasn't sure. He hadn't mated with his own species since he'd become male, and so the instinct to become passive after mating was new to him. He just didn't feel like eating the warmblood. She had made him feel better, and for some reason, he could see the pictures of her thoughts instead of just sending his own signals. He sensed no fear in her, and no need to send the signal to draw her to him. Strange for a warmblood.

He lay his head down on the bed of cypress needles to sleep and let his wounds heal. He could eat her later. Somewhere in the back of his brain, as he fell asleep, a fear alarm went off. In five thousand years of life, he had never conceived of the concept of later or before, only now. His DNA had rechained itself many times, adapted to changes without waiting for the life cycles of generations—he was a unique organism in that way—but the concept of time, of memory beyond the cellular level, was a new adaptation. Through his contact with Molly he was evolving consciousness, and like the pragmatic mechanism that it is, nature was trying to warn him. The nightmare was about to have a nightmare.

Val

Is this a date? Val sat alone at a table in the back of H.P.'s Cafe. She'd ordered a glass of a local chardonnay and was trying to form an opinion about it that would reflect the appropriate disgust, but unfortunately, it was quite good. She was wearing light evening makeup and an understated raw silk suit in indigo with a single string of pearls so as not to clash too badly with her date, who she knew would be in jeans or cotton khaki. Her date? If this is a date, how far have I sunk? she asked herself. This tacky little cafe in this tacky little town, waiting for a man who had probably never worn a tux or a Rolex, and she was looking forward to it.

No, it's not a date. It's just dinner. It's sustenance. It's, for once, not eating alone. Slumming in the land of the folksy and the neighborly, that's what it is. It's a satirical performance art experience; call it *The Bourgeois Fried Chicken Follies*. It was one thing to read her journals over coffee in the local cafe, but dinner?

Gabe Fenton came through the front door and Val felt her pulse quicken. She smiled in spite of herself as she watched the waitress point to her table. Then Theo Crowe was following Gabe across the restaurant and a bolt of anxiety shot up her spine. This definitely isn't a date.

Gabe smiled and the lines around his eyes crinkled as if he were about to burst out laughing. He extended his hand to her. "Hi, I hope you don't mind, I asked Theo to join us." His hair was combed, as was his beard, and he was wearing a faded but clean chambray shirt. Not exactly dashing, but a pretty good-looking guy in a lumberjack sort of way.

"No, please," Val said. "Sit down, Theo."

Theo nodded and pulled a chair up to the table, which had been set for two. The waitress breezed in with another place setting before they were seated. "I'm sorry to intrude," Theo said, "but Gabe insisted."

"No, really, you're welcome, Constable."

"Theo, please."

"Theo then," Val said. She forced a smile. What now? The last time she had talked to this man it had thrown her life for a loop. She found herself building a resentment for Gabe that was usually reserved for relationships that were years old.

Theo cleared his throat. "Uh, can we go on the doctor-patient confidentiality plan again, Doctor?"

Val nodded to Gabe, "That usually implies a session. Not dinner."

"Okay, then, don't say anything, but Joseph Leander killed his wife."

Val didn't say, "Wow." Almost, but she didn't. "And you know this because . . ."

"Because he told me so," Theo said. "He gave her tea made from foxglove. Evidently, it can cause heart failure and is almost undetectable. Then he hung her in the dining room."

"So you've arrested him?"

"No, I don't know where he is."

"But you've put a warrant out for his arrest or whatever it is that you do?

"No, I'm not sure that I'm still the constable."

Gabe broke in. "We've been talking about it, Val. I say that Theo is an elected official, and therefore the only way he can lose his job is through impeachment, even if his immediate superior tries to kill him. What do you think?"

"Kill him?"

"Smooth," Theo said, grinning at Gabe.

"Oh, maybe you should tell her about the crank lab and stuff, Theo."

And so Theo explained, telling the story of his kidnapping, the drug lab, Joseph Leander's disappearance, and Molly Michon setting him free, but leaving out any theories he had about a giant creature. During the telling, they ordered (fried chicken for Theo and Gabe, a Greek salad for Val) and were halfway through dinner before Theo stopped talking.

Val stared at her salad and silence washed over the table. If there was going to be a murder investigation, she could be found out. And if they found out what she had done to her patients, her career was over. She might even go to jail. It wasn't fair, she really had tried to do the right thing for once. She resisted the urge to blurt out a confession—to throw herself on the mercy of a court born of sheer paranoia. Instead she raised her eyes to Gabe, who took the signal to break the silence.

Gabe said, "And I still don't know the significance of the low serotonin levels in the rats' brains."

"Huh?" said not only Val and Theo, but the waitress, Jenny, who had been eavesdropping from the next table and joined the confusion at Gabe's non sequitur.

"Sorry," Gabe said to Val. "I thought you might have a take on the brain chemistry of those rats I had tested. You said you were interested."

"And I am," Val said, lying through her teeth, "but I'm a little overwhelmed by the news about Bess Leander."

"Right, anyway, the group of rats that didn't take part in the mass migration all had unusually low levels of serotonin. The brain chemistry of the larger group, the group that ran, was all in normal ranges. So I'm thinking that . . ."

"They were depressed," Val said.

"Pardon me?" Gabe said.

"Of course they're depressed, they're rats," Theo said. Gabe glared at him.

"Well, imagine waking up to that every morning," Theo continued. " 'Oh, it's a great day, crap, I'm still a rat. Never mind.' "

"Well, I don't know about rats," Val said, "but serotonin levels in humans affect a lot of different things, predominantly mood. Low levels of serotonin can indicate depression. That's how Prozac works. It basically keeps serotonin in the brain to keep the patient from getting depressed. So maybe Gabe's rats were too depressed to run."

Gabe stroked his beard. "I never thought of that. But it doesn't help that much. It doesn't tell me why the majority of the rats did run."

"Well, duh, Gabe," Theo said. "It's the fucking monster."

"What?" Val said.

"What?" said Jenny, who was lingering nearby.

"Can we get some dessert menus?" Gabe asked, sending Jenny backing across the restaurant.

"Monster?" Val said.

"Maybe you'd better explain, Gabe," Theo said. "I think your scientific skepticism will make it sound more credible."

Val's jaw dropped visibly as she listened to Gabe talk about the tracks at the ranch, the mutilated cattle, and Theo's theory for the disappearances of Joseph Leander, Mikey Plotznik, and perhaps Les from the hardware store. When Gabe brought up Molly Michon, Val stopped him.

"You can't believe what she tells you. Molly is a very disturbed woman."

"She didn't tell me anything," Theo said. "I just think she knows something about all this."

Val wanted to call up Theo's drug history to sweep the story aside, then she remembered what Estelle Boyet had told her in therapy. "I'm not going to say who, but one of my patients mentioned a sea monster in session."

Gabe asked. "Who?"

"I can't say," Val said.

"Estelle Boyet," Jenny said as she came up to get the dessert order.

"Damn," Val said. "I wasn't the one who told you," she said to Theo.

"Well, she was talking about it over breakfast with that Catfish guy," Jenny added.

"No dessert," Val snapped at Jenny.

"I'll bring the check."

"So Estelle has seen it?" Theo asked.

"No, she says she's heard it. She's not the type to propagate a hoax, but I wouldn't put it past Molly Michon. Perhaps that's where the rumor started. I can ask Estelle."

"Do that," Theo said. "But it's not a hoax. My car is smashed. That's evidence. I'm going to Molly's tonight and wait for her. The door was unlocked when I checked earlier and I can't go home."

"You think it's that dangerous?" Val asked.

"I know it is." Theo stood and started to pull some bills from his pocket. Gabe waved him off. Theo said, "Doctor, can you give Gabe a ride?"

"Sure, but . . ."

"Thanks," Theo said. "I'll call you, Gabe. Thanks for letting me join you, Doctor. I thought you'd want to know about Bess. I'm afraid I've ruined your date."

I'll say, Val thought as she watched Theo leave the restaurant. A sense of alert exhaustion washed over her like an espresso fog bank.

"He just quit smoking pot," Gabe said. "He's feeling the stress."

"He has a right to. You don't believe any of that stuff about a monster, do you?"

"I have some theories."

"Would you like to come up to the house and explain them over a bottle of wine?"

"Really? I mean, sure, that would be nice."

"Good," Val said. "I think I need to get hammered and I'd like your company." Had she used the term "hammered" since college? She didn't think so.

"I'll get the check," Gabe said.

"Of course you will."

"I hope you don't mind having a dog in your car," Gabe said.

I'm not slumming, she thought. I've moved to the slums.

twenty-two

Theo

The walls of Molly's trailer were plastered with movie posters. He stood in the middle of the living room among the scattered videotapes, magazines, and junk mail and slowly turned. It was her, Molly. She hadn't been lying all this time. Most of the posters were in foreign languages, but every one featured a younger Molly in various states of undress, holding weapons or fighting off bad guys, her hair flying in the wind, a nuked-out city or a desert littered with human skulls and burned-out cars in the background.

The adolescent male part of Theo, the part that every man tries to bury but carries to his grave, reared up. She was a movie star. A hot movie star! And he knew her, had in fact put handcuffs on her. If there was only a locker room, a street corner, or a second-period study hall where he could brag about it to his friends. But he didn't really have any friends, except for Gabe maybe, and Gabe was a grown-up. The prurient moment passed and Theo felt guilty about the way he had treated Molly: patronizing her and condescending to her; the way many people treated him when he tried to be something besides a pothead and a puppet.

He kneeled down to a bookshelf filled with videotapes, found one labeled KENDRA: WARRIOR BABE OF THE OUT-

LAND (ENGLISH), and slipped it into the VCR and turned on the television. Then he turned off the lights, laid his guns on the coffee table, and lay down on Molly's couch to wait. He watched as the Crazy Lady of Pine Cove battled mutants and Sand Pirates for half an hour before he drifted off to sleep. His mind needed a deeper escape from his problems than the movie could provide.

"Hi, Theo."

He came awake startled. The movie was still casting a flickering light over the room, so he couldn't have been sleeping that long. She stood in the doorway, half in shadow, looking very much like the woman on the television screen. She held an assault rifle at her side.

"Molly, I've been waiting for you."

"How'd you like it?" She nodded toward the television.

"Loved it. I never realized. I was just so tired . . ."

Molly nodded. "I won't be long, I just came to get some clean clothes. You're welcome to stay here."

Theo didn't know what to do. It didn't seem like the time to grab one of the pistols off the table. He felt more embarrassed than threatened.

"Thanks," he said.

"He's the last one, Theo. After him there aren't any more of his kind. His time has passed. I think that's what we have in common. You don't know what it is to be a has-been, do you?"

"I think I'm what they call a never-was."

"That's easier. At least you're always looking up the ladder, not down. Coming down is scarier."

"How? Why? What is he?"

"I'm not sure, a dragon maybe. Who knows?" She leaned back against the doorway and sighed. "But I can kinda tell what he's thinking. I guess it's because I'm nuts. Who would have thought that would come in handy, huh?"

"Don't say that about yourself. You're saner than I am."

Molly laughed, and Theo could see her movie-star teeth shine in the light of the television. "You're a neurotic, Theo. A neurotic is someone who thinks something is wrong with him, but everyone else thinks he is normal; a psychotic thinks she is normal, but everyone else thinks something's wrong with her. Take a poll of the locals, I think I'd come out in the latter category, don't you?"

"Molly, this is really dangerous stuff you're messing with."

"He won't hurt me."

"It's not just that. You could go to jail just for having that machine gun, Molly. People are getting killed, aren't they?"

"In a manner of speaking."

"That's what happened to Joseph Leander, and the guys working the drug lab, right? Your pal ate them?"

"They were going to hurt you, and Steve was hungry. Seemed like great timing to me."

"Molly, that's murder!"

"Theo! I'm nuts. What are they going to do to me?"

Theo shrugged his shoulders and sat back on the couch. "I don't know what to do."

"You're not in a position to do anything right now. Get some rest."

Theo cradled his head in his hands. His cell phone, still in the pocket of his flannel shirt, began ringing. "I could sure use a hit right now."

"There's some Smurfs of Sanity in the cupboard over the sink—neuroleptics Dr. Val gave me, antipsychotics—they've done wonders for me."

"Obviously."

"Your phone is ringing."

Theo pulled out the phone, flipped it open, hit the answer button and watched as the incoming number appeared on the display. It was Sheriff Burton's cell phone number. Theo hit disconnect.

"I'm fucked," Theo said.

Molly picked up Theo's .357 Magnum from the table, held it on Theo, then picked up Joseph Leander's automatic. "I'll give these back before I go. I'm going to get some clean clothes and some girlie things out of my bedroom. You be okay here?"

"Yeah, sure." His head was still hung. He spoke into his lap.

"You're bumming me out, Theo."

"Sorry."

Molly was gone from the room for only five minutes, in which time Theo tried to get a handle on what had happened. Molly returned with a duffel bag slung over her shoulder. She was wearing the Kendra costume, complete with thigh-high boots. Even in the dim light from the television, Theo could see a ragged scar over her breast. She caught him looking.

"Ended my career," she said. "I suppose now they could fix it, but it's a little late."

"I'm sorry," Theo said. "I think you look beautiful."

She smiled and shifted both of the pistols to one hand. She'd left the assault rifle by the door and Theo hadn't even noticed. "You ever feel special, Theo?"

"Special?"

"Not like you're better than everyone else, just that you're different in a good way, like it makes a difference that you're on the planet? You ever feel that way?"

"I don't know. No, not really."

"I had that for a while. Even though they were cheesy B movies and even though I had to do some humiliating things to get into them, I felt special, Theo. Then it went away. Well, now I feel that way again. That's why."

"Why what?"

"You asked me why before. That's why I'm going back to Steve."

"Steve? You call him Steve?"

"He looked like a Steve," Molly said. "I have to go. I'll leave your guns in the bed of that red truck you stole. Don't try to follow, okay?"

Theo nodded. "Molly, don't let it kill anybody else. Promise me that."

"Promise to leave us alone?"

"I can't do that."

"Okay. Take care of yourself." She grabbed the assault rifle, kicked open the door, and stepped out.

Theo heard her go down the steps, pause, then come back up. She popped her head in the door. "I'm sorry you never felt special, Theo," she said.

Theo forced a smile. "Thanks, Molly."

Gabe

Gabe stood in the foyer of Valerie Riordan's home, looking at his hiking boots, then the white carpet, then his boots again. Val had gone into the kitchen to get some wine. Skinner was wandering around outside.

Gabe sat down on the marble floor, unlaced his boots, then slipped them off. He'd once been into a level-nine clean room at a biotech facility in San Jose, a place where the air was scrubbed and filtered down to the micron and you had to wear a plastic bunny suit with its own air umbilical to avoid contaminating the specimens. Strangely, he'd had a similar feeling to the one he was feeling now, which was: I am the harbinger of filth. Thank God Theo had made him shower and change before his date.

Val came into the sunken living room carrying a tray

with a bottle of wine and two glasses. She looked up at Gabe, who was standing at the edge of the stairs as if ready to wade into molten lava.

"Well, come on in and have a seat," Val said.

Gabe took a tentative step. "Nice place," he said.

"Thanks, I still have a lot to do on it. I suppose I should just hire a decorator and have done with it, but I like finding pieces myself."

"Right," Gabe said, taking another step. You could play handball in this room if you didn't mind destroying a lot of antiques.

"It's a cabernet from Wild Horse Vineyard over the hill. I hope you like it." Val poured the wine into stemmed bubble glasses. She took hers and sat down on the velvet couch, then raised her eyebrows as if to say, "Well?"

Gabe joined her at the other end of the couch, then took a tentative sip of the wine. "It's nice."

"For a local cheapie," Val said.

An awkward silence passed between them. Val made a show of tasting the wine again, then said, "You don't really believe this stuff about a sea monster, do you, Gabe?"

Gabe was relieved. She wanted to talk about work. He'd been afraid that she would want to talk about something else—anything else—and he didn't really know how. "Well, there are the tracks, which look very authentic, so if they are fake, whoever did them studied fossil tracks and replicated them perfectly. Then there's the timing of the rat migration, plus Theo and your patient. Estelle, was it?"

Val set down her wine. "Gabe, I know you're a scientist, and a discovery like this could make you rich and famous, but I just don't believe there's a dinosaur in town."

"Rich and famous? I hadn't thought about it. I guess there would be some recognition, wouldn't there?"

"Look, Gabe, you deal in hard facts, but every day I deal with the delusions and constructions of people's minds. They are just tracks on the ground, probably like that Bigfoot hoax in Washington a few years ago. Theo is a chronic drug user, and Estelle and her boyfriend Catfish are artist types. They all have overactive imaginations."

Gabe was put off by her judgment of Theo and the others. He thought for a second, then said, "As a biologist, I have a theory about imagination. I think it's pretty obvious that fear—fear of loud noises, fear of heights, the capacity to learn fear—is something that we've adapted over the years as a survival mechanism, and so is imagination. Everyone thinks that it was the big strong caveman who got the girl, and for the most part, that may have been true, but physical strength doesn't explain how our species created civilization. I think there was always some scrawny dreamer sitting at the edge of the firelight, who had the ability to imagine dangers, to look into the future in his imagination and see possibilities, and therefore survived to pass his genes on to the next generation. When the big ape men ended up running off the cliff or getting killed while trying to beat a mastodon into submission with a stick, the dreamer was standing back thinking, 'Hey, that might work, but you need to run the mastodon off the cliff.' And, then he'd mate with the women left over after the go-getters got killed."

"So nerds rule," Val said with a smile. "But if fear and imagination make you more highly evolved, then someone with paranoid delusions would be ruling the world." Val was getting into the theory of it now. How strange to talk to a man who talked about ideas, not property and personal agendas. Val liked it. A lot.

Gabe said, "Well, we didn't miss that by far with Hitler, did we? Evolution takes some missteps sometimes.

Big teeth worked pretty well for a while, then they got too big. Mastodons' tusks got so large they would snap the animal's neck. And you've probably noticed that there are no saber-toothed cats around anymore."

"Okay, I'll buy that imagination is an evolutionary leap. But what about depression?" Talking about mental conditions, she couldn't help thinking about what she'd done to her patients. Her crimes circled in her mind, trying to get out. "Psychiatry is looking more and more at mental conditions from a physical point of view, so that fits. That's why we're treating depression with drugs like Prozac. But what evolutionary purpose is there for depression?"

"I've been thinking about that since you mentioned it at dinner," Gabe said. He drained his wineglass and moved closer to her on the couch, as if by being closer, she would share in his excitement. He was in his element now. "A lot of animals besides humans get depressed. Higher mammals like dolphins and whales can die from it, but even rats seem to get the Blues. I can't figure out what purpose it serves. But in humans it might be like nearsightedness: civilization has protected a biological weakness that would have been weeded out by natural dangers or predators."

"Predators? How?"

"I don't know. Depression might slow the prey down, make it react less quickly to danger. Who knows?"

"So a predator might actually evolve that preyed on depressed animals?" Right and it's me, Val thought. If I haven't been preying on depressed people, what have I been doing? She suddenly felt ashamed of her home, of the pure materialism of it. Here was an incredibly bright man who was concerned with the pure pursuit of knowledge, and she had sold her integrity for some antiques and a Mercedes.

Gabe poured himself another glass of wine and sat

back now, thinking as he spoke. "Interesting idea. I suppose there could be some sort of chemical or behavioral
stimulus that would trigger preying on the depressed.
Low serotonin levels tend to raise libido, right? At least
temporarily?"

"Yes," Val said. That's why the entire town has turned
into horndogs, she thought.

"Therefore," Gabe continued, "you'd have more animals mating and passing on the depression gene. Nature
tends to evolve mechanisms to remain in balance. A predator or a disease would naturally evolve to keep the depressed population down. Interesting, I've been feeling
especially horny lately, I wonder if I'm depressed." Gabe's
eyes snapped open wide and he looked at Val with the
full-blown terror of what he had just said. He gulped his
wine, then said, "I'm sorry, I . . ."

Val couldn't stand it anymore. Gabe's faux pas opened
the gate, and she stepped through it. "Gabe, we have to
talk."

"I'm really sorry, I didn't mean to . . ."

She grabbed his arm to stop him. "No, I have to tell
you something."

Gabe braced himself for the worst. He'd fallen out of
the lofty world of theory into the awkward, gritty world
of first dates, and she was going to drop the "Don't get
the wrong idea" bomb on him.

She gripped his arm and her nails dug into his bicep
hard enough to make him wince.

She said, "A little over a month ago, I took almost a
third of the people in Pine Cove off antidepressants."

"Huh?" That wasn't at all what he'd expected. "My
God, why?"

"Because of Bess Leander's suicide. Or what I thought
was her suicide. I was just going through the motions in
my practice. Writing prescriptions and collecting fees."
She explained about her arrangement with Winston

Krauss and how the pharmacist had refused to put everyone back on the drugs. When she finished, to wait for his
judgment, there were tears welling up in her eyes.

He put his arms around her tentatively, hoping it was
the right thing to do. "Why tell me this?"

She melted against his chest. "Because I trust you and
because I have to tell someone and because I need to
figure out what to do. I don't want to go to jail, Gabe.
Maybe all my patients didn't need to be on antidepressants, but a lot of them did." She sobbed on his shoulder
and he began to stroke her hair, then pushed up her chin
and kissed her tears.

"It'll be okay. It will."

She looked up into his eyes, as if looking for a hint of
disdain, then not finding it, she kissed him hard and
pulled him on top of her on the couch.

A Higher Power

And they worshipped the dragon which gave power unto the beast: and they worshipped the beast, saying, Who is like unto the beast?

—Revelation 13:4

twenty-three

Steve

What horrors can a dragon dream? A creature who has, in his own way, ruled the planet for millions of years, a creature for whom the mingy man mammals have built temples, a creature who has known no predator but time—what could he possibly dream that would frighten him? Call it the knowing?

Under a stand of oak trees, sexually satisfied and with a bellyful of drug dealers, the dragon dreamed a vision of time past. The eternal now that he had always known suddenly had history. In the dream he saw himself as a larva, tucked into the protective pouch under his mother's tongue until it was safe to venture out under her watchful eye. He saw the hunting and the mating, the forms he had learned to mimic as his mercurial DNA evolved not through generations, but through regeneration of cells. He saw the mates he had eaten, the three young he had borne as a female, the last killed by a warmblood who sang the Blues. He remembered the changing, not so long ago, from female to male, and he remembered all of it in pictures, not in mere instinctual patterns and conditioned responses.

He saw these pictures in the dream, brought on by the strange mating with the warmblood, and he wondered why. For the first time in his five thousand years, he asked, *Why?* And the dream answered with a picture of all the oceans and swamps, the rivers and bogs and trenches and mountains beneath the sea, and they were all empty of his kind. As sure as if he were floating through the cold black at the end of the universe, where light gives up hope and time chases its tail until it dies from exhaustion, he was alone.

Sex does that to some guys.

Val

"Oh my God, the rat brains!" Gabe shouted.

It was a different response to lovemaking. Val wasn't sure that she might not be hurt, feeling vulnerable as she was, with her knees in the vicinity of her ears, a biologist on top of her, and her panty hose waving off one foot like a tattered battle flag.

Gabe collapsed into her arms and she looked over his shoulder to the coffee table to check that they hadn't kicked the wineglasses off onto the carpet.

"Are you okay?" she asked, a little breathless.

"I'm sorry, but I just realized what's going on with this creature."

"That's what you were thinking about?" Yes, her feelings were definitely hurt.

"No, not during. It came to me in a flash right after. Somehow the creature can attract mammals with lower than normal serotonin levels. And you've got, what, a third of the population running around in antidepressant withdrawal?"

She was pissed now, not hurt. She dumped him off her onto the floor, stood up, pulled her skirt down, and stepped away. He scrambled into his pants and looked around for his shirt, which lay in shreds behind the couch.

He had a tan that ended at the neckline and just below the shoulders; the rest of him was milk white. He looked up at her from the gap between the couch and the coffee table with a pleading in his eyes, as if he were looking up from a coffin in which he was about to be buried alive.

"Sorry," he said.

He wasn't looking her in the eye, and Val suddenly realized that he was talking to her exposed breasts. She pulled her blouse closed, and a battery of insults rose in her mind, ready to be fired, but all of them were mean-spirited and would serve to do nothing but make them both feel ashamed. He was who he was, and he was honest and real, and she knew that he hadn't meant to hurt her. So she cried. Thinking, Great, crying is what got me into this in the first place.

She plopped down on the couch with her face in her hands. Gabe moved to her side and put his arm around her. "I'm really sorry. I'm not very good at this sort of thing."

"You're fine. It's just too much."

"I should go." He started to stand.

She caught his arm in a death grip. "You go and I'll hunt you down and kill you like a rabid dog."

"I'll stay."

"No go," she said. "I understand."

"Okay, I'll go."

"Don't you dare." She threw her arms around him and kissed him hard, pulling him back down onto the couch, and within seconds they were all over each other again.

That's it, she thought, no more crying. It's the crying that does it. This guy is aroused by my pain.

But soon they lay in a panting sweaty pile on the floor and the idea of crying was light-years away.

And this time Gabe said, "That was wonderful."

Val noticed a wineglass overturned by her head, a

cabernet stain bleeding over the carpet. "Is it salt or club soda?"

Gabe pulled away far enough to look into her eyes and saw that she was looking at the stained carpet. "Salt and cold water, I think. Or is that blood?" A drop of sweat dripped off his forehead onto her lips.

She looked at him. "You weren't thinking about that creature that doesn't exist, were you?"

"Just you."

She smiled. "Really?"

"And a weed-whacker, for some reason."

"You're kidding."

"Uh, yes, I'm kidding. I was only thinking of you."

"So you don't think I'm a horrible person for what I've done?"

"You were trying to do what you thought was right. How could that be horrible?"

"I feel horrible."

"It's been a long time. I'm out of practice."

"No, not about this. About my patients. You really think something could be preying on them?"

"It's just a theory. There may not even be a creature."

"But what if there is? Shouldn't we call the National Guard or something?"

"I was thinking of calling Theo."

"Theo isn't even a real cop."

"He deserves to know."

They lay there in silence for a few minutes, staring at the spreading stain on the carpet, feeling the sweat run down their ribs, and listening to the beat of each other's hearts.

"Gabe?" Val whispered.

"Yes."

"Maybe we should go to couples' counseling."

"Should we get dressed first?"

"You were serious about the weed-whacker, weren't you?"

"I don't know where that image came from."

"There's supposed to be a good couples' guy in San Junipero, unless you'd rather go to a woman counselor."

"I thought we were going to call the National Guard."

"Only if it comes to that," Val said. Thinking, When we tell the shrink about this, I'm leaving out the part about the wine spilling.

Theo

Is there anything more irritating than people who have just been laid? Especially when you have not. Not for a long time.

Oh, it was obvious as soon as they came through Molly's front door, waking Theo for the second time that night: Gabe's grin looking like the oversized grill on an old Chrysler, Val Riordan wearing jeans and almost no makeup; the both of them giddy and giggling and blushing like children. Theo wanted to puke. He was happy for them, but he wanted to puke.

"What?" Theo said.

Gabe was obviously amped and trying not to show it. He put his hands in his pockets to keep from waving them around. "I"—he looked at Val and smiled—"we think that this creature, if it exists, may be attracted to prey with low serum serotonin levels."

Gabe bounced on the balls of his feet as he waited for his statement to sink in. Theo sat there, staring at him, with no discernible change in expression from the weariness he'd worn since they came through the door. He guessed that he was supposed to say something now.

"Molly was here," Theo said. "The creature exists. It

ate Mikey Plotznik, and Joseph Leander, and who knows who else? She said it's a dragon."

Gabe's grin dropped. "That's great. I mean, that's horrible, but it's great from a scientific point of view. I have another theory about this species. I think it has some specialized mechanism to affect its prey. Have you been horny lately?"

"There's no need to be arrogant, Gabe. I'm glad you two had a good time, but there's no need to rub it in."

"No no, you don't get it." Gabe went on to explain about Val Riordan's decision to take her patients off antidepressants and how the lowering of serotonin levels could lead to increased libido. "So Pine Cove has been full of horny people."

"Right," Theo said. "And I still can't get a date."

Val Riordan laughed and Theo glared at her. Gabe said, "The rats I found alive near this trailer, where we think the creature might have been, were mating when I found them. There are some species of carnivorous plants that give off a sex pheromone that attracts their prey. In some species, the behavior of the male—a display, a dance, a scent—will stimulate the ovaries in the female of the species without any physical contact. I think that's what's happened to us."

"Our ovaries are being stimulated?" Theo rubbed sleep from his eyes. "I gotta be honest with you, Gabe. I'm not feeling it."

Val turned to Gabe. "That's not very romantic."

"It's incredibly exciting. This may be the most elegant predator that the world has ever seen."

Theo shook his head. "I have no home, no job, no car, there's probably a warrant out for my arrest, and you want me to be excited over the fact that we have a monster in town that makes you horny so he can eat you? Sorry, Gabe, I'm missing the positive side of this."

Val chimed in, "It may be the reason that you've been able to quit smoking pot so easily."

"Pardon me? Easily?" Theo wanted to jump off the couch and bitch-slap them both.

"Were you ever able to go this long before?"

"She could be right, Theo," Gabe said. "If this thing affects serotonin, it could affect other neurotransmitters."

"Oh good," Theo said. "Let's open a detox clinic. We'll feed half of the patients to the monster and the other half will recover. I can't wait."

"There's no need to be sarcastic," Gabe said. "We're just trying to help."

"Help? Help with what? Bar fight? I can handle it. Skateboard theft? I'm on it. But my law enforcement experience hasn't prepared me for dealing with this."

"That's true, Gabe," Val said. "Theo's little more than a rent-a-cop. Maybe we should call the sheriff or the FBI or the National Guard."

"And tell them what?" Theo asked. Rent-a-cop? I'm not even that now, he thought.

"He has a point." Gabe said. "We haven't seen anything."

"That old Blues singer has," Val said.

Theo nodded. "We need to find him. Maybe he'll . . ."

"He's living with Estelle Boyet," Val said. "I have her address in my office."

twenty-four

The Sheriff

Sheriff John Burton stood by the ruins of Theo's Volvo, pounding the keys of his cell phone. He could smell the cow shit he'd stepped in coming off his Guccis and the damp wind was blowing cowlicks in his gelled silver hair. His black Armani suit was smudged with the ashes he'd poked through at Theo's cabin, thinking there might be a burned body underneath. He was not happy.

Didn't anybody answer their goddamn phone anymore? He'd called Joseph Leander, Theophilus Crowe, and Jim Beer, the man who owned the ranch, and no one was answering. Which is what had brought him to Pine Cove in the middle of the night in a state of near panic in the first place. The second shift of crank cookers should be working in the lab right now, but there was no one around. His world was falling down around him, all because of the meddling of a pothead constable who had forgotten that he was supposed to be incompetent.

Crowe's line was ringing. Burton heard a click, then was immediately disconnected. "Fuck!" He slammed the cell phone shut and dropped it into the pocket of his suit jacket. Someone was answering Crowe's phone. Either he was still alive or Leander had killed him, taken his phone, and was fucking with him. But Leander's van had been parked at Crowe's cabin? So where was he? Not at home,

Burton had already checked, finding nothing but a sleepy baby-sitter and two groggy little girls in nightgowns. Would Leander run and not take his daughters?

Burton pulled out the phone and dialed the data offices at the department. The Spider answered.

"Nailsworth," the Spider said. Burton could hear him chewing.

"Put down that Twinkie, you fucking tub of lard, I need you to find me a name and an address."

"It's a Sno Ball. Pink. I only eat the marshmallow covers."

Burton could feel his pulse rising in his temples and made an effort to control his rage. In the rush to get to Pine Cove, he'd forgotten to take his blood pressure medication. "The name is Betsy Butler. I need a Pine Cove address."

"Joseph Leander's girlfriend?" the Spider asked.

"How do you know that?"

"Please, Sheriff," the Spider said with a snort. "Remember who you're talking to."

"Just get me the address." Burton could hear Nailsworth typing. The Spider was dangerous, a constant threat to his operation, and Burton couldn't figure out how to get to him. He was immune to bribes or threats of any kind and seemed content with his lot in life as long as he could make others squirm. And Burton was too afraid of what the corpulent information officer might really know to fire him. Maybe some of that foxglove tea that Leander had used on his wife. Certainly, no one would question heart failure in a man who got winded unwrapping a Snickers.

"No address," Nailsworth said. "Just a P.O. box. I checked DMV, TRW, and Social Security. She works at H.P.'s Cafe in Pine Cove. You want the address?"

"It's five in the morning, Nailsworth. I need to find this woman now."

The Spider sighed. "They open for breakfast at six. Do you want the address?"

Burton was seething again. "Give it to me," he said through gritted teeth.

The Spider gave him an address on Cypress Street and said, "Try the Eggs-Sothoth, they're supposed to be great."

"How would you know? You never leave the goddamn office."

"Ah, what fools these mortals be," the Spider said in a very bad British accent. "I know everything, Sheriff. Everything." Then he hung up.

Burton took a deep breath and checked his Rolex. He had enough time to make a little visit to Jim Beer's ranch house before the restaurant opened. The old shit kicker was probably already up and punching doggies, or whatever the fuck ranchers did at this hour. He certainly wasn't answering his phone. Burton climbed into the black Eldorado and roared across the rutted ranch road toward the gate by Theo's cabin.

As he headed out to the Coast Highway to loop back to the front of the ranch (he'd be damned if he'd take his Caddy across two miles of cow trails), someone stepped into his headlights and he slammed on the brakes. The antilocks throbbed and the Caddy stopped just short of running over a woman in a white choir robe. There was a whole line of them, making their way down the Coast Highway, shielding candles against the wind. They didn't even look up, but walked past the front of his car as if in a trance.

Burton rolled down the window and stuck his head out.

"What are you people doing? It's five in the morning."

A balding man whose choir robe was three sizes too small looked up with a beatific smile and said, "We've been called by the Holy Spirit. We've been called." Then he walked on.

"Yeah, well, you almost got to see him early!" Burton yelled, but no one paid attention. He fell back into the seat and waited as the procession passed. It wasn't just people in choir robes, but aging hippies in jeans and Birkenstocks, half a dozen Gen X'ers dressed in their Sunday best, and one skinny guy who was wearing the saffron robes of a Buddhist monk.

Burton wrenched his briefcase off the passenger seat and popped it open. False passport, driver's license, Social Security card, stick-on beard, and a ticket to the Caymans: the platinum parachute kit he kept with him at all times. Maybe it was time to bail.

Skinner

Well, the Food Guy finally got a female, Skinner thought. Probably because he had the scent of those mashed cows on him. Skinner had been tempted to roll in the goo himself, but was afraid the Food Guy would yell at him. (He hated that.) But this was even better: riding in the different car with the Food Guy and his female and the Tall Guy who always smelled of burning weeds and sometimes gave him hamburgers. He looked out the window and wagged his tail, which repeatedly smacked Theo in the face.

They were stopping. Oh boy, maybe they would leave him in the car. That would be good; the seats were chewy and tasted of cow. But no, they let him out, told him to come along with them to the small house. An Old Guy answered the door and Skinner said hi with a nose to the crotch. The Old Guy scratched his ears. Skinner liked him. He smelled like a dog who'd been howling all night.

Being near him made Skinner want to howl and he did, one time, enjoying the sad sound of his own voice.

The Food Guy told him to shut up.

The Old Guy said, "I guess I know how you feel."

They all went inside and left Skinner there on the steps. They were all nervous, Skinner could smell it, and they probably wouldn't be inside long. He had work to do. It was a big yard with a lot of shrubs where other dogs had left him messages. He needed to reply to them all, so each could only get a short spray. Dog e-mail.

He was only half-finished when they came back out.

The Tall Guy said, "Well, Mr. Jefferson, we're going to find the monster and we'd like your help. You're the only one who has seen it."

"Oh, I think you'll know him when you see him," said the old guy. "Y'all don't need my help."

Everyone smelled sad and afraid and Skinner couldn't help himself. He let loose a forlorn howl that he held until the Food Guy grabbed his collar and dragged him to the car. Skinner had a bad feeling that they might be going to the place where there was danger.

Danger, Food Guy, he warned. His barking was deafening in the confines of the Mercedes.

Estelle

Estelle was fuming as she cleared the teacups from the table and threw them into the sink. Two broke and she swore to herself, then turned to Catfish, who was sitting on the bed picking out a soft version of "Walkin' Man's Blues" on the National steel guitar.

"You could have helped them," Estelle said.

Catfish looked at the guitar and sang, "Got a mean old woman, Lawd, stay angry all the time."

"There's nothing noble in using your art to escape life. You should have helped them."

"Got a mean old woman, Lawd, Lawd, Lawd. She just stay angry all the time."

"Don't you ignore me, Catfish Jefferson. I'm talking to you. People in this town have been good to you. You should help them."

Catfish threw back his head and sang to the ceiling, "She gots no idea, Lawd, what's hers and what's mine."

Estelle snagged a skillet out of the dish rack, crossed the room, and raised it for a rocketing forehand shot to Catfish's head. "Go ahead, sing another verse about your 'mean old woman,' Catfish. I'm curious, what rhymes with 'clobbered'?"

Catfish put the guitar aside and slipped on his sunglasses. "You know, they say a woman was the one poisoned Robert Johnson?"

"Do you know what she used?" Estelle wasn't smiling. "I'm making my shopping list."

"Dang, woman, why you talk like that? I ain't been nothin but good to you."

"And me to you. That's why you keep singing that mean old woman song, right?"

"Don't sound right singin 'sweet old woman.' "

Estelle lowered the pan. Tears welled up in her eyes. "You can help them and when it's over you can stay here. You can play your music, I can paint. People in Pine Cove love your music."

"People here sayin hello to me on the street, puttin too much money in the tip jar, buying me drinks—I ain't got the Blues on me no more."

"So you have to go wreck your car, or pick cotton, or shoot a man in Memphis, or whatever it is that you have to do to put the Blues on you? For what?"

"It's what I do. I don't know nothin else."

"You've never tried anything else. I'm here, I'm real.

Is it so bad to know that you have a warm bed to sleep in with someone who loves you? There's nothing out there, Catfish."

"That dragon out there. He always be out there."

"So face it. You got away from it before."

"Why you care?"

"Because it took a lot for me to open my heart to you after what I've been through, and I don't have much tolerance for cowards anymore."

"Call it like you sees it, Mama."

Estelle turned and went back to the kitchen. "Then maybe you better go."

"I'll get my hat," Catfish said. He snapped the National back into its case, grabbed his hat from the table, and in a moment he was gone.

Estelle turned and stared at the door. When she heard his station wagon start, she fell to the floor and felt a once warm future bleed a black stain around her.

Meanwhile, Back at the Ranch

The cave lay under a hillside, less than a mile from the ranch road at Theo's cabin. The narrow mouth looked down over a wide, grassy marine terrace to the Pacific, and the interior, which opened into a huge cathedral chamber, echoed with the sound of crashing waves. Fossilized starfish and trilobites peppered the walls and the rocky floor was covered with a patina of bat guano and crystallized sea salt. The last time Steve had visited the cave it had been underwater, and he had spent a pleasant autumn there feeding on the gray whales that migrated down the coast to Baja to bear their young. He didn't remember the cave consciously, of course, but when he sensed that Molly was searching for a hiding place, the map in his mind that had long ago gone to instinct led them there.

Since they'd arrived at the cave, a dark mood had fallen on Steve and, in turn, over Molly. She'd used the weed-whacker on the Sea Beast several times to try to cheer him up, but now the sex machine was out of gas and Molly was developing a heat rash on the inside of her thighs from repeated tongue lashings. It had been two days since she had eaten, and even Steve refused to touch his cows (Black Angus steers, now that Molly knew he couldn't tolerate dairy).

Since the coming of the Sea Beast, Molly had been in a state of controlled euphoria. Worries about her sanity had melted away and she had joined him in the Zen moment that is the life of an animal, but since the dream and the horrible self-consciousness that had descended on Steve, the notion of their incompatibility had begun to rise in Molly's mind like a trout to a fly.

"Steve," she said, leaning on her broadsword and staring him squarely in one of his basketball eyes, "your breath could knock a buzzard off a shit wagon."

The Sea Beast, rather than go on the defensive (which was fortunate for Molly, because the only defense he could think of was to bite her legs off), let out a pathetic whimper and tried to tuck his huge head under a forelimb. Molly immediately regretted her comment and tried to patch the damage.

"Oh, I know, it's not your fault. Maybe someone sells Tic Tacs the size of easy chairs. We'll get through it." But she didn't mean it, and Steve could sense her insincerity. "Maybe we need to get out more," she added.

Dawn had broken outside and a beam of sunlight was streaming into the cathedral like a cop's flashlight in a smoky bar. "Maybe a swim," Molly said. "Your gills seem to be healing." How she knew the treelike growths on his neck were gills, she wasn't sure—perhaps more of the unspoken communication that passes between lovers.

Steve lifted his head and Molly thought that she might have gotten his attention, but then she noticed that a shadow had come over the entrance to the cave. She looked up to see half a dozen people in choir robes standing at the opening of the cathedral.

"We've come to offer sacrifice," one woman managed to say.

"And not a breath mint among you, I'll bet," Molly said.

twenty-five

Theo

H.P.'s Cafe was crowded with early morning old guys drinking coffee. Theo downed three cups of coffee quickly, which only served to make him anxious. Val and Gabe had ordered a cinnamon roll to share, and now Val was feeding a piece of it to Gabe as if the man had somehow managed to reach middle age and earn two Ph.D.s without ever having learned to feed himself. Theo just wanted to blow the bitter chunks of indignation.

Val said, "I certainly hope that the presence of this creature isn't responsible for how I feel right now." She licked icing from her fingers.

Right, Theo thought, the fact that you've fucked up all the previously fucked-up people in town and committed a string of felonies in the process shouldn't be the rain on your little love parade. However, Theo did subscribe to the "honest mistake" school of law enforcement, and he honestly believed that she was trying to right a wrong by taking her patients off their medication. So although Val was currently irritating him like a porcupine suppository, he was honest enough to realize that he was merely jealous of what she had found with Gabe. That realized, Gabe started to irritate him as well.

"What do we do, Gabe? Tranquilize this thing? Shoot it? What?"

"Assuming it exists."

"Assume it," Theo spat. "I'm afraid if you wait for enough evidence to be sure, we'll have to find you an ass donor, because this creature will have bitten yours off."

"No need to be snotty, Theo. I'm just being sensibly skeptical, as any researcher would."

"Theo," Val said, "I can write you a scrip for some Valium. Might take the edge off your withdrawal symptoms."

Theo scoffed. He didn't scoff often, so he wasn't good at it, and it appeared to Gabe and Val that he might be gacking up a hair ball.

"You all right?" Gabe asked.

"I'm fine. I was scoffing."

"At what?"

"At Dr. Feelgood here wanting to give me a prescription for Valium so Winston Krauss can fill it with M&Ms."

"I'd forgotten about that," Val said. "Sorry."

"It would appear that we have multifarious problems with which to deal, and I don't have a clue where to start," Theo said.

"Multifarious?" Gabe said.

"A shitload," said Theo.

"I know what it means, Theo. I just can't believe it came out of your mouth."

Val laughed gaily at Gabe's kinda-sorta humor. Theo glared at her.

Jenny, who was almost as cranky as Theo for having had to close H.P.'s the night before and then open the restaurant in the morning when the morning girl called in sick, came by to refill their coffees.

"That's your boss pulling up, isn't it, Theo?" she asked, nodding toward the front. Out the window Theo could see Sheriff John Burton crawling out of his black Eldorado.

"Back door?" Theo said, urgent pleading in his eyes.

"Sure, through the kitchen and Howard's office."

Theo was up in a second and halfway to the kitchen when he noticed that Val and Gabe had missed the entire exchange and were staring into each other's eyes. He ran back and slapped the table with his open palm. They looked at him as if they'd been dragged out of a dream.

"Attention," Theo said, trying not to raise his voice. "Sheriff coming in? My boss? Deadly drug dealer? We're criminals. We'll be making a break for the back door? Now? Hello?"

"I'm not a criminal," Gabe said. "I'm a biologist."

Theo grabbed him by the front of the shirt and made for the kitchen, dragging the biologist behind him. The criminal shrink brought up the rear.

The Sheriff

"I'm looking for Betsy Butler," Burton said, flipping open a badge wallet as if everyone in the county didn't immediately recognize his white Stetson-over-Armani look.

"What's she done?" Jenny asked, putting herself between the sheriff and the door to the kitchen.

"That's not your affair. I just need to talk to her."

"Well, I'm on the floor alone, so you have to follow me if you want to talk or I'll get behind."

"I don't want to talk to you."

"Fine." Jenny turned her back on the sheriff and went to the waitress station behind the counter to start a fresh pot of coffee.

Burton followed her, suppressing the urge to put her in a choke hold. "Do you know where she lives?"

"Yes," Jenny said. "But she's not home." Jenny glanced back through the kitchen window to make sure that Theo and his bunch had made it through to Howard's office.

Burton's face was going red now. "Please. Could you tell me where she is?"

Jenny thought she could jerk this guy around for another ten minutes or so, but it didn't look as if it was necessary. Besides, she was pissed at Betsy for calling in anyway. "She called in this morning with a spiritual emergency. Her words, by the way. The flu I can understand, but I'm working a double after closing last night over her spiritual emergency—"

"Where is Betsy Butler?" the sheriff barked.

Jenny jumped back a step. The man looked as if he might go for his gun any second. No wonder Theo had bolted out the back. "She said she was going with a group up to the Beer Bar Ranch. That they were being called by the spirit to make a sacrifice. Pretty weird, huh?"

"Was Joseph Leander going with her?"

"No one's supposed to know about Betsy and Joseph."

"I know about them. Was he going with her?"

"She didn't say. She sounded a little spaced out."

"Does Theo Crowe come in here?"

"Sometimes." Jenny wasn't volunteering anything to this creep. He was rude, he was mean, and he was wearing enough Aramis to choke a skunk.

"Has he been in here today?"

"No, haven't seen him."

Without a word, Burton turned and stormed out the door to his Cadillac. Jenny went back to the kitchen, where Gabe, Val, and Theo were standing by the fryers, trying to stay out of the way of the two cooks, who were flipping eggs and thrashing hash browns.

Gabe pointed to the back door. "It's locked."

"He's gone," Jenny said. "He was looking for Betsy and Joseph, but he asked about you, Theo. I think he's going up to the Beer Bar to find Betsy."

"What's Betsy doing at the ranch?" Theo asked.

"Something about making a sacrifice. That girl needs help."

Theo turned to Val. "Give me the keys to your car. I'm going after him."

"I don't think so," the psychiatrist said, holding her purse away from him.

"Please, Val. I've got to see what he's up to. This is my life here."

"And that's my Mercedes, and you're not taking it."

"I have guns, Val."

"Yeah, but you don't have a Mercedes. It's mine."

Gabe looked at her as if she'd squirted a grapefruit in his eyes. "You really won't let Theo use your car?" His voice was flat with disappointment. "It's just a car."

They all stared at her, even the two cooks, burly Hispanic men who had until now refused to acknowledge their existence. Val reached into her purse, brought out the keys, and handed them to Theo as if she were giving up a child for sacrifice.

"How will we get home?" Gabe asked.

"Go to the Head of the Slug and wait. I'll either pick you up or call you from my cell phone and let you know what's going on. It shouldn't take long." With that, Theo ran out of the kitchen.

A few seconds later Valerie Riordan cringed at the sound of squealing tires as Theo pulled out of the restaurant parking lot.

Skinner

Skinner liked chasing cars as much as the next dog, and they didn't get away as easily when you chased them in another car, but despite the excitement of the chase, Skinner was anxious. When he had seen the Tall Guy come out to the car, he thought that the Food Guy was coming too. But now they were driving away from the Food Guy and toward the danger. Skinner could feel it. He whined and ran back and forth across the backseat of the Mercedes, leaving nose prints on the window, then jumped into the front seat and stuck his head out the passenger window. There was no joy to the turbo-charged smells or the wind in his ears, only danger. He barked and scratched at the door handle to warn the Tall Guy, but all he got for his efforts was a perfunctory ear scratching, so he crawled into the Tall Guy's lap, where it felt at least a little safer.

The Sheriff

Burton first noticed the Mercedes behind him when he turned onto the access road to the Coast Highway. A week ago he might not have thought twice about it, but now he was seeing an enemy in every tree. DEA wouldn't use a Mercedes, and neither would FBI, but the Mexican Mafia could. Except for his operation, they ran the meth trade out of the West; perhaps they'd decided that they wanted the whole trade. That would explain the disappearance of Leander, Crowe, and the guys at the lab, except that it had been a little too clean. They would have left bodies as a warning, and they would have burned down all of Crowe's cabin, not just the pot patch.

He pulled his Beretta 9 mm. out of its holster and placed it on the seat next to him. He had a shotgun in the trunk, but it might as well be in Canada for all the good it would do him. If there were two or less in the car, he might take them. If more, they probably had Uzis or Mac 10 machine guns and he would run. The Mexicans liked to have a crowd in on their hits. Burton made a quick right off the highway and stopped a block up a side street.

Theo

Why hadn't he let Skinner out at the cafe? He hadn't been able to figure out the electric seat adjustment on the Mercedes, so he was driving with his knees up around the wheel anyway, but now he had an eighty-pound dog in his lap and he had to whip his head from side to side to keep Burton's Caddy in sight.

The Caddy made an abrupt turn off the highway and it was all Theo could do to get the Mercedes around the corner without screeching the tires. By the time he could see around Skinner's head again, the Caddy was stopped only fifty yards ahead. Theo ducked quickly onto the passenger seat and tried to call on THE FORCE to steer as they passed the Caddy.

The Sheriff

Sheriff John Burton was prepared for a confrontation with DEA agents, he was prepared for a high-speed escape, he was even prepared for a shoot-out with Mexican drug dealers, if it came to that. He prided himself on being tough and adaptable and thought himself superior to other men because of his cool response to pressure. He was, however, not prepared to see a Mercedes cruise by with a Labrador retriever at the wheel. His *Ubermensch* arrogance shriveled as he stared gape-jawed at the passing Mercedes. It made an erratic turn at the next corner, bouncing off a curb before disappearing behind a hedge.

He wasn't the sort of man who doubted his own perceptions—if he saw it, he saw it—so his mind dropped into politician mode to file the experience. "That right there," he said aloud, "is why I will never support a bill to license dogs to drive."

Still, political certainties weren't going to count for much if he didn't get to Betsy Butler and find out what had happened to his prized drug mule. He pulled a U-turn and headed back to the Coast Highway, where he found himself looking a little more closely than usual at the drivers in oncoming cars.

Molly

There were thirty of them all together. Six stood side by side at the cave entrance; the rest crowded behind them, trying to get a look inside. Molly recognized the one doing the talking, she was the ditzy waitress from H.P.'s cafe. She was in her mid-twenties, with short blonde hair and a figure that promised to go pear-shaped by the time she hit forty. She wore a white choir robe over jeans and aerobics shoes.

"You're Betsy from H.P.'s, right?" Molly asked, leaning on her broadsword.

Betsy seemed to recognize Molly for the first time, "You're the craz—"

Molly held up her sword to hush the girl. "Be nice."

"Sorry," said Betsy. "We've been called. I didn't expect you to be here."

Two women stepped up beside Betsy, the pastel church ladies that Molly had chased away from the dragon trailer. "Remember us?"

Molly shook her head. "What exactly do you all think you are doing here?"

They looked to each other, as if the question hadn't occurred to them before this. They craned their necks and squinted into the cathedral chamber to see what was behind Molly. Steve lay curled up in the dark at the back of the chamber, sulking.

Molly turned and spoke to the back of the chamber. "Steve, did you bring these people here? What were you thinking?"

A loud and low-pitched whimper came out of the dark. The crowd at the entrance murmured among themselves. Suddenly a man stepped forward and pushed Betsy aside. He was in his forties and wore an African dashiki over khakis and Birkenstocks, his long hair held out of his face with a beaded headband. "Look, man, you can't stop us. There's something very special and very spiritual happening here, and we're not going to let some crazy woman keep us from being part of it. So just back off."

Molly smiled. "You want to be a part of this, do you?"

"Yeah, that's right," the man said. The others nodded behind him.

"Fine, I want you all to empty your pockets before you come in here. Leave your keys, wallets, money, everything outside."

"We don't have to do that," Betsy said.

Molly stepped up and thrust her sword into the ground between the girl's feet. "Okay then, naked." Molly said.

"What?"

"No one comes in here unless they are naked. Now get to it."

Protests arose until a short Asian man with a shaved head shrugged off his saffron robes, stepped forward, and bowed to Molly, thus mooning the rest of the group.

Molly shook her head dolefully at the monk. "I thought you guys had more sense." Then she turned to the back of the cave and shouted, "Hey, Steve, cheer up, I brought home Chinese for lunch."

twenty-six

Val and Gabe entered the bar, then stepped out of the doorway and stood by the blinking pinball machine while their eyes adjusted to the darkness. Val wrinkled her nose at the hangover smell of stale beer and cigarettes; Gabe squinted at the sticky floor, looking for signs of interesting wild life.

Morning was the darkest part of a day at the Head of the Slug Saloon. It was so dark that the dingy confines of the bar seemed to suck light in from the street every time someone opened the door, causing the daytime regulars to cringe and hiss as if a touch of sunshine might vaporize them on their stools. Mavis moved behind the bar with a grim, if wobbly, determination, drinking coffee from a gargoyle-green mug while a Tarryton extra long dangled from her lips, dropping long ashes down the front of her sweater like the smoking turds of tiny ghost poodles. She went about setting up shots of cheap bourbon at the empty curve of the bar, lining them up like soldiers before a firing squad. Every two or three minutes an old man would enter the bar, bent over and wearing baggy pants—leaning on a four-point cane or the last hope of a painless death—and climb onto one of the empty stools to wrap an arthritic claw around a shot glass and raise it to his lips. The shots were nursed, not tossed back, and by the time Mavis had finished her first cup of coffee, the curve of the bar looked like the queue to hell: crooked, wheezing geezers all in a row.

Refreshments while you wait? The Reaper will see you now. Occasionally, one of the shots would sit untouched, the stool empty, and Mavis would let an hour pass before sliding the shot down to the next daytime regular and calling Theo to track down her truant. Most often, the ambulance would slide in and out of town as quiet as a vulture riding a thermal, and Mavis would get the news when Theo cracked the door, shook his head, and moved on.

"Hey, cheer up," Mavis would say. "You got a free drink out of it, didn't you? That stool won't be empty for long."

There had always been daytime regulars, there always would be. Her new crop started coming in around 9 A.M., younger men who bathed and shaved every third day and spent their days around her snooker table, drinking cheap drafts and keeping a laser focus on the green felt lest they get a glimpse of their lives. Where once were wives and jobs, now were dreams of glorious shots and clever strategies. When their dreams and eyesight faded, they filled the stools at the end of the bar with the daytime regulars.

Ironically, the aura of despair that hung over the daytime regulars gave Mavis the closest thing to a thrill she'd felt since she last whacked a cop with her Louisville Slugger. As she pulled the bottle of Old Tennis Shoes from the well and poured it down the bar to refill their shot glasses, a bolt of electric loathing would shoot up her spine and she would scamper back to the other end of the bar and stand there breathless until her stereo pacemakers brought her heartbeat back down from redline. It was like tweaking death's nose, sticking a KICK ME sign on the head of a cobra and getting away with it.

Gabe and Val watched this ritual without moving from their spot by the pinball machine. Val was cautious, just waiting for the right moment to move to the bar and ask if Theo had called. Gabe was, as usual, just being socially awkward.

Mavis retreated to her spot by the coffeepot, presumably out of death's reach, and called down to the couple. "You two want something to drink, or you just window-shopping?"

Gabe led them down the bar. "Two coffees please." He looked quickly to Val for her approval, but she was fixated on Catfish, who was seated across from Mavis near the end of the bar. Just beyond him was another man, an incredibly gaunt gentleman whose skin was so white it appeared translucent under the haze of Mavis's cigarette smoke.

"Hello, uh, Mr. Fish," Val said.

Catfish, who was staring at the bottom of a shot glass, looked up and forced a smile through a face betraying hangdog sorrow. "It's Jefferson," he said. "Catfish is my first name."

"Sorry," Val said.

Mavis made a mental note of the new couple. She recognized Gabe, he'd been in with Theophilus Crowe a number of times, but the woman was a new face to her. She put the two coffees in front of Gabe and Val. "Mavis Sand," Mavis said, but she didn't offer her hand. For years she'd avoided shaking hands because the grip often hurt her arthritis. Now, with her new titanium joints and levers, she had to be careful not to crush the delicate phalanges of her customers.

"I'm sorry," Gabe said. "Mavis, this is Dr. Valerie Riordan. She has a psychiatric practice here in town."

Mavis stepped back and Val could see the apparatus in the woman's eye focusing—when the light from over the snooker table caught it right, the eye appeared to glow red.

"Pleased," Mavis said. "You know Howard Phillips?" Mavis nodded to the gaunt man at the end of the bar.

"H.P.," Gabe added, nodding to Howard. "Of H.P.'s Cafe."

Howard Phillips might have been forty, or sixty, or seventy, or he might have died young for all the animation in his face. He wore a black suit out of the nineteenth century, right down to the button shoes, and he was nursing a glass of Guinness Stout, although he didn't look as if he'd had any caloric intake for months.

Val said, "We just came from your restaurant. Lovely place."

Without changing expression, Howard said, "As a psychiatrist, does it bother you that Jung was a Nazi sympathizer?" He had a flat, upper-class British accent, and Val felt vaguely as if she'd just been spat upon.

"Ray of sunshine, Howard is," Mavis said. "Looks like death, don't he?"

Howard cleared his throat and said, "Mavis has come to mock death, since most of her mortal parts have been replaced with machinery."

Mavis leaned into Gabe and Val as if guarding a secret, even as she raised her voice to make sure Howard could hear. "He's been cranky for some ten years now— and drunk most of that time."

"I had hoped to develop a laudanum habit in the tradition of Byron and Shelley," Howard said, "but procurement of the substance is, to say the least, difficult."

"Yeah, that month you drank Nyquil on the rocks didn't help either. He'd drop off at the bar stool sittin' straight up, sit there asleep sometimes for four hours, then wake up and finish his drink. I have to say, though, Howard, you never coughed once." Again Mavis leaned into the bar. "He pretends to have consumption sometimes."

"I'm sure the good doctor is not interested in the particulars of my substance abuse, Mavis."

"Actually," Gabe said, "we're just waiting for a call from Theo."

"And I think I'd prefer a Bloody Mary to coffee," Val said.

"Ya'll ain't goin to talk me into chasin no monster, so don't even try," Catfish said. "I got the Blues on me and I got some drinkin to do."

"Don't be a wuss, Catfish," Mavis said as she mixed Val's cocktail. "Monsters are no big deal. Howard and me got one, huh, Howard?"

"Walk in the proverbial park," Howard said.

Catfish, Val, and Gabe just stared at Howard, waiting.

Mavis said, "Course your drinking started right after the last one, didn't it?"

"Nonstop," Howard said.

Theo

It occurred to Theo, as he tried to keep a safe distance from the sheriff's Caddy turning into the ranch, that he had never been trained in the proper procedure for tailing someone. He'd never really followed anyone. Well, there was a sixth-month period in the seventies when he had followed the Grateful Dead around the country but with them, you just followed the trail of tie-dye and didn't have to worry about them killing you if they found out you were behind them. He also realized that he had no idea why, exactly, he was following Burton, except that it seemed more aggressive than curling into a ball and dying of worry.

The black Caddy turned through a cattle gate onto the section of the ranch adjacent the ocean. Theo slowed to a stop under a line of eucalyptus trees beside the ranch road, keeping the sheriff in sight between the tree trunks. The grassy marine terrace that dropped to the shoreline was too open to go onto without Burton noticing. He would have to let the Caddy pass over the next hill, nearly half a mile off the road, before he dared follow. Theo watched the Caddy bump over the deep ruts in the road, the front wheels throwing up mud as it climbed the hill, and suddenly he regretted not having driven the red four-wheel-drive truck. The rear-wheel-drive Mercedes might not be able to follow much farther.

When the Caddy topped the hill, Theo pulled out and gunned the Mercedes through the cattle gate and into the field. Tall grass thrashed at the underside of the big German car as rocks and holes jarred Theo and threw Skinner around like a toy. Momentum carried them up the side of the first hill. As they approached the crest, Theo let off the gas. The Mercedes settled to a stop. When he applied the gas again, the back wheels of the Mercedes dug into the mud, stuck.

Theo left Skinner and the keys in the car and ran to the top of the hill. He could see more than a mile in every direction, east to some rock outcroppings by the tree line, west to the ocean, and across the marine terrace to the north, which curved around the coastline and out of sight. South, well, he'd come from the south. Nothing there but his cabin and beyond that the crank lab. What he could not see was the black Cadillac.

He checked the battery in his cell phone and both pistols to see that they were loaded, then he set out on foot toward the rocks. It was the only place the Caddy could have gotten out of sight. Burton had to be there.

Twenty minutes later he stood at the base of the rock outcroppings, sweating and trying to catch his breath. At least maybe he'd get some lung capacity back, now that he wasn't smoking pot anymore. He bent over with his hands on his knees and scanned the rocks for any movement. These were no gentle sedimentary rocks formed over centuries of settling seas. These craggy bastards looked like gray teeth that had been thrust up through the earth's crust by the violent burp of a volcano and the rasping shift of a fault line. Lichen and seagull crap covered their surfaces and here and there a creosote bush or cypress tried to gain a foothold in the cracks.

There was supposed to be a cave around here somewhere, but Theo had never seen it, and he doubted that it was big enough to park a Cadillac in. He stayed low, moving around the edge of the rocks, expecting to see the flash of a black fender at every turn. He drew his service revolver and led around each turn with the barrel of the gun, then changed his strategy. That was like broadcasting a warning. He bent over double before peeking around the next corner, figuring that if Burton heard him or was waiting, he would be aiming high. The vastness of what Theo didn't know about surveillance and combat techniques seemed to be expanding with every step. He just wasn't a sneaky guy.

He skirted a narrow path between two fanglike towers of rock. As he prepared to take a quick peek around the next turn, his foot slipped, sending a pile of rocks skittering down the hill like broken glass. He stopped and held his breath, listening for the sound of a reaction somewhere in the rocks. There was only the crashing surf in the distance and a low whistle of coastal wind. He ventured a quick glance around the rock and before he could pull back, the metallic click of a gun cocking behind his head sounded like icicles being driven into his spine.

Molly

Molly was sorting through the piles of clothing the pilgrims had left by the cave entrance. She had come up with two hundred and fifty-eight dollars in cash, a stack of Gold Cards, and more than a dozen vials of antidepressants.

A voice in her head said, "You haven't seen this many meds since you were on the lock-down ward. They have a lot of gall calling you crazy." The narrator was back, and Molly wasn't at all happy about it. For the last few days, her thinking had been incredibly clear.

"Yeah, you're helping a lot with my mental health self-image," she said to the narrator. "I liked it better when it was just me and Steve."

None of the pilgrims seemed to notice that Molly was talking to herself. They were all in some trancelike state, stark naked, seated in a semicircle around Steve, who lay in the back of the cave, where it was dark, with his head tucked under his forelegs, flashing sullen colors across his flanks: olive drab, rust, and blue so dark that it appeared more like an afterimage on the back of the eyelid than an actual color.

"Oh yeah, you and Steve," the narrator said snidely. "There's a healthy couple—the two greatest has-beens of all time. He's sulking, and you're robbing people who are even nuttier than you are. Now you're going to feed them to old lizard lick over there."

"Am not."

"Looks like none of these people has had any sun or exercise since high school gym class. Except for that guy who came in Birkenstocks, and he has that Gandhi-tan vegetarian starvation stare that looks like he'd slaughter a whole kindergarten for a Pink's foot-long with sauerkraut. You feel okay about making them strip and prostrate themselves before the big guy?"

"I thought it would make them go away."

"The lizard is using you."

"We care about each other. Now just shut up. I'm trying to think."

"Oh, like you've been thinking so far."

Molly shook her head violently to try and dislodge
the narrator from her mind. Her hair whipped about her
face and shoulders and stood out in a wild mess. The
narrator was quiet. Molly pulled a compact out of one of
the pilgrims' purses and looked at herself in the mirror.
She certainly couldn't have looked much crazier. She
braced for the narrator's comment, but it didn't come.

She tried to get in touch with the warm feeling that
had been running through her since Steve had appeared,
but it just wasn't there. Maybe the pilgrims were using
up his energy. Maybe the magic had just passed.

She remembered sitting on a deck in Malibu, waiting
for a producer who had just made love to her, only to
have his Hispanic maid show up with a glass of wine and
an apology that "The mister had to go to the studio, he
very sorry, you call him next week please." Molly had
really liked the guy. She'd broken her foot kicking his
spare Ferrari as she left and had to eat painkillers through
the filming of her next movie, which eventually put her
in detox. She never heard from the producer again.

That was being used. This was different.

"Right," said the narrator sarcastically.

"Shhhhh," Molly said. She heard someone scuffling
on the rocks outside the cave. She snatched up the assault
rifle and waited just inside the cave mouth.

twenty-seven

Val

Val was wishing she had a video recorder to preserve the gargantuan lie that Mavis Sand and Howard Phillips had been telling over the last hour. According to them, ten years ago the village of Pine Cove had been visited by a demon from hell, and only through the combined effort of a handful of drunks were they able to banish the demon whence it came. It was a magnificent delusion, and Val thought that she could at least get an academic paper on shared psychosis out of it. Being around Gabe had ignited her enthusiasm for research.

When Mavis and Howard wrapped up their story, Catfish started in with his tale of being pursued through the bayou by a sea monster. Soon Gabe and Val were spouting the details of Gabe's theory that the monster had evolved the ability to affect the brain chemistry of its prey. Tipsy after a few Bloody Marys and taken by the momentum of the tale, Val confessed her replacement of Pine Cove's supply of antidepressants with placebos. Even as she unburdened herself, Val realized that her and Gabe's stories were no more credible than the fairy tale Mavis and Howard had just told.

"That Winston Krauss is a weasel," Mavis said. "Comes in here every day acting like his shit don't stink, then overcharges the whole town for something they ain't even gettin. Should'a known he was a fish-fucker."

"That's in strictest confidence," Val said. "I shouldn't have mentioned it."

Mavis cackled. "Well, it ain't like I'm gonna run tell Sheriff Burton on you. He's a weasel with a capital Weas. Besides, girl, you increased my business by eighty percent when you took the wackos off their drugs. And I thought it was old Mopey down there." Mavis shot a bionic thumb toward Catfish.

The Bluesman put down his drink. "Hey!"

Gabe said, "So you believe that there really is a sea monster on that ranch?"

"What reason would you have to lie?" said Howard. "It would seem that Mr. Fish is an eyewitness as well."

"Jefferson," Catfish said. "Catfish Jefferson."

"Shut up, you chickenshit," Mavis spat. "You could have helped Theo when he asked you. What's that boy think he's doing following that sheriff out to the ranch anyway? It's not like he can do anything."

Gabe said, "We don't know. He just left and told us to come here and wait for his call."

"Ya'll some heartless souls," Catfish said. "I lost me a good woman because of all this."

"She's smarter than she looks," Mavis said.

"Theo has my Mercedes," Val added, feeling out of place even as she said it. Suddenly she felt more ashamed of looking down on these people than she did about all of her professional indiscretions.

"I'm getting worried," said Gabe. "It's been over an hour."

"I don't suppose you thought about calling *him*?" Mavis asked.

"You have his cell phone number?" Gabe asked.

"He's the constable. It's not like he's unlisted."

"I suppose I should have thought of that," said Howard.

Mavis shook her head and one of her false eyelashes

sprung up like a snare trap. "What, you three got thirty years of college between you and not enough smarts to dial a phone without a blueprint?"

"Astute observation," Howard said.

"I ain't got no college," Catfish said.

"Well, cheers to you for being just naturally stupid," Mavis said, picking up the phone.

The daytime regulars at the end of the bar had snapped out of their malaise to have a laugh at Catfish. There's nothing quite so satisfying to the desperate as having someone to look down on.

Theo

The gun barrel was pushed so hard into the spot behind Theo's ear that he thought he could hear bone cracking. Burton reached around and took the .357 and tossed it aside, then he took the automatic from Theo's waistband and did the same.

"On the ground, facedown." Burton kicked Theo's feet out from under him, then put his knee in the constable's back and handcuffed him. Theo could taste blood where his lip had split hitting the rock. He turned his head to the side, raking his cheek on some lichen. He was terrified. Every muscle in his body ached with the need to run.

Burton smacked him across the back of the head with his pistol, not hard enough to knock him out, but when the white-hot light of the blow faded, Theo could feel blood oozing into his right ear.

"You fucking stoner. How dare you fuck with my business?"

"What business?" Theo said, hoping ignorance might buy his life.

"I saw your car at the lab, Crowe. The last time I

talked to Leander he was on his way to see you. Now where is he?"

"I don't know."

The pistol smacked Theo on the other side of the head.

"I don't fucking know!" Theo shrieked. "He was at the lab, then he was gone. I didn't see him leave."

"I don't care if he's alive or dead, Crowe. And it doesn't make any difference to you either. But I need to know. Did you kill him? Did he run? What?"

"I think he's dead."

"You think?"

Theo could feel Burton rearing back to hit him again.

"No! He's dead. He's dead. I know it."

"What happened?"

Theo tried to think of a plausible explanation, something that would buy him a minute, a few more seconds even, but he couldn't clear his head. "I'm not sure," he said. "I—I heard gunfire. I was in the shed. When I came out, he was gone."

"Then how do you know he's dead?"

Theo couldn't see any advantage to telling Burton that Molly had told him. Burton would track her down and put her in the same shallow grave that he was going to end up in.

"Fuck you," Theo said. "Figure it out."

The pistol whipped across the back of Theo's head and he nearly passed out this time. He heard a ringing in his ears, but a second later he realized that it wasn't in his ears at all. His cell phone was ringing in his shirt pocket. Burton rolled him over and put the barrel of the gun on Theo's right eyelid.

"We're going to answer this, Crowe. And if you fuck up, the calling party is going to hear a very loud disconnect." The sheriff bent down until his face was almost touching Theo's and reached for the phone.

Suddenly a series of deafening explosions went off a few feet away and bullets whined off the rocks like angry wasps. Burton rolled off Theo and into a shallow crevice just below them. Theo felt someone grab his collar and pull him to his feet. Before he could see who it was, a dozen hands closed on him and dragged him out of the sun. He fell hard on his back and the gunfire stopped. His phone was still ringing. A cloud of bats was swirling above him.

He looked up to see Molly Michon standing over him with a smoking assault rifle, and in that second, she looked like what he had always imagined an avenging angel might look like, except for the six naked white guys standing behind her.

"Hi, Theo," she said.

"Hi, Molly."

Molly pointed to the phone in his shirt pocket with the barrel of her rifle. "You want me to get that?"

"Yeah, it might be important," Theo said.

There was a gunshot and a bullet whined off the edge of the cave entrance and ricocheted into the darkness. Theo could feel the roar that rose up out of the back of the cave vibrating in his ribs.

The Sheriff

Burton reached over the edge of the crevice and fired a shot in the general direction of the cave, then braced himself for return fire from the AK-47, but instead he heard a roaring that sounded like someone had dropped the entire cast of *The Lion King* in a deep fryer. Burton was not a coward, not by any means, but a man would have to be insane not to be frightened by that noise. Too much weirdness, too fast. A woman in a leather bikini and thigh-high boots firing an AK-47 while six naked guys dragged Crowe into a cave. He needed time to regroup, call in backup, drink a fifth of Glenlivet.

It seemed safe here for the time being. As long as he didn't move, no one could get a firing angle on him without making a target of himself. He pulled his cell phone from his jacket pocket, then paused, trying to figure out who to call. A general officer-in-trouble call could bring anyone, and the last thing he needed was television helicopters hovering around. Besides, his goal wasn't to arrest the suspects, he needed them silenced for good. He could call in the guys from the crank lab, if he could get hold of them, but the vision of a bunch of untrained illegal immigrants running around on this hill with automatic weapons didn't seem like the best strategy either. He had to call SWAT, but only his guys. Eight of the twenty men on the SWAT team were in his pocket. Again, he couldn't go through dispatch. They'd have to be called in on private lines. He dialed the number that rang into the information center deep in the basement of the county justice building. The Spider picked up on the first ring.

"Nailsworth."

"It's Burton. Listen, don't talk. Call Lopez, Sheridan, Miller, Morales, O'Hara, Crumb, Connelly, and LeMay. Tell them to come in full SWAT to the Beer Bar Ranch north of Pine Cove, the northern access road. There's a cave here. Pull up whatever maps you need and give them directions. Do not use open channels. They are not to log in or report to anyone where they are going. There are at least two suspects in the cave with automatic weapons. I'm pinned down about ten yards from the west-facing entrance. Have them meet south of the rocks, they'll see them, then have Sheridan call me. No aircraft. Find out if there's another entrance to this cave. I need everyone in place ASAP. Can you do it?"

"Of course," the Spider said. "It's going to take them

a minimum of forty minutes, maybe more if I can't find them all."

Burton could hear the Spider's fat fingers blazing on his keyboard already. "Send whoever you can find. Tell them to come in separate cars. Tell them to avoid sirens if possible on the way up, definitely once they hit the ranch."

"Do you have descriptions of the suspects?"

"It's Theophilus Crowe and a woman, five-eight, one twenty, twenty-five to forty years old, gray hair, wearing a leather bikini."

"Twenty-five to forty? Pretty specific," the Spider said sarcastically.

"Fuck you, Nailsworth. How many women do you think are running around these hills wearing a leather bikini and shooting an AK? Call me when they are on the way." Burton disconnected and checked the battery on the phone. It would last.

Since the roaring sound had come from the cave, it had been quiet, but he didn't dare peek over the edge of the crevice. "Crowe!" he shouted. "It's not too late to work this out!"

Theo

The naked guys were standing over Theo, wearing dazed smiles, as if they'd all just shared a big pipe of opium. "Jesus, was that it?" Theo asked, Steve's roar still ringing in his ears.

"Him," Molly corrected, holding up a finger to shush Theo as she pressed the answer button on his phone. "Hello," she said into the phone. "None of your business. Who is this?" She covered the mouthpiece and said, "It's Gabe."

"Tell him I'm okay. Ask him where he is."

"Theo says he's okay. Where are you?" She listened for a second, then covered the mouthpiece again. "He's at the Slug."

"Tell him I'll call him right back."

"He'll call you back." She disconnected and tossed the phone in the pile of clothing by the door.

Theo looked up at the naked guys. He thought he recognized a couple of them, but didn't want to acknowledge that he did. "Would you guys back off a little?" Theo said. They didn't move. Theo looked at Molly. "Can you tell them to go somewhere? They're making me nervous."

"Why?"

"Molly, I don't know if you've notice, but all these guys are in a—a state of arousal."

"Maybe they're just glad to see you."

"Would you tell them to back off, please?"

Molly motioned for the naked guys to move away. "Go. Go. Back to the back of the cave, guys. Go. Go. Go." She poked at a couple of them with the assault rifle. Slowly they turned and ambled farther back into the cave.

"What in the hell is wrong with them?"

"What do you mean, wrong? They're acting like all guys do, they're just being more honest about it."

"Molly, seriously, what did you do to them?"

"I didn't do anything. That's how they've been acting since they saw Steve back there."

Theo looked to the back of the cave, but could only see the partially lit backs of a group of people sitting on the cave floor. "It's like they're in a trance or something."

"Yeah, isn't it cool? They came to help me get you when I asked, though. So they're not total zombies. I'm, like, in charge."

Blood was dripping out of Theo's scalp, matting his

hair and leaving spots on his shirt. "That's great, Molly. Could you get these handcuffs off me?"

"I was going to ask you about those. Every time I see you, you're in handcuffs. Do you have a fetish or something?"

"Please, Molly, there's a key in my front pocket."

"He gave you the key?"

"It's my key."

"I see," Molly said with a knowing smile.

"Handcuffs all use the same key, Molly. Please help me get out of these."

She knelt and reached into his pocket, keeping her eyes locked on his through the process. His head throbbed when he rolled over so she could get to the cuffs.

As she pulled them off, they heard Burton call from outside. "Crowe! It's not too late to work this out!"

Once his hands were free, Theo threw his arms around Molly and pulled her close. She dropped her rifle and returned his embrace. Another roar emanated from the back of the cave. A couple of the pilgrims shrieked and Molly let go of Theo and stood up, gazing back into the darkness.

"It's okay, Steve," she said.

"What in the hell was that?" Burton shouted from outside.

"That was Steve," Molly shouted back. "You were asking what happened to Joseph Leander. Well, that was it. Steve ate him."

"How many of you are in there?" Burton asked.

Molly looked around. "A bunch."

"Who in the hell are you?"

"I am Kendra, Warrior Babe of the Outland." She shot a silly grin at Theo, who was trying to follow what was going on up here, while listening to some disturbing stirring noises going on in the back of the cave.

"What do you want?" Burton asked.

Without a beat, Molly said, "Ten percent of the gross on all my films, retroactive fifteen years, an industrial-strength weed-whacker with gas, and world peace."

"Seriously. We can work this out."

"Okay. I want sixty peanut butter and jelly sandwiches, a couple of gallons of Diet Coke, and . . ." She turned to Theo, "You want anything?"

Theo shrugged. Hell, as long as they were stalling. "A new Volvo station wagon."

"And a new Volvo station wagon," Molly shouted. "And we want it with two cup holders, you bastard, or the deal's off." She turned and beamed at Theo.

"Nice touch."

"You deserve it," Molly said. Suddenly her eyes went wide as she looked past Theo. "No, Steve!" she screamed.

Theo rolled over to see a huge pair of jaws descending over him.

twenty-eight

The Sheriff

To Burton, it sounded like there could be thirty or forty people wailing in the cave, let alone whatever was making the roaring noise. It might not be as easy to get rid of witnesses as he'd thought. If all the people he'd passed on the road earlier were in the cave, the SWAT snipers were going to have their work cut out for them. One thing was for sure, he couldn't let Crowe and this woman, whoever she was, leave the ranch alive.

His cell phone rang and he pushed the answer button. "What?" He set his gun down and covered his ear to shut out the noise from the cave.

"Nailsworth here," the Spider said. "They're on the way. Give it forty minutes. And there's no other entrance to that cave."

Burton was not happy, having to lie in this crevice for another forty minutes, but once the SWAT team arrived, it would be over. "Nailsworth, shot in the dark here, but have you ever heard of someone calling themselves Kendra, Warrior Babe of the Wasteland?"

"The Outland," the Spider corrected. "Warrior Babe of the Outland. Of course, only the finest series of nuked-out future movies ever made. Kendra's a huge star. Was a huge star. Molly Michon was the actress's name. Why?"

"Never mind. One of the suspects thinks she's a comedian."

"If you want some of the cassettes, I can let you have some copies for twenty bucks apiece. I've got almost the whole collection."

"Nailsworth, you're a pathetic piece of shit." Burton disconnected. The wailing was still coming from the cave and the woman was screaming something he couldn't make out.

Molly

Theo's sneakers were still showing, sticking out between Steve's teeth. Molly grabbed her broadsword, ran up the Sea Beast's foreleg, and leapt onto his broad neck. She brought the broadsword down hard between his eyes and the impact made her hands go numb. "Spit him out! Spit him out!"

Steve tossed his head, trying to throw her off, but she gripped him with her thighs and hacked away at his head. Chunks of his scales flew off and the blade sparked. "Spit him out! Spit him out!" Molly screamed, punctuating the panicked chant with blows from the sword. She'd seen this before. She knew that if she heard a crunch, Theo was finished.

The Sea Beast opened his jaws to deliver the coup de grace and Molly could hear a gurgling scream come from Theo. She leapt to her feet on Steve's forehead, put the tip of the broadsword in the corner of his eye, and prepared to leap on the hilt to drive it into his eye socket. "Spit him out! Now!"

Steve went cross-eyed trying to see his attacker, then made a grunting noise and hacked the constable out on the cave floor. He whipped his head and Molly went flying, hitting her back hard on the cave wall ten feet away and sliding down.

The pilgrims' wails turned to sobs as Steve slunk to the back of the cave.

Theo, mired in a puddle of blood, bat guano, and dragon spit, pushed himself up on his hands and knees and looked to Molly. "You okay?" he gasped.

She nodded. "I think so. You?"

Theo nodded and looked down to make sure his legs were still there. "Yeah." He crawled over to her and sat back against the cave wall beside her, still heaving to get his breath back. "Nice friends you have. Why'd he stop?"

"I think his feelings are hurt."

"Sorry."

"He'll get over it. He's a big boy."

Despite himself, Theo started laughing, and before long he and Molly were leaning against each other, giggling uncontrollably.

"Steve, huh?" Theo said.

"He looks like a Steve, don't you think?" Molly said.

Theo wiped the dragon spit from his mouth and leaned over to kiss her. She caught his chin in her hand and pushed him away. "Bad idea."

Another roar rose from the back of the cave, this one less angry and more sad than the last.

"I guess so," Theo said.

"What in the hell is going on in there, Crowe?" Burton called from outside. "You don't have a lot of time to dick around here. There's a SWAT team on the way. What do you want?"

"I don't even know what the hell you're talking about," Theo shouted.

"What do you want to walk away from this? Leave the state. Forget everything. How much? Give me a figure."

Theo looked at Molly as if she might have the answer. She said, "I thought we made our demands pretty clear."

"He's not going to let me go, Molly. And now he's not going to let you go either. If there's a SWAT team on the way, we're in big trouble."

"I need to go talk to Steve." Molly stood and walked between the sobbing pilgrims to the back of the cave. Theo watched her fade into the dark where the Sea Beast was pulsing with dim spots of green and blue. Theo rubbed his eyes to try to clear his vision.

"Well, Crowe? What'll it be?"

"Make me an offer," Theo said, trying to figure out some kind of insurance. Something that would keep him alive more than two seconds after he stepped out of the cave.

"I'll give you a hundred thousand. It's a fair offer, Crowe. You can't prove anything anyway, not if Leander is dead. Take the money and walk away."

"I'm dead," Theo said to himself. The size of the bluff offer itself betrayed Burton's seriousness. There was no way he was letting Theo get away alive. "We'll talk it over!" Theo shouted. His head was throbbing from the pistol whipping he'd taken and the vision in his left eye was blurry. His cell phone chirped from within the pile of pilgrims' clothing and he scrambled through the clothes and pill bottles to find it. His vision went black with the movement and he had to steady himself until it cleared. He found the phone nestled in a pair of panty hose and hit the answer button.

Steve

He knew an enemy when he saw one. He could sense waves of aggression and fear coming from them, and he had felt those things coming from his warmblood lover. He could feel the fear even now as she approached him through the feeder people. Why, if she was going to find another mate, did she go to the trouble of unwrapping the feeder people for him?

He didn't mind being hit with the sharp thing, that felt good, he thought she wanted to mate again, but when she put it in his eye, he knew she would have killed him. He felt it. She had turned her loyalties to another. He considered biting off her head to show her how badly he felt.

He tucked his head under his foreleg as she approached. She rubbed his gill tree and he sent a bolt of scarlet over his back to tell her to stop.

"I'm sorry, Steve. I don't have many friends. I couldn't let you eat Theo."

He could sense benevolence in her tone, but he didn't trust her now. Maybe he would just bite off an arm as a test. His back pulsed magenta and blue.

"You have to go, Steve. There's a SWAT team coming. You can get past that guy outside without a problem. In fact, you can eat that guy outside if you want. In fact, I'd really appreciate it if you'd eat that guy outside."

She stepped back from him. "Steve, you have to get out of here or they're going to kill you."

He pulsed a dull olive drab to her and tucked his head farther under his foreleg. She wanted him to go away, he could feel it. And he wanted to go away, but he didn't want her to want him to go away. He knew she could never be what he wanted, and he understood never now, but he didn't want the warmblood to have her either. Colors ran like sorrow over his scales.

"I'm not rejecting you," Molly said. "I'm trying to save your life."

She pushed through the pilgrims, who were all on their knees sobbing, and one woman, a thirtyish redhead with gravity-defying fake breasts, grabbed her arm. "I can sacrifice," the woman said. "I can."

Molly pulled her arm away from the woman. "Fuck off, lady," Molly said, "Martyrdom's easy, it comes with the plumbing."

Theo

It was only when he answered the cell phone that Theo realized one of Burton's blows had caught him on the ear. "Ouch! Goddamn it. Ouch!" Theo limped around in a circle, despite the fact that his limbs weren't injured at all.

"Theo?" Gabe said, his voice tinny in the receiver.

"Yeah, it's me." Theo changed the phone to his other ear, but still held it a few inches away, now that it had bitten him once.

"Where are you? Who answered your phone?"

"That was Molly Michon. We're in that cave up on the ranch where the mushroom farm used to be. Burton has us pinned in here and he's called in a SWAT team."

"Have you seen it?"

"Yeah, I've seen it, Gabe. I think you were right about the brain chemistry thing. There's a bunch of people here all tranced out, saying they were called to give sacrifice. They all have prescriptions written by Val."

"Wow," Gabe said. "Wow. What's it look like?"

"It's large, Gabe."

"Could you be more specific?"

"Look, Gabe, we need some help. Burton is going to kill us. I need witnesses up here so he can't claim that we fired on his men. Call the TV station and the paper. Get a news helicopter up here."

Theo felt Molly grab his shoulder. He turned to see

her shaking her head. "Just a second, Gabe." He covered the mouthpiece with his hand.

"No reporters, Theo."

"Why not?"

"Because if they find out about Steve, they'll put him in a cage or kill him. No reporters. No cameras." She gripped his shoulder until it hurt and tears welled up in her eyes. "Please."

Theo nodded. "Gabe," he said into the phone, "Forget the reporters. No news people. No cameras. You guys come, though. I need witnesses here that don't work for Burton."

"You said there were a bunch of people there?"

"They're all out of it, I don't think they're worth a damn. Besides, they're naked."

There was a pause. Gabe said, "Why are they naked?"

Theo looked to Molly, "Why are they naked?"

"To deter them from coming into the cave."

"To deter them from coming into the cave," Theo said into the phone.

"Well, that didn't work very well, did it?" Gabe said. "Why didn't she scare them off with the creature?"

"That's what I've been telling you, Gabe. They're here to *be* with the creature."

"Fascinating. And Molly has control over him?"

Theo looked at the dragon spit running down his jeans. "Not exactly. Gabe, please, bring Val and get your ass up here. You can claim to be here for scientific reasons or something. Val can say she's a trained hostage negotiator. These people are her patients; that should help her credibility. Bring as many people as you can."

Molly grabbed Theo's arm again and shook her head. "Just the people who already know."

Theo cursed under his breath. "Scratch that, Gabe. Just you and Val. Don't tell anyone else."

"Mavis and Howard and Catfish know already."

"Just them. Please, Gabe, borrow Mavis's car and get up here."

"Theo, this isn't going to help you much. We might keep you from getting killed, but Burton is still going to arrest you guys. You know it. And once he gets you in his jail, well, you know."

"One thing at a time."

"Theo, we've got to preserve that creature. This is the greatest . . ."

"Gabe," Theo interrupted. "I'm trying to preserve my ass. Get going, please."

"You've got to get that creature out of there, Theo. They might not shoot you if there are witnesses, but they won't let the creature go."

"He won't move. He's in the back of the cave, sulking."

"Sulking?"

"I don't know, Gabe. Just come, okay." Theo disconnected and sat down. To Molly he said, "Gabe's right. We may just be delaying the inevitable by bringing in witnesses. Maybe we should rush Burton before SWAT gets here."

Molly picked up the AK-47 from the floor, released the clip and tilted it so Theo could see it was empty. "Bad idea."

The Head of the Slug

"Hostage negotiator?" Val Riordan said. "I did my residency in eating disorders. The closest I've ever come to a hostage negotiation is talking a sugar-jagged actress out of purging fourteen quarts of Ben & Jerry's Monkey Chunks after she lost her part on 'Baywatch.' "

"That counts," said Gabe. He'd related everything that

Theo had told him and was ready to run to the rescue, but Val was reluctant.

"I believe the flavor is Chunky Monkey," H.P. said.

"Whatever," said Val. "I don't see why Theo needs us if he's got a whole cave full of my patients."

Gabe was trying to be patient, but he could feel a clock ticking in the back of his brain, each tick taking away his chance to save his friend and lay eyes on a living specimen from the Cretaceous period. "I told you, Theo says they're out of it."

"Perfectly logical," said H.P.

"How so?" asked Val, obviously irritated at the stuffy restaurateur's tone.

"The tradition of making sacrifice is as old as man. It may be more than just a tradition. The Babylonians sacrificed to the serpent, Tiamet, the Aztecs and Mayans sacrificed to serpent gods. Perhaps this creature was the serpent to which they sacrificed."

"That's ridiculous," Val said. "This thing eats people."

H.P. chuckled, "People have been loving vengeful gods for thousands of years. Who's to say it isn't the vengeance that inspires that love? Perhaps, as Dr. Fenton has pointed out, there is some symbiotic relationship between the hunting habits of this creature and the brain chemistry of its prey. Perhaps it inspires love as well as sexual stimulation. That feeling needn't be reciprocal, you know. He could be as oblivious to his worshippers as any other god. He takes the sacrifices as his due, with no responsibility on his part."

"That's a steamin bag of dog snot if I ever heard it," Catfish spouted. "I been near this thing and it ain't never done nothin but scare the daylights out of me."

"Is that right, Mr. Fish?" H.P. said. "Isn't it true that your fear of this creature has inspired a lifelong career in music? Perhaps you owe thanks to this beast."

"I owe ya'll a ride to the booby hatch, thass what I owe."

"Enough!" Gabe shouted. "I'm going. You can come or you can stay, but I'm going to help Theo and see if I can keep that creature alive. Mavis, can I borrow your car?"

Mavis threw her keys on the bar. "Wish I was going with you, kid."

"May I join you?" H.P. asked.

Gabe nodded and looked at Val. "They are your patients."

She pressed her back against the bar. "This is all going to blow up, and when it all comes out, I'm going to go to jail. I should help with that?"

"Yes," said Gabe.

"Why?"

"Because it's the right thing to do, and because it's important to me and you love me."

Val stared at him, then dragged her purse off the bar. "I'll go, but you will all be getting hate mail from me when I'm in jail."

Mavis looked at Catfish. "Well?"

"Ya'll go on. I got the Blues on me."

They started out the door. "Don't you worry, honey," Mavis called after them. "You're not going to jail. Mavis will see to it."

twenty-nine

Gabe

Up until the time that Steve had come to town, the most fearsome prehistoric beast on the Central Coast was Mavis Sand's 1956 Cadillac convertible. It was lemon-pie yellow with a great chrome grill that seemed to slurp at the road as it passed and gold-plated curb feelers that vibrated in the wind like spring-loaded whiskers. The daytime regulars called it the "Banana" and in a fit of ambition had once even fashioned a giant blue Chiquita emblem, which they stuck on the trunk lid while Mavis was working. "Well," Mavis said, more than somewhat surprised by their efforts, "it ain't the first banana I've rode, but it takes the size record by at least a foot."

Even in his youth, Gabe had never driven anything like the Banana before. It steered like a barge and it rocked and lurched over dips and potholes like a foundering scow. Gabe had activated the electric top when they'd first climbed in and hadn't figured out how to put it back up.

Gabe spotted Val's Mercedes parked on the side of a hill off the main ranch road. There were six other vehicles parked next to it, all four-wheel-drive sport utility vehicles: two Blazers and two larger Suburbans. A group of men in black jumpsuits were standing by the vehicles, the tallest watching them through binoculars and talking on a radio or cell phone.

"Maybe we should have taken a more inconspicuous vehicle," Gabe said.

"Why didn't we take your car, Howard?" Val asked. She was slouched in the passenger seat.

Howard sat in the back, as stiff as a mannequin, squinting as if this was his first exposure ever to sunlight. "I own a Jaguar. Superior coach works, none like them in the world outside of Bentley and Rolls. Walnut burl on all the interior surfaces."

"Doesn't run, huh?"

"Sorry," said Howard.

Gabe stopped the Banana at the cattle gate. "What should I do? They're watching us."

"Go on up there," Val said. "That's why we're here." She had gotten brave all of a sudden.

Gabe wasn't quite so self-assured. "Someone tell me again why the sheriff won't just shoot us along with Theo and Molly?"

Val was getting into the spirit of the thing, realizing that this might be the only way to atone for what she'd done to her patients. "I'm a psychiatrist, Gabe, and you have a Ph.D. The police don't shoot people like us."

"You're kidding, right?"

Howard said, "Does one require an advanced degree to be immune to gunfire, or does a life of scholarship count as well?"

"Go, Gabe," Val said. "We'll be fine."

Gabe looked over at her and she smiled at him. He smiled back, sort of, and pulled the Banana into the pasture toward five heavily armed men who did not look happy to see them.

Theo

Theo had searched the rest of the cave, using the disposable lighter he'd forgotten to abandon with the rest of his pot habit. The cathedral chamber was closed, except for the entrance where Burton waited. Theo gave the Sea Beast a wide clearance on his way back to Molly, who stood just inside the cave mouth.

Burton shouted from outside, "Crowe, we've got your friends locked up! This is your last chance to make a deal! I'll give you five minutes, then we're using gas!"

Theo turned to Molly in a panic. "We've got to get these people out of here, Molly. As soon as the first gas grenade comes in, it's all over."

"Don't we need hostages?"

"For what? He's not going to negotiate. The only thing he wants is me—and probably you—dead."

"Why don't you call someone and tell them what you know? Then Burton won't have a reason to kill us."

"All I know is what I've seen. With Leander dead, there's no one to connect him to the labs. I've already told Val and Gabe. Now he's got them. I was an idiot to bring them into this."

"Sorry," Molly said.

"Wait." Theo flipped open his phone and dialed. The phone rang eight times and Theo was glancing at the battery gauge, which showed only a quarter-charge, when a man answered.

"Nailsworth," the Spider said, leaving the caller to guess that they had contacted the Sheriff's Department's information officer.

"Nailsworth, it's Theo Crowe. I need your help."

"Having a bad day, Theo?"

What a prick, Theo thought. "Listen, I'm trapped . . ."

"I know where you are, Theo. Remember, I know everything. Actually, I'm glad you called. I had something I wanted to ask you about."

Theo fought the urge to scream at the megalomaniacal geek. "Please, Nailsworth, I don't know how long this battery is going to hold out. I need you to do me a favor."

"Me first."

"Go," Theo barked.

"Well, when Burton called me, he mentioned that your accomplice said she was Kendra, Warrior Babe of the Outland. So I started looking around. Turns out there was a Molly Michon admitted to county psychiatric a few times. She left a Pine Cove address. I wondered if . . ."

"It's her," Theo said.

"Wow, you're kidding! No way!"

"She's right here." Theo looked at Molly and shrugged. "Look, you warned me not to go on the ranch. You know about Burton's crank network."

"I might," Nailsworth said.

"Don't be coy. You know everything. But what I need to know is do you have access to information that could be used as evidence—money transfers, checks, offshore accounts, phone records, and such—stuff you could give to the state attorney?"

"Why, Theo, you're starting to sound like a cop."

"Can you get it?"

"Theo, Theo, Theo, don't be silly. Not only can I get it, but I've had it. I've been compiling a file for years."

"Can you get it to the attorney general's office right now?"

"What's in it for me?"

"Nailsworth, he's going to kill us."

"Kendra is right there with you, huh? I can't believe it."

Theo shuddered, halfway between panic and anger. He held the phone out to Molly. "Say something Kendra-like."

Molly cleared her throat and said, "Die, you scum-sucking mutant pig. The only thing of mine you'll feel is cold steel!"

"Oh my God! It's her!" the Spider said.

"Yeah, it is," Theo said. "Now will you help?"

"I want a copy of the Norwegian *Battle Babes*. Can I get one?"

Theo covered the receiver and looked at Molly. "Norwegian *Battle Babes?*"

Molly smiled. *"Kendra VI: Battle Babes in the Hot Oil Arena.* The Norwegian version is the only version that has full nudity in all the arena scenes. It's very rare."

Theo's mouth had dropped open. His survival had come down to this? "So do you have a copy?"

"Sure."

"You got it," Theo said into the phone. "I'll bring Kendra naked and in person to your office if you get moving now."

"I don't think so," said Molly.

"I'll send the file to Sacramento," the Spider said, "but that won't do you any good. Even if you tell Burton about it, he's got you in a perfect situation to kill you anyway. You need media."

"Media? Helicopters? We're too far north to get anyone here in time," Theo said.

"No!" Molly shouted.

"I'll call them," the Spider said. "Hold them off for twenty minutes, maybe twenty-five."

"We don't have anything but naked people and a jealous sea monster to hold them off with."

"Is that more of your drug nomenclature?" the Spider asked.

"It's what it is. If they use gas, we won't have twenty minutes."

"They won't."

"How do . . ."

"Twenty-five minutes. And *Battle Babes* better be in the original box." The Spider hung up. Theo clicked his phone closed.

"I said no helicopters, Theo," Molly said. "Even if we get out, you know they'll hurt Steve. You need to call him and tell him no helicopters."

Theo felt he was close to losing it. He clenched his fists and tried very hard not to scream in her face. His voice went to a whisper. "Molly, even with a warrant out for Burton, he will kill us. If you want your dragon to live, then you've got to get him out of here before they get here."

"He won't leave. He won't listen to me. Look at him. He doesn't care about anything anymore."

Sheridan

Sergeant Rich Sheridan was six-three, two-thirty, with dark hair, a mustache, and a long, hooked nose that had been broken several times. Like the other men on the hill, he was wearing body armor and a radio headset, as well as a weapons belt. He was the only one not holding his M-16. Instead he was talking on a cell phone. He had been a cop for ten years and working for Burton on the side for eight. If this had been an official activation of Special Weapons and Tactics he would have been second in command, but as the real commander wasn't in Burton's pocket, Sheridan was in charge.

He let the binoculars dangle around his neck and waited while his men got firing angles on all of the yellow Cadillac's passengers before he approached. Sheriff Burton was screaming at him on the cell phone.

"I'm pinned down up here, Sheridan. Handle this and get your ass up here. Now!"

"Yes, sir. What do you want me to do with them?"

"Find out who they are, then cuff them and leave them there. And hurry."

Sheridan hung up. "Get out of the car. Keep your hands where I can see them."

The two men and a woman did as they were told and submitted to pat-downs from Sheridan's men. When they were handcuffed, Sheridan spun the younger man around.

"Who are you?"

"Gabe Fenton. I'm a biologist." Gabe smiled weakly. "Nice headsets. You guys could all be standing by to take my subscription order for *Corruption Weekly*."

Sheridan didn't react. "What are you doing here?"

"Endangered species protection. There's a very rare creature in that cave up there."

Val winced. "Were you supposed to tell him that?" she whispered.

"How did you know to come here?" Sheridan asked.

"This is the habitat of the California red-legged frog, very endangered. I saw your SWAT vehicle go by and the driver had that 'I want to kill some rare frogs' look in his eye." Gabe looked at one of the other SWAT guys, a stocky Hispanic man who was glaring at him over the sights of his M-16. "See, there's that look right there."

"We didn't bring the SWAT vehicle," Sheridan said flatly.

"Actually," Val jumped in, "I'm a clinical psychologist. I have experience in hostage negotiation. I heard the SWAT team being dispatched on my scanner at home, and since you're so far north, I thought you might need some help. Dr. Fenton agreed to ride along with me."

"We weren't dispatched over the radio," Sheridan said, dismissing Val as if she were an insect. He looked at Howard. "And you?"

"Howard Phillips. I'm merely here to observe a hideous ancient creature that has arisen from the darkest Stygian depths to wreak havoc on civilization and feast on human flesh." Howard smiled (the smile of an undertaker at the news of a big bus crash, but a smile nonetheless).

Sheridan stared blankly at H.P., saying nothing.

"He's the caterer," Gabe said quickly. "We brought him along to get your order. I'll bet none of you guys remembered to pack a lunch, did you?"

"Who did you tell you were coming here?"

Gabe looked at Val and Howard for some clue as to the right answer. "No one," he said.

Sheridan nodded. "We are going to put you in the back of that truck over there for your own safety," he said. Then to the others he said, "Lock them in the K-9 unit. We've got to go."

 **thirty**

Theo

"Listen," Theo said, cocking his ear toward the cave mouth. "Vehicles. The SWAT team is here."

Molly glanced to the back of the cave. From the light of the colors Steve was flashing she could see that the pilgrims had surrounded the Sea Beast and were stroking his scales. She turned back to Theo. "You've got to stop the helicopters. Call them and stop it."

"Molly, it's not the news helicopters that will hurt him, or us. It's those guys who just pulled up." Theo peeked out the mouth of the cave and saw two four-wheel-drives parking down on the marine terrace, about a hundred yards from the cave mouth. Of course, he thought, they still think they need cover.

Molly brandished her broadsword, holding it only inches from Theo's stomach. "If he's hurt, I'll never forgive you, Theo Crowe. I'll track you down to the ends of the earth and kill you like the radioactive scum that you are."

"That Kendra or Molly talking?"

"I mean it," she screamed, almost hysterical now. Steve roared from the back of the cave.

"Don't go nuts on me, Molly. I'm doing my best. But the only thing your pal seems likely to do is eat me. He doesn't seemed real motivated by anything else."

Molly slumped to her knees and hung her head as if someone had sucked the energy out of her through a valve in her boot. Theo fought the urge to comfort her, afraid that if he even touched her shoulder the Sea Beast might attack him.

Then it hit him. He flipped open his cell phone and dialed the Head of the Slug.

Mavis

Mavis Sand had spent a lifetime making mistakes and learning from them, and that perspective made her feel as if she knew what was good for people better than they knew themselves. Consequently, Mavis was a meddler. Most of the time she was content to use information as her tool of choice and rumor as her means of delivery. What someone knew—and when they knew it—controlled what they did. (The Spider, pulling digital strings from his basement web, had exactly the same philosophy.) Today she'd had a heap of problems dumped on her, none of them directly hers, and she had been pondering them all morning without much luck in coming up with a way to manipulate the information to solve them. Then the call came from Theo, and it all clicked: Theo was right, they could use the monster's instincts to get them out of the cave, but if she played the mix right, she could solve a couple of other problems as well.

She put down the phone and Catfish said, "Who that?"

"It was Theo."

"That ol' dragon ain't et him yet? Boy must be livin a charmed life."

Mavis leaned over the bar, close to Catfish, took his hand in hers, and began squeezing. "Sweetie, put on your

Winston Krauss turned and scowled at Catfish. "Was that really necessary?"

"Man's got to look after his reputation," Catfish said.

The Sheriff

Burton had them cover him while he moved down through the rocks and across the marine terrace to the Blazers. He found Sheridan crouched behind the fender, his M-16 trained on the cave entrance.

"Rough morning, Sheriff?" Sheridan said, showing a hint of a smile at Burton's disheveled suit.

Burton looked around at the other team members, who were all staring through rifle scopes at the cave entrance. "So we only have five?"

"Morales is coaching Pee-Wee Football today. The others are on regular duty. We couldn't pull them off."

Burton scowled. "As far as I know, they only have the one weapon, but it's a fully automatic AK. I want two men on either side of the cave mouth, one down in that crevice where I was pinned down can deliver the gas, followed by concussion grenades. I'll stay here with a sniper rifle to take out anyone who gets past the entry crew. Shoot anything that moves. Let's go, five minutes. On my mark."

"No gas," Sheridan said.

"What?"

"No gas and no concussion. You wanted us here without checking in. That stuff is kept in the locker at County Justice. We just have the body armor and our own personal weapons."

Burton looked around at the other men again. "You guys all have your own personal M-16s, but no grenades?"

friendly persuasion hat. I need you to run down to the pharmacy and pick up something for me."

"Yes, ma'am," Catfish said, wincing as the bones in his fingers compressed under her grip.

When the Bluesman was gone, Mavis made a quick phone call, then went to the back room and dug through boxes and filing cabinets until she came up with what she was looking for: a small black box attached to a long cord with a cigarette lighter plug on the end. "Don't worry, Theo," she said to herself. "I put my life in the hands of machinery a long time ago, and I'm doing just fine." She giggled and it came out sounding like the starter cranking on a fuel dry Ford.

Catfish

A Bluesman hates to be told what to do. Authority rankles him, inspires his rebellion, and plays to his need to self-destruct. A Bluesman doesn't take to having a boss unless he's on a chain gang (for the chain gang boss ranks below only a mean old woman and a sweet young thing in the hierarchy of the Blues Muse, followed closely by bad liquor, a dead dog, and the Man). Catfish had a boss who *was* a mean old woman: a distinct and disconcerting turn of the Blues screw that might have driven a lesser Bluesman to shoot hisself, get shot, get hold of some bad liquor, or bust up his guitar and take a job down to the mill. But Catfish hadn't taken nigh unto eighty trips around that cruel, cruel sun without gaining some perspective, so he would go to the pharmacy as he was told. He would talk to the fish-fucking white boy with the combed-over hair that waved in the air like the sprung lid on a bean can. And when he was done, he would pick up his pay from the mean old woman who was holding it hostage and he would get his wrinkly Black ass out of this town and go nurse his heartbreak on the moving trap that was, is, and always shall be the road.

So Catfish strolled a rolling Delta moonwalk of a stroll (redolent of sassafras and jive) into Pine Cove Drug and Gift, and the four blue-haired chicken women behind the counter nearly tumbled over each other trying to get to the back room. Imagine it: a person of the Dark persuasion in their midst. What if he should ask for a vial of Afro-Sheen or some other ethnically oriented product with which they were totally unfamiliar? Why, the smoke alarms would melt, screaming like dying witches, when their collective minds steamed to a stop. Do we look like thrill-seekers? Wasn't it enough that we had to put up that sign reading NO HABLA ESPANOL and acknowledge the existence of thirty percent of the population, even in the negative? No, we shall err on the side of safety, thank you, and in lieu of sand in which to bury our heads, we shall head into the back room.

Winston Krauss, who was counting fake Zolofts behind his glass wall, looked up and saw Catfish coming down the aisle toward the counter and immediately regretted that he hadn't installed bulletproof glass. Still, Winston was a man of the world, and you don't indulge the fantasy of molesting dolphins without becoming familiar with the ways of people of color, for that is who dolphins prefer to hang out with, when they aren't hanging out with the Cousteaus, or so it appeared on the Discovery Channel. He stepped out of his booth and met Catfish as he reached the counter.

"Good day, me brother-mon, ye," Winston said in his best island dialect. "What can I be gettin for ye?" And there was that welcoming smile, only a dreadlock and a white sand beach short of a travel poster.

Catfish squinted, removed his fedora, ran a hand over his shining scalp, stepped back, turned his head to the

side and studied the pharmacist for a moment, then said, "I *will* slap the shit out of you. You know that?"

"Sorry," Winston said, coughing somewhat, as if trying to dislodge the errant Jamaican from his throat. "What can I do for you, sir?"

"Mavis down to the Slug sent me up to ax you somethin."

"I'm familiar with her medical records," Winston said, "You can have her call me if she has a question."

"Yeah, she don't want to call you. She want you to come down to see her."

Winston adjusted his bolo tie. "I'm sorry, but you'll have to have her call me. I can't leave the store."

Catfish nodded. "That what she thought you'd say. She say to ax you if she can have a big jar of them sugar pills you selling instead medicine."

Winston glanced at the back room where his staff was huddled like Anne Frank and family, peering out through the crack in the door. "Tell her I'll be right over," Winston said.

"She said to wait and come with you."

Winston was visibly sweating now; oily beads rose on his scalp. "Let me tell the staff where I'll be."

"Hurry up, Flipper. I ain't got all day," Catfish said.

Winston Krauss shuddered, hitched up his double knits, and waddled around the counter. "Ladies, I'll be back in few minutes," he called over his shoulder.

Catfish leaned over the counter to where he could see the row of eyes peering out of the crack and said, "I be back in a few minutes my own self, ladies. I needs some medicine what can help me with this huge black dick I have to carry around. The weight of it like to break my back."

There was a collective intake of breath so abrupt that the drop in pressure sprung the barometer on the wall and made Catfish's ears pop.

"Yes, sir."

"So I have a standoff? I had a standoff before, Sheridan. A standoff doesn't do me any good. Come with me." He pushed a fresh clip into his 9 mm. and turned to the others. "Cover us."

Burton led the SWAT commander to a spot in the rocks just below the cave mouth. "Crowe?" Burton called. "You've had enough time to consider my offer!"

"Offer?" Sheridan asked.

Burton shushed him.

"I haven't decided yet!" Theo shouted. "We've got thirty people in here to discuss it with and they're not being cooperative."

Sheridan looked at Burton. "Thirty people? We can't shoot thirty people. I'm not shooting any thirty people."

"Five minutes, Crowe," Burton said. "Then you have no more options."

"What's the offer?" Sheridan whispered to the sheriff.

"Don't worry about it. I'm just trying to get the subject separated from the hostages so we can take him out."

"Then we'd better have a description of the suspect, don't you think?"

"He's the one in handcuffs," Burton said.

"Well, aren't you the fucking hero?" Sheridan shot back.

Skinner

Skinner watched from the front seat of the Mercedes as the Food Guy was loaded into the back of the Suburban with the cage in it. The Bad Guys hadn't even left the windows cracked. How would the Food Guy breathe? He wouldn't be able to sit in the front seat and put his head out the window either. Skinner was sad for the Food Guy.

He crawled in the backseat of the Mercedes and lay down to nap away his anxiety.

The Head of the Slug

The first thing Catfish saw when he came through the doors of the Head of the Slug was Estelle standing at the bar, and he could feel the crust peeling off his heart like old paint. Her hair was down. Brushed out, it hung to her waist. She was wearing a pair of pink overalls that had been splattered with paint over a man's white T-shirt—his T-shirt, he realized. She looked to him like what he always thought home was supposed to look like, but as a Bluesman, he was bound by tradition to be cool.

"Hey, girl, what you doin' here?"

"I called her," Mavis said. "This is your driver."

"What I need a driver for?"

"I'll tell you." Estelle took his hand and led him to a booth in the corner.

Winston Krauss came through the door a second later and Mavis waved him over to the bar. "Son, I'm about to make you the happiest man in the whole world."

"You are? Why?"

"Because I like to see people get what they want. And I have what you want."

"You do?"

Mavis stepped up to the bar and in low, conspiratorial tones, began telling Winston Krauss the most titillating, outrageously erotic tale that she had ever told, trying the whole time to remember that the man she was talking to wanted to have sex with marine animals.

Over in the corner booth, Catfish's modicum of cool had melted. Estelle was smiling, even as tears welled up in her eyes. "I wouldn't ask you to do it if I thought it would put you in danger. Really."

"I know that," Catfish said, a gentleness in his voice that he usually reserved for kittens and traffic cops. "It just that I been runnin from this my whole life."

"I don't think so," Estelle said. "I think you've been running *to* this."

Catfish grinned. "You gonna take them old Blues off me for good, ain't you?"

"You know it."

"Then let's go." Catfish stood up and turned to where Mavis and Winston stood.

"We ready? Y'all ready?" He noticed that the front of Winston's trousers had become overly tight. "Yeah, you ready. You sick, but you ready."

Mavis nodded, a slight mechanical ratcheting noise coming from her neck, "Take the second turn out, not the first," Mavis said to Estelle. "From there it hugs the coast, so there's no hills."

"I have to go get my mask and fins," wailed Winston.

 *thirty-one*

Molly

"Has it been five minutes yet?" Molly was sitting cross-legged, her sword held across her knees. Theo jumped as if he'd been poked with an ice pick, then checked his watch. He crouched by the cave mouth, listening for the sound of either salvation or death.

"About a minute left. Where the hell are they? Molly, maybe you should find some cover."

"What cover?" She looked around the cave. It was an open chamber; the only cover would be the darkness in the back of the chamber.

"Get behind Steve."

"No," Molly said. "I won't do that." She heard a voice come from the back of her mind. "Get to cover, you daffy broad. What, do you have a death wish?"

"I have abandonment issues. I'm not going to turn around and abandon someone else," Molly said.

"What?" Theo said.

"I wasn't talking to you."

"Fine, die. What do I care?" said the narrator.

"Bastard," Molly said.

"What?" said Theo.

"Not you!"

"Molly, how did you get those guys to come out and drag me into the cave before?"

"I just told them to."

"Well, take their clothes back to them and tell them to get dressed."

"Why?"

"Just do it. And tell them to hang on to Steve's sides and not let go, no matter what he does."

"Now who's nuts?"

"Molly, please, I'm trying to save him."

The Sheriff

Burton checked his watch. "That's it. Get into position. We're going in."

Sergeant Sheridan wasn't so sure. "They have thirty hostages and we don't have any recon of their positions and we don't have a full team. You want to take this guy out with thirty witnesses?"

"Goddamn it, Sheridan, get your men in position. We go on my signal."

"Sheriff Burton." Theo's voice from the cave.

"What?"

"I'll take your offer," Theo said. "Give me five more minutes and I'll come out. We can all leave together. The others will come out after you're gone."

"You just want him anyway, right?" Sheridan said. "He's the only one that can hurt the operation."

Burton turned it over in his mind. He'd been determined to take out the constable and the woman, but now he had to rethink things. If he could get Crowe away from the others, he could dispose of him with no witnesses.

Burton's cell phone rang. He flipped it open. "Burton," he said.

"You shouldn't have made disparaging comments about my weight, Sheriff," the Spider said.

"Nailsworth, you piece of sh—" The line went dead.

Suddenly the sound of a wailing Blues guitar came screaming over the marine terrace. Burton and the SWAT team turned to see an old white station wagon driving along the edge of the terrace, next to where it dropped to the beach.

An inhuman roar rose up out of the cave, and when Burton looked back to the cave all he saw was a huge reptilian face coming at him.

Winston Krauss

Winston sat in the back of the station wagon, steadying the Marshall amplifier that was screaming out the notes from Catfish's Stratocaster. The amp was plugged into Mavis's black box and a cord ran over the seats into the cigarette lighter, next to where Catfish was playing. After the first few notes, Winston's hearing had shut down due to temporary deafness, but he didn't care. He could hardly believe his luck. Mavis had promised him the biggest sexual thrill of his life, and he had doubted her. But now he saw it. It was the most gorgeous creature he'd ever seen.

Steve

The feelings of self-pity, jealousy, and heartbreak were new to him, but the response that welled up in him when he heard the sound of his enemy was more deeply imprinted on his lizard brain and it displaced all the newer feelings with rage and the imperative to attack.

He stormed out of the cave with pilgrims hanging on

his back by the ridge of armored plates that ran down his spine. Two layers of protective covering slid over his eyes, shortening his vision, but it was the sound that guided him anyway, the sound that carried the strongest association with the enemy. He flashed bright crimson and yellow as he charged over the rocks, kicking aside the vehicles and shedding pilgrims as he made his way to his enemy at the shore.

Theo

Molly stood in the cave entrance, screaming for Steve to stop. Theo grabbed her around the waist and pulled her away just as the Sea Beast, dangling pilgrims, charged past them. She elbowed Theo in the forehead, stunning him for a second, and she made for the cave entrance. Theo caught her outside on the rocks and held her.

"No!"

Theo wrapped his arms around her, pinning her arms to her side, and lifted her off the ground, then held her kicking as he braced for gunfire. But none came.

Burton was climbing to his feet just below them, focused on the Sea Beast as it passed. "Shoot that thing! Shoot it! Shoot it!"

The SWAT commander had rolled out of the way and come up with his weapon ready, but with people hanging all over the beast, he didn't know where to shoot, so instead let his weapon fall to his side as he stared in amazement.

Burton drew a pistol and began running after the Sea Beast. Below, two of the SWAT team had already broken into a run from behind the Blazers just as the Sea Beast bowled them over. The other two were pinned underneath one of the crushed vehicles. As they fell, each pilgrim jumped to his feet and ran after the Sea Beast, who was making a beeline across the grassy terrace toward the white station wagon.

Theo watched as the car stopped, Blues slide notes still screaming out of the back, and Estelle Boyet crawled out of the driver's seat and ran around to the back. The guitar playing stopped for a second as the passenger side opened, and out stepped Catfish Jefferson, holding a Fender Stratocaster.

"Let me go!" Molly screamed. "I've got to save him! I've got to save him!"

Theo yanked her back toward the cave. When he was able to look again, someone he didn't immediately recognize had crawled out of the station wagon, and Catfish handed him the guitar.

Sheriff Burton was running after the Sea Beast, waving his weapon around, trying to get an angle to shoot without hitting one of the pilgrims. He stopped, dropped to one knee, steadied his aim, and fired. The Sea Beast roared and whipped around, throwing the last of the pilgrims into a tumble in the grass.

Molly whipped her head back into Theo's chin at the same time she drove a heel into his knee. Theo let go of her and she rushed over the rocks and down toward the monster.

Catfish

Estelle had brought the car right to the edge of the drop-off to the rocky beach. Catfish looked at the surf beating on the rocks below, then at his guitar cords coiled in the front seat, then at the rocks again. They just might be long enough. But the dragon was going to get to them before he could find out.

"Hurry!" Estelle shouted.

Catfish stood mesmerized by the charging monster, not a hundred yards away.

"Go," he said weakly, "get yourself out of here."

"No!" said Winston Krauss. "You promised."

There was a gunshot and the Sea Beast whipped around in his tracks, bringing Catfish to his senses. "Let's go," he said to Winston. Then he looked at Estelle over the top of the car and winked. "You go on. This ain't your time."

Catfish played a few notes on the Stratocaster and then ambled after Winston to the surf. The pharmacist ran into the water up to his knees, then turned around. Catfish was having trouble climbing over the rocks to the water while keeping the guitar cord from catching.

"That's far enough," Catfish said. He walked into the surf and stood next to Winston, keeping the guitar high to keep any spray off of it.

"Give it," Winston demanded.

"You ain't got a lick a sense, do you?"

"Give it," Winston repeated.

Catfish played four bars of "Green Onions" on the Strat, the notes still blaring out of the amp in the station wagon, then draped the strap around Winston's neck and handed him a guitar pick. "Have fun," Catfish said.

"Oh, I will," Winston said, a lascivious grin crossing his face. "You know I will."

"Play!" Catfish said as he turned and ran up the beach. He saw Estelle already making her way away down the shore away from the commotion. Behind him, the sour, rattling notes began to emanate from the amp in the station wagon as gunshots filled the air.

Molly

The sheriff fired three more times as he backed away from the Sea Beast, missing not only the monster but the entire North American continent. Molly threw herself sideways from a full run into the back of Burton's knees and cut his legs out from under him. She came up in a crouch, putting herself between Burton and the Sea Beast. The sheriff thought he heard the song "Green Onions" and shook his head to clear a hallucination. The Sea Beast roared again and the sheriff vaulted into a crouch, ready to fire, but instead of a sea monster in front of him, he saw a woman in a leather bikini. He looked over his shoulder and watched the Sea Beast snap up the white station wagon in its jaws and toss it aside. The guitar sounds stopped and the Sea Beast slid over the bluff to the beach. Seeing that the danger was gone, he trained his sights on the woman. People were streaming by him on either side after the monster, wailing like a crowd of banshees.

Molly looked over her shoulder and saw Steve going into the water, then turned back to Burton. "Go ahead, you prick. I don't care."

"You got it," Burton said.

Winston Krauss

He was just beating on the guitar strings now, but it didn't matter. The amplifier wasn't working anymore and this beautiful creature was coming to him. Winston was so turned on he thought he'd explode. She was coming to him, his dream lover, and he yanked the guitar from around his neck, ready to receive her.

"Oh, come on, baby. Come to papa," he said.

The Sea Beast charged into the water, throwing spray fifty feet in the air, then snapped his jaws over Winston, severing the pharmacist's body into two sleazy pieces. The Sea Beast swallowed Winston's legs and roared, then snapped up the remaining piece and dove under the sea.

The Sheriff

"I don't think so, Sheriff," Sheridan said.

Burton looked over his shoulder without taking the gun off Molly. Sheridan had his M-16 trained on the sheriff's back. "Don't fuck with me, Sheridan. You're in this with me."

"I'm not in *this*. Lower your weapon, sir."

Burton lowered the pistol and turned toward Sheridan. Molly started to leap forward and the SWAT commander pointed the M-16 at her. "Right there," he said. She stopped.

The pilgrims were all standing at the shore now, wailing as they looked out. Molly gestured in that direction and Sheridan nodded. She ran toward the shoreline.

"What now?" Burton asked.

"I don't know," said Sheridan, "but no one has been shot here, and I have a feeling that there's going to be a lot of attention around this event, so no one is going to get shot."

"You wimp."

"Whatever," Sheridan said.

"Hey, Burton!" Theo Crowe was running down the hill toward them. "You hear that?"

When they looked up, Theo ducked behind one of the wrecked Blazers and pointed toward the southern sky. "Film at eleven."

Burton could hear them now: helicopters. He looked

to the south and saw the two dots coming over the horizon. Two of the SWAT team members were topping the next hill. They had started running when the monster first came out of the cave. The other two were still pinned under one of the overturned Blazers. He turned back to Sheridan. The big cop was watching the approaching helicopters. "Game over," Sheridan said. "Guess it's time to start thinking about my deal with the D.A."

Burton shot him in the face, then broke for the far side of the rocks to his Eldorado before the others had time to figure out what had happened.

Theo

Theo came up behind Molly and touched her lightly on the shoulder. When she turned, he could see tears streaming down her cheeks. Then she returned to staring out to sea with the others. She said, "All I ever wanted is to feel special. To feel like something set me apart."

Theo put his arm around her. "Everyone wants that."

"But I had it, Theo. More by having Steve in my life than when I was making movies. These people felt it, but not like me."

The two helicopters were coming in close now and Theo had to speak right into her ear to be heard over the thumping blades. "No one's like you."

There was a stirring in the water just past the surf line, and something was rising in the kelp bed. Theo could see the purple gill trees standing out on the Sea Beast's neck. He was heading toward shore. Theo tried to pull Molly closer, but she broke loose from him, jumped off the bluff, and ran into the surf, scooping up two baseball-sized rocks as she went.

Theo went after her and was halfway across the beach

when she turned and looked at him with eyes filled with such pleading and desperation that it stopped him in his tracks. The helicopters were hovering only a hundred feet over the beach now. The wash from the blades kicked up sand in the faces of the onlookers.

As the Sea Beast approached shore, only his eyes and gills above the water, Molly threw one of the stones. "No, go away! Go!" The second stone hit the Sea Beast's eye, and he stopped. "Don't come back!" Molly screamed.

Slowly the Sea Beast sank below the surface.

The Sheriff

The speedometer on the Eldorado was approaching sixty when Burton topped the last hill before the cattle guard. He had to get to the airport and use the open ticket in his briefcase to join his money in the Caymans before anyone could figure out where he had gone. He'd planned for this all along, knowing he might have to make a run for it at some point, but what he hadn't planned was that there would be two Suburbans and a Mercedes parked just over the top of the hill.

Before he could stop himself, he hit the brakes and wrenched the wheel to the left. The tires dug into the pasture and sent the Eldorado up on two wheels, then over. There was none of the slowing of time or compression of events that often happens in accidents. He saw light and dark, felt his body being beaten around the Caddy, and then the crash of smashing metal and breaking glass. Then there was a pause.

He lay on the ceiling of the overturned Eldorado, peppered with pieces of safety glass, trying to feel if any of his limbs were broken. He seemed okay, he could feel his feet, and it didn't hurt when he breathed. But he smelled gas. It was enough to remind him to move.

He grabbed the briefcase with his escape kit and slithered out the broken back window to find the Eldorado half-perched, half-smashed over the front of a white Suburban. He climbed to his feet and ran to the truck. It was locked. Sheridan, you prick, you would lock your truck, he thought. He didn't notice the people handcuffed inside the K-9 cage in the back.

The Mercedes was his last chance. He ran around it and yanked opened the driver's side door. The keys were in the ignition. He climbed in and took a deep breath. He had to calm down now. No more mistakes, he told himself. He started the Mercedes and was turning to back it down the hill when the dog hit him.

thirty-two

Catfish and Estelle

"That was a good guitar," Catfish said. He had his arms around Estelle, who had pressed her face to his chest when the monster attacked Winston Krauss.

"I didn't realize," Estelle said. "I didn't think it would do that."

Catfish stroked her hair. "That was a good car too. That car never broke."

Estelle pushed Catfish away and looked in his eyes. "You knew, didn't you?"

"What I knew is that boy wanted to get up close to a sea monster and that's what he got. Case you didn't notice, he was happy when it happened."

"What now?"

"I think we ought to get you home, girl. You got some paintings gonna come out of this."

"Home? Are you coming with me?"

"I ain't got no car to go anywhere. I guess I am."

"You're going to stay? You're not afraid of losing the Blues and getting content?"

Catfish grinned, and there was that gold tooth with the eighth note cut in it, glistening in the morning sunshine. "Dragon done ate my car, my guitar, my amp—girl, I got me enough Blues to last a good long time. I'm thinkin I'll write me some new songs while you makin your paintings."

"I'd like that," Estelle said. "I'd like to paint the Blues."

"Long as you don't go cuttin your ear off like old Vincent. A man finds a one-eared woman stone unattractive."

Estelle pulled him tight. "I'll do my best."

"Course, there was a woman I knowed down Memphis way, name of Sally, had only one leg. Called her One Leg Sally . . ."

"I don't want to hear it."

"What you wanna hear?"

"I want to hear the door closing behind us, the fire crackling in the stove, and the teakettle just coming to a whistle while my lovin man picks out 'Walkin' Man's Blues' on a National steel guitar."

"You easy," Catfish said.

"I thought you liked that," she said, and she took his spidery hand in hers and led him up over the bluff to find a ride home.

Theo and Molly

Theo had never felt quite so overwhelmed in his entire life. He sensed that the excitement and the danger of it all was over, but he still felt as if a beast every bit as intimidating as the one that had just sunk into the sea was looming over him. He didn't know if he had a job, or for that matter a home, since his cabin had been part of his pay. He didn't even have his bong collection and victory garden to crawl into. He was confused and horrified by what had just happened, but not relieved that it was over. He stood there, not ten feet from where Molly Michon was standing in the surf, and he had no idea what the rest of his life had to offer him.

"Hey," he called. "You okay?"

He watched her nod without turning around. The waves were breaking in front of her and foam and seaweed was splashing up over her thighs, yet she stood there solid, staring out to sea.

"You going to be okay?"

Without turning, she said, "I haven't been okay for years. Ask anybody."

"Matter of opinion. I think you're okay."

Now she looked over her shoulder at him, her hair in a tangle from the wind, tear tracks down her face. "Really?"

"I'm a huge fan."

"You had never heard of my movies until you came to my trailer, had you?"

"Nope. I'm a huge fan, though."

She turned and walked out of the surf toward him, and a smile was breaking there on her face. A smile with too much history to it, but a smile nonetheless.

"The narrator says you did good," she said.

"The narrator?" Theo found himself smiling too, as close to crying as he had come since his father had died, but smiling nonetheless.

"Yeah, it's this voice I hear when I don't take my meds for a while. He's kind of a prick, but he's got a better sense of judgment than I do."

She was right there in front of him now—looking up at him, a hand on her hip, a challenge in that movie-star smile—looking more like Kendra the Warrior Babe than she ever had in the posters, the five-inch-long scar standing glorious over her left breast, seawater and grime streaking her body, a look in her eyes that comes from watching your future get nuked—repeatedly. She took his breath away.

"Do you think the three of us could go out to dinner sometime?"

"I'm on the rebound, you know?"

His heart sank. "I understand."

She walked around him and started up the bluff. He followed her, understanding for the first time how the pilgrims had felt following the Sea Beast to the cave.

"I didn't say no," Molly said. "I just thought you ought to know. The narrator is warning me not to talk about my ex over dinner."

His heart soared. "I think a lot of people are going to be talking about your ex."

"You're not intimidated?"

"Of course. But not by him."

"The narrator says it's a bad idea. Says the two of us put together might make one good loser."

"Wow, he *is* a prick."

"I'll get some meds from Dr. Val and he'll go away."

"You're sure that's a good idea?"

"Yeah," she said, turning back to him again before climbing up to where the pilgrims waited. "I'd like to be alone with you."

Skinner

What the man in the driver's seat didn't seem to understand was that as far as this Mercedes was concerned, Skinner was the alpha male. The man smelled of fear and anger and aggression, as well as gunpowder and sweat, and Skinner didn't like him from the moment he got into the car: Skinner's new mobile territory. So Skinner had to show him, and he did so in the traditional way, by clamping his jaws over the Challenger's throat and waiting for him to take a submissive posture. The man had struggled and even hit Skinner, but hadn't said bad-dog, bad-dog, so Skinner just growled and tightened his jaws until he tasted blood and the man was still.

Skinner was still waiting for the Challenger to submit when the Tall Guy opened the car door.

"Good dog, Skinner. Good dog," Theo said.

"Get this fucking animal off me," the Challenger said.

Skinner wagged his tail and tightened his jaws until the Challenger made a gurgling sound. The Tall Guy scratched his ears and put some metal on the Challenger's paws.

"Let go now, Skinner," the Tall Guy said. "I've got him."

Skinner let go and licked Theo's face before the constable dragged the sheriff out onto the ground and stood on the back of his neck with one foot.

The Tall Guy tasted like lizard spit. That was strange. Skinner considered it a moment, then his doggie attention span ran out and he bounded out of the car to go see what the Food Guy was doing in the back of the truck. The Tall Guy's female was breaking out the back window of the truck with a metal stick. Skinner barked at her, trying to tell her not to hurt the Food Guy.

Good Guys

"Is the creature still there?" Gabe asked Molly as he climbed out of the back of the Suburban. Skinner was frisking and jumping on him, and with the handcuffs he couldn't ward off the damp affection. "Down, boy. Down."

"No, he's gone," Molly said as she helped Val and Howard out of the Suburban. She nodded to Val. "Hi, Doc. I think I've had an episode or something. You'll have to debrief me in session or something."

Valerie Riordan nodded. "I'll check my calendar."

Theo came around the back of the Mercedes. "You guys okay?"

"You have your key?" Gabe asked, turning his back to Theo to show the handcuffs.

"We heard shots," Val said. "Did . . . ?"

"One of the SWAT team is dead. Burton shot him. A few of your patients are scraped and bruised, but they'll be okay. Winston Krauss was eaten."

"Eaten?" The color ran out of Val's face.

"Long story, Val," Theo said. "Mavis set it all up after you guys left. Catfish and Estelle came in and drew the monster out. Winston was sort of the bait."

"Oh my god!" Val said. "She said something about my not being in trouble."

Theo held his finger to his lips to shush her, then nodded to where Sheriff Burton lay on the ground. "It never happened, Val. None of it. I don't know a thing." He spun her around and unlocked her handcuffs. Then did the same for Gabe and Howard.

The gaunt restaurateur seemed more morose than usual. "I had really hoped to lay eyes on the creature."

"Me too," said Gabe, putting his arm around Valerie.

"Sorry," Theo said. To Val he said, "The reporters from those helicopters are going to be here in a few minutes. If I were you, I'd get out of here." He handed her the keys to the Mercedes. "The district attorney is sending a deputy to pick up Burton, so I'm going to stay here. Will you give Molly a ride back into town?"

"Of course," Val said. "What are you going to tell the reporters?"

"I don't know," Theo said. "Deny everything, I guess. It depends on what they ask and what they got on tape. Having lived most my life in denial, I may be perfectly suited for dealing with them."

"I'm sorry I was—I'm sorry I doubted your abilities, Theo."

"So did I, Val. I'll call you guys and let you know what's going on."

Gabe called Skinner and they loaded into the Mercedes, leaving Theo and Molly facing each other. Theo looked at his shoes. "I guess I'll be seeing you."

She stretched up and kissed him on the cheek. Then without a word she crawled into the back of the Mercedes with Howard and Skinner and closed the door.

Theo watched them back away, then turn and head across the pasture and out of the cattle gate.

"You're going down with me, Crowe!" Burton screamed from the ground.

Theo spotted something shiny lying in the grass near the back of the Suburban and went over to it. It was Molly's broadsword. He felt a smile breaking out as he picked it up and went over to where Burton was lying.

"You have the right to remain silent," Theo said. "I suggest you exercise that right. Immediately." Theo plunged the sword into the ground half an inch from Burton's face and watched the sheriff's eyes go wide.

thirty-three

Winter

Winter in Pine Cove is a pause, a timeout, an extended coffee break. A slowness comes over the town and people stop their cars in the street to talk with a passing neighbor without worrying about a tourist honking his horn so he can get on with his relaxing vacation (damn it!). Waiters and hotel clerks go to part-time shifts and money slows to a creep. Couples spend their nights at home in front of the fireplace as the smell of rain-washed wood smoke fills the air, and single people resolve to move somewhere where life is a full-time sport.

Winter near the shore is cold. The wind kicks up a salty mist and elephant seals come to shore to trumpet and rut and birth their pups. Retired people put sweaters on their lap dogs and drag them down the street on re-tractable leashes in a nightly parade of doggie humilia-tion. Surfers don their wetsuits against the chill of storm waves and white sharks adjust their diets to include shrink-wrapped dude-snacks on fiberglass crackers. But the chill is crisp and forgiving and settles in a way so that the town's collective metabolism can slow into semihiber-nation without a shock.

At least that's the way it is most winters.

After the coming of the Sea Beast, winter was a jugger-naut, a party, an irritation and a windfall. News footage from the helicopters was beamed out over satellites and Pine Cove displaced Roswell, New Mexico, as the number one crackpot travel destination. There wasn't much on the tapes, just a crowd of people gathered on the shore and the fuzzy image of something large in the water, but with the footprints and the eyewitness accounts, it was enough. Shops filled with cheesy serpent souvenirs and H.P.'s Cafe added to the menu a sandwich called the Theosaurus, which was the official scientific name of the Sea Beast (coined by biologist Gabriel Fenton). The hotels filled, the streets congested, and Mavis Sand actually had to hire a second bartender to help serve the imported wackos.

Estelle Boyet opened her own gallery on Cypress Street where she sold her new series of paintings enigmatically entitled *Steve*, as well as the new Catfish Jefferson CD entitled *The What Do I Do Now That I'm Happy? Blues.*

As the story of the Sea Beast spread and was sensationalized, interest rose in an obscure B-movie actress named Molly Michon. Discs and videocassettes of the *Warrior Babe* series were remastered and rereleased to an enthusiastic audience, and the Screen Actors Guild came down on the producers like an avenging accountant angel to capture a piece of the profits for Molly.

Valerie Riordan's practice stabilized as she struck a balance between therapy and medication and she was able to schedule a sabbatical to join her fiancé, Gabe Fenton, on an oceanographic expedition aboard a Scripps vessel to look for evidence of the Theosaurus in the deep trenches off California.

After he testified against John Burton, putting him away for life, winter settled on Theophilus Crowe like a warm blessing. In the second month of his recovery, he realized that his addiction to marijuana had been nothing more than a response to boredom. Like the child who whines away a summer day because there's nothing to do, but makes no effort to actually do anything, Theo had simply lacked the ambition to entertain himself. Sharing his life with Molly solved the problem, and Theo found that although he was often exhausted by the demands of his job and his lover, he was never bored. Molly's trailer was moved to the edge of the ranch by his cabin. Every morning they shared a hearty breakfast pizza at her place. In the evening, they ate dinner on his cable spool table. She answered his calls while he was at work, and he ran interference with the geeky fans who were rabid enough to seek her out at the ranch. Not a day passed that he did not tell Molly how special she was to him, and as time passed, the narrator in her head fell silent and never spoke again.

There was no winter in the deep submarine trench off California, two miles down. Everything was as it had been: a dark pressurized sameness where the Sea Beast lay by his black smoker, grieving for love lost. He stopped grazing on deep water worms that grew on the rocks and his great body began to waste away under the weight of the water and the years. He had resolved never to move again—to lie there until his great heart stopped and with it the throb of heartbreak—when sensor cells along his flanks picked up a signal. Something he had not felt for half a century, the signature of a creature he thought he would never feel again. He flipped his tail and shook off the crust of loneliness that had settled over him, and that organ buried deep beneath his reptile brain picked up a message coming from the female. Roughly translated, it said, "Hey, sailor, want to get lucky?"

About the Author

Christopher Moore is the author of four previous novels: *Practical Demonkeeping, Coyote Blue, Bloodsucking Fiends,* and *Island of the Sequined Love Nun.* He lives in Northern California with a mysterious woman and thirty-nine goldfish named Steve. You can e-mail him at BSFiends@aol.com, or check out the silliness on the official Christopher Moore web page at chrismoore.com